A Shattered Peace

A Cameron Ballack mystery

by Luke H. Davis

Permission to quote in critical reviews with citation:
A Shattered Peace
By Luke H. Davis

Print ISBN 978-0-9984000-4-4

www.dunrobin.us

To my parents,

Ralph and Barbara Davis,

who have taught by word and example

that peace is never shattered

if it is joined together with truth.

AUTHOR'S NOTE

There is simultaneously both ease and challenge to writing a murder mystery. The ease comes by seeing how much of a mystery reflects life itself. The faith tradition in which I swim tends to see life through the interpretive lens of creation, ruin, redemption, and restoration. A world is formed, humans bring tragic circumstances into it by their corrupt choices, and then astoundingly there is hope that the original wonder can be recaptured. I am struck how a murder mystery presents us this environment writ small. The reader may encounter an environment marked by peace, initial quietude, and relative virtue. But soon that locale is ravaged by the vices of jealousy, obsession, or revenge, followed by the violence of life taken in cold blood. And the whole micro-world is stained, as the sin of murder makes suspects out of ordinary citizens. Enter the literary imprint of the divine redeemer—the protagonist detective, who seeks to put this broken world back together with the resources before him or her. And so the reader follows, not truly satisfied until redemption and restoration are accomplished by bringing the guilty to justice.

And yet there is a challenge for the mystery writer, that of making this template seem at once alive, readable, realistic, and creative. Nobody wants to read the same old thing. And thus, I am constantly back at the drawing board, figuring out another angle for a unique detective—the wheelchair-bound Cameron Ballack—to use his agnostic leanings to solve a spiritually contoured case. That calls for revised settings, unique characters, malleable relationship angles, and distinct justifications from a new murderer. It means I have to figure out a fresh manner for Ballack to display his detective generalship while facing significant physical barriers himself. Yes, there were moments in writing and re-shaping *A Shattered Peace* when I felt like I was climbing in the Rockies on a sprained ankle. But I wouldn't accept the craft of writing without the challenges. They do exist for a reason.

Naturally, I would be the worst of sinners if I didn't thank those who helped and empowered my efforts in grand fashion during this season. Lester Stuckmeyer and John Bauer have given counsel on how to make legal affairs both realistic and vivid. Theresa Robinson again came to the rescue on many details of police protocol and investigation. And I was thinking it is about time I recognize a worthy group of supporters from over the years—my former students from numerous years of teaching. Several of them have given overwhelming encouragement at critical moments, inspiring me to stay on the literary path and never swerve away. Also, my wife Christy and our children have given love and remarkable patience throughout this entire process. Additionally, I benefited from wonderful teamwork for the cover design. My daughter Lindsay photographed the grave at Bellerive Cemetery in St. Louis, upon which Ciarra Peters did her usual excellent work in drawing the final cover image. A heartfelt thank-you to both ladies!

A murder mystery set in a counseling clinic carries with it the chance of questioned motives. Let me state immediately that all events and characters in this novel are fictitious and exist only in my imagination. But even with that reality in place, readers might wonder if licensed professional counselors or their clients are closer to a more chilling and permanent peace than that for which they aim. This story is not meant to dissuade others from seeking professional help for life's struggles, mental health, or emotional wellbeing. Murders, however, do happen in space and time. This tale serves to highlight the fundamental irony of danger in a safe spiritual haven, thus keeping in line with the tension of my previous works—*Litany of Secrets* and *The Broken Cross*.

A quick thank-you also must go to several counselors I've known and encountered in various settings over the years. Their activity has been invaluable, helping me to understand the world of the licensed professional counselor, whether or not they've realized their assistance in the roles of colleagues, professors, or family. Many thanks to Sherry Blough, Kathy Karigan, Dan Zink, and my late uncle Robert Herron for their insight into these particulars.

Residents of the St. Louis area will recognize familiar landmarks and thoroughfares interspersed throughout the book, ideally laid out with precision and detail. The locations of the Dayspring Community Church and Dayspring Counseling Center are, of course, fictitious. I must give sincere apologies to the parishioners at Trinity Evangelical Lutheran Church for reshaping their property as if their church didn't exist, but I felt it was too prime a location to pass up!

Above all, it is my hope that in life's journey—no matter how shattered you may feel—you will experience peace that endures and be lifted up from the shards of despair.

Ascension Day 2017

CONTENTS

"Part of every misery is, so to speak, the misery's shadow or
reflection: the fact that you don't merely suffer
but have to keep on thinking about the fact that you suffer.
I not only live each endless day in grief,
but live each day thinking about living each day in grief."
(C.S. Lewis, *A Grief Observed*)

"Crown Him the Son of God, before the worlds began,
And ye who tread where He hath trod, crown Him the Son of Man,
Who every grief hath known that wrings the human breast
And takes and bears them for His own, that all in Him may rest."
("Crown Him With Many Crowns", by Matthew Bridges)

"This is not peace. This is an armistice for twenty years."
(Ferdinand Foch, French Marshall and Supreme Commander during
World War I, upon seeing the final draft of the Treaty of Versailles)

PROLOGUE
A Time to Tear …

(Years before)

They were practically an eternity from Chicago, and that was a good thing. To Peter Van Sluys, any place was better than the Windy City, its memories, and its suburbs that sprawled endlessly into places like Deerfield, Batavia, Lansing, Wheaton, and South Barrington. Better to catch a Cubs game on radio here, where the glorious waters were only a few yards away, rather than having to meander through asphyxiating traffic for nine innings of staring at Wrigley's vines.

Saturdays on the shores of Lake Michigan were hardly docile affairs. Peter's work as a lifeguard meant he had to be especially watchful on a day like this. During the week, he could bring along a book and sneak it under his towel, whiling away the hours. Or he might think about what his friends were up to. Perhaps Doug was beefing up his political science degree, grunting away as a summer page for Representative McAuliffe far away in Springfield. Maybe Greg was crumbling under the thought of actually having a class before noon next semester and was drowning his superficial sorrows by getting hammered cheaply, thanks to a seemingly endless supply of Milwaukee's Best Light.

Lately though, Peter couldn't keep a straight line of thought with either a good book or thoughts about his friends. This had been a building scenario for several years now. He craned his neck and scanned the beach, wondering where his aunt, the completely professional—yet beautiful and stunningly single—Angela DeHaan might be. Normally in summer weekends of the past, when the temperatures would soar past ninety degrees, she would accompany Peter's younger sister and brother to the beach.

She also happened to be Peter's one perpetual beacon of happiness and sweetness for the past few years. His had been the typical Dutch family upbringing in Chicago's suburbs—traditional, hard working, and emotionally reserved. His education, and that of his siblings, took place in the same Christian school system from kindergarten through his senior year. Sundays meant church, mouthing away the creeds and liturgies that he knew by heart before he turned twelve. Summers as a young boy were normally spent on a constant shuttle of camp, sports, volunteering with his mother at the public library, and the occasional hours assisting his father at the shop. That was little wonder. His gruff patriarch spent an inordinate amount of time at work, likely assuming that Peter's ken would be to seek employment at Voyager's Heating and Cooling. The elder Van Sluys was the owner of the shop, a cash cow in Chicagoland during both extremes of summer and winter.

Peter's great frustration was the god they worshipped. Try as he faked it Sunday after Sunday, he soon discerned that deity was not the Trinity of Father, Son, and Holy Spirit. It was the Divine Essence of Predictability. Routine marked their days, weeks, and years. Didactic commands took precedence over precocious queries. Order trumped spontaneity, steadiness triumphed over variance, and discipline always won out over any ounce of tenderness. Even interest in the ways of youth seemed not to penetrate his parents. Mom would attend Peter's basketball games and cross-country meets, but she would never compliment him or comment on his performance unless Dad gave her some invisible liberty to speak at the dinner table. That community's most grievous sin, thought Peter, would be to mix in any flavor with the vanilla ice cream of existence.

The meteor of delight that crash-landed in his universe was his aunt Angela. Six years younger than Peter's mother, she was a licensed professional counselor, having done the expected route through Calvin College and, later, Calvin Seminary in Grand Rapids, Michigan. She settled in a community on the shores of Lake Michigan, latching on with a Christian counseling center that also sponsored summer camps and sports clinics as a full-service model of personal wellness. There was plenty to do in the area, and ever since Peter turned twelve, he, his sister, and his brother would spend a six-week stretch each summer at Aunt Angela's. While she saw clients during the day, Peter would walk his siblings to the camp. Later in the evening, they'd gather on the back deck at Angela's house, enjoying a different sort of cookout each night of the week. As the years passed, Peter graduated from the camp scene and became a licensed lifeguard at the beach. Yet the evening scene remained the same, the four of them picnicking behind Angela's three-bedroom house, looking up into the starry sky. Peter was always amazed by the flood of contentment that saturated these days, with much of that happiness due to the love and trustworthiness emanating from Angela. No one he knew—especially his own one-dimensional parents—showed the tender compassion that Angela did. He could not fathom any higher form of grace and joy.

What he also could not possibly fathom was how the coming years would change everything.

Following one's heart can be a ride like no other. Spurning caution yet again, Peter headed back to Lake Michigan after his sophomore year of college. This year he would do so alone. Katie was headed off for her first days at the University of Illinois, and so she had already moved into an apartment there in Champaign, working for an Urbana catering company to supplement her bank account. Garrett had given up on the summer scene at the lake and begun working full time at the HVAC shop. It wasn't as if Peter minded. He felt that staying with Angela alone during the summer brought an extra edge of happiness. He swore his pulse doubled as he set himself toward what he hoped was a season of joy.

On the surface, it was a summer like any other. He was at the lake during the day, then cooking out with Angela in the evenings. The common thread was processing his studies with her, talking shop as it were. As June moved into July, Peter sensed her opening up more than usual, confessing her fear of being alone, connecting it with the irony of healing the relationships and marriages of others when she remained single. He listened to her, gesturing and responding with kind words and understanding nods, wondering all the time why she was opening up to him.

It was in on the twenty-third of July that year that the dam burst. After a long day on the beach, he tossed down three hot dogs before telling Angela he was going to head to the neighborhood pool for a cool dip to clear his head. She was otherwise occupied, finishing a presentation on her recently published book on the fusion of religion and multi-generational dynamics. She had told Peter this could be her big break for exposure. He had not yet read her *opus* despite his promises to do so, and he reiterated his intentions to glance it over once he returned from the pool.

"Of course you will," Angela exasperated humorously as he disappeared into the dark. She picked up the mail, looking with sudden concern at a psychological journal. "I'm going to bed early, so be quiet coming back in."

His swim took longer than he intended. He lingered in the hot tub, staring unnoticed at two girls he remembered from the beach. Senior year in high school, he recalled. Closer to his age. He dallied longer than normal, exploring the line of carnality that youthful charm can provide, but he concluded his evening by asking for their phone numbers instead. He emitted a jaunty whistle as he toweled himself off, his pores opened due to the muggy soak he had just endured for twenty minutes. He wanted to get back to the house and crack open another Michelob in the sanctity of his own room.

In the years that followed, even he could not explain why he went around to the back door, clad only in his swim trunks and flip-flops. He could only chalk it up to some esoteric cosmic force that drew him that way, softly hopping the stone path and not making a sound. He wanted to go through the screened porch and into the kitchen, just to snatch a bag of Ruffles to go with his beer. But this night, just as he looked up at the back yard's towering sugar maple tree, he noticed something was awry. A soft, flickering light illuminated the porch. He peered from behind the sarvisberry bushes, peering through and discovering that Angela was bathing herself in the comfort of a classic celluloid love story. Breathing silently yet steadily, Peter noticed it was *An Affair to Remember.* Old school, he mused. Turner Classic Movies was at it again. He became so engrossed in the movie that it was several minutes before his eyes turned toward Angela, nearing causing himself to gasp.

In the silent gloom, he knew something of the horror he would see. He looked through the bushes and saw her sprawled on the sofa, clad in a black tee shirt and red lounge pants. The ceiling fan was dead still, the television's picture flickering off its recently polished blades, and her right hand was cold and still. Her left arm dangled off the sofa, barely touching one of three empty bottles of wine that surrounded an overturned bottle of Diazepam pills. It was a new bottle, thought Peter, who had not noticed an anxiety relapse within her the entire summer. But new bottle or not, he was too late. Her glassy eyes appraised him with emptiness, and her entire body was as cold as a Minnesota blizzard. That was what caused him to run into the kitchen and vomit into a sink laden with dirty dishes.

The battery of invasions that evening fazed him little. Police came, dusted for prints, questioned him repeatedly, and left seemingly satisfied with his innocence. Words like "no note" and "accidental overdose" lingered well after the chief detective left Peter a calling card, encouraging him to call if he happened to remember anything from that day. Peter nodded and gave the expected promise that he would break anyway. His parents arrived the next day, set about the grim activity of planning her funeral, and were strangely kind for the remainder of the summer until he returned to college near the end of the month.

It was what awaited him in the college mailroom on his return to school that brought his abject grief full circle. There was a package there for him, complete with a compact disc file inside, and a single index card with the words "PASSWORD: PETERV1." It was when he opened the drive that he saw the awful truth. He thanked God his roommates were not there to see his reaction to this evil, the hijacking and destruction of the one soul in the universe he loved and desired more than any other. He noted the comments, line by line, and committed every transgression to memory. He would have his vengeance, thought Peter, and by God, no one would see it coming. He reached forward and touched Angela's picture on his computer screen, and through a pained sigh he elicited a tortured benediction he prayed would pursue her to eternal repose.

BOOK ONE
A Saddened World

(April 2-10)

1

The office phone beeped loudly, jolting Susanna Delcliffe from her routine of setting out the files she would need for her clients' appointments that day. Even though her first session wasn't for another thirty minutes, she had been in the office since seven-thirty. Her husband Phil was on a sales trip three states away, so there had been no reason to stay around the house for a cozy breakfast in his absence. It had taken her less than five minutes to commute from their two-story house off Weidman Road to her parking spot at Dayspring Counseling Center at the intersection of Clayton Road and Highway 141. She usually had the office to herself Monday mornings. Karissa Emerson, the center's vivacious and petite receptionist, would not be in for another fifteen minutes. Rarely did Susanna expect a phone call before Dayspring officially opened for the day. Yet what caused her brow to crease with wonderment was that this was a call patched through the front desk line. She looked at the number on the caller ID. Someone had beaten her to work today, and there was no question who it was. She reached out with anxious curiosity and pulled the handset off the receiver and to her ear.

"Good morning, Trent. What are you doing here?"

"Hi, Susanna," responded Trent Fogarty, director of Dayspring Counseling Center. His voice, while certainly a soothing invitation to clients to tell him their stories of grief, abuse, and need, always struck Susanna as packed full of consternation and uncertainty whenever he spoke to her. Fogarty had been elevated to the position of director four years before, leapfrogging Susanna in the process and turning a stable working environment into an atmosphere fraught with low-grade agitation. The official explanation for the masculine tilt came from the center's supervising organization, Dayspring Community Church, whose grounds were no more than fifty yards from Susanna's office. The church's board of elders had pushed for Fogarty's directorship, and the initial impetus for this declaration had come from the church's senior pastor, the affable yet intrusive Paul Merriwether. Susanna had retrospectively noticed the obsequious nature of the relationship between Fogarty and Merriwether. The midweek golf outings had no doubt cemented a growing friendship that flowered while she herself shouldered much of the behind-the-scenes leadership of the counseling work. While she had resigned herself to Fogarty's presence there, she deplored the sycophantic and intentional progression of his rapport with the church's head man. At times, she could feel the director's manipulative force frothing around her, and she was sure it meant he was up to no good.

"I need to speak with you at some point in the next few minutes," he continued. "Are you free now? I could come to your office."

"You actually surprised me by calling, Trent," she replied. "We can talk over the phone. Where are you calling from? Your car's not in the lot."

"I'm over here at the church. It's about my clients this morning. I was over in Paul's office ..."

I'll bet you were, Susanna thought cynically.

"… and he asked me to come along to the regional conference in town today. We have a few things to discuss before the board meeting next week and he's approached me about switching from being an assistant pastor to being an associate pastor on staff. He was wanting to chat about these things and he thought …"

"Trent," Susanna interrupted, "perhaps you'd better come on over and finish this." She had no intention of discussing it over the phone if he was going to ramble. At that precise moment, the beep of the security system let her know the basement door had opened.

"That was me," Fogarty said, chuckling. "On my cell. One second and I'll be up."

Furious and not wanting it to show, Susanna shoved the last file out of her cabinet and tossed the pile on her desk. She pulled a bottle of Snapple out of a stash beneath her desk and took a few labored sips. When she put the bottle down, Trent Fogarty's form came through the doorway.

The center's director was a tall, athletic individual with dark brown hair that soaked up its share of styling gel. Susanna swore his coif never moved even on the windiest days. Fogarty was wearing a light blue shirt with a red sweater vest, khakis, and docksiders. He rubbed his hands as if warming them up for a difficult manual task. He cocked his head to the right whenever he got nervous, or when he believed confrontation was going to go badly, and his head was cocked extremely far right now.

"What did you need, Trent?" Susanna asked, a thinly veiled level of pique in her voice.

Fogarty paused before skittishly venturing ahead. "Given what I had just mentioned, being out today and all, I'm going to need my clients called or re-directed to others here. I know this is last minute, but the good news is that several of them have met with you or Ethan or Seg or Audrey before. I'm sure we can spread them out and make the load manageable."

Susanna closed her eyes, then turned her head away before facing him again. "Trent, you're right. This is last minute. Not to mention unprofessional. You've done this three times in the last six months, and every time has something to do with the church or some discussion you need to have with Paul. I don't mind helping others out in a time of need, but not when those moments are self-inflicted. Plus, you've had a habit of running late over the past year. I've had to run most of the staff meetings. It feels as if I've been filling some of the gaps but you're the one reaping the benefits."

"Benefits?" Fogarty responded, his head still apprehensively off-center. "Look, I'm sorry, but not everyone can multi-task a counseling office to success during a recession when most people are wanting to save money and deal with their own problems. Not to mention Debbie and I are coming out of our own low points in our marriage. The way you've jumped in on these matters," he slowed down, as if building the suspense, "might look as if you are angling for my position."

The statement, enveloping a hidden accusation, hung in the air as clumsily as an obese hummingbird. The vibe had simmered between the two of them for some time now. Susanna had been patient with Trent Fogarty, playing the role of the loyal soldier despite what she perceived to be some clear misogynistic actions behind the scenes. She gathered herself for her response.

"Listen, Trent, I can sympathize with your plight with Debbie. For heaven's sake, we deal with people's issues every day. But my larger point is that if you are the director of this center, you should conduct yourself that way. I don't think this is a time when we get your appointment list for the day and coordinate who gets what. Discuss this with Karissa at the front desk about how you'd like this done, but don't expect us to do this for you. A last-minute decision to leave for the day isn't our duty to repair."

Fogarty straightened his head and glared at her. "Do you have a problem with me, Susanna? Because you seem to enjoy giving that impression."

Susanna was adept enough at interpreting body language to realize this was exactly where Fogarty had been steering her all along. He was beginning to exude some confidence. His only goal had been to come in here and provoke a fight, and she had played into his hands.

"Tell you what," he said, "Let's set that aside. You're right. I'll call my clients. It'll be a stretch to get them notified before I leave, but I'm sure Karissa can do the rest. But I'm really unsettled by your tone, Susanna. We obviously have neither the time nor the cool heads to discuss this now. But we do need to have some coffee and work through this sometime, sooner rather than later. Our staff looks to us to work through conflict, so we need to hash this out."

"Coffee?" Susanna responded, nearly sarcastically.

"I was thinking we meet for breakfast," he replied smoothly. "Just someplace close by. Nothing wrong with making amends over java and a bagel."

Not satisfied with this new angle to their conversation, Susanna ventured, "Making amends?"

"I should have rephrased that, Susanna. I'm sorry. There are obviously some matters between us, but nothing that can't be worked out."

Susanna crossed her arms and looked out the window, feeling trapped.

She heard Fogarty speak, almost pleadingly, "It's my treat."

She turned toward him. "And just you and me?"

He exhaled slowly, as if she was frustrating some elaborate scheme of his. "Well, if you want someone there to make sure everything goes smoothly, we can have a third party involved. Would you mind if Paul joined us?"

His suggestion sounded canned, as if the entire dialogue had been set up to get to this gauche destination, like a political talk show host slanting the interview toward a question designed to trap the guest. She saw through it and shook her head.

"Trent, I don't think that's wise. It's not that I don't trust him," she swallowed hard at the ease of her own lie. "But I think we need someone who is a little more detached and not on the church staff."

"But doesn't it make sense to have someone from Dayspring Church be part of this, since the center is a ministry of the church?" Fogarty seemed desperate to get his way.

"I'm not saying someone from outside of the church. It makes sense to have a leader involved in this meeting," she replied, her mind whirring frantically to come up with some alternative. The fact she wasn't a member of Dayspring Community Church was a strike against her more often than not. "Maybe an elder on the church board. Someone we both trust."

"Okay," Fogarty hedged uneasily. "Who do you suggest?"

She thought for a second. "Dave Slayden. He's a seasoned leader. Objective. Understands the vision of our counseling program. He'd be a good one. Do you want me to call him?"

Fogarty looked at his watch and said, "No, that's fine. Dave's a good choice." He lifted his wrist closer to his face before saying, "And don't worry about calling him. I'll email him or call him and set it up. How about at Six North Café, say, early morning on Wednesday?"

Susanna wondered where this was going, but against her better judgment found herself saying, "That'll work, Trent. I'll write it down to remind myself. Thanks."

"Actually, thank you," he said with a wide grin, "and now I need to head out. Have a great day and I'll see you Wednesday." He turned to head out her door when he said, "And we also need to prep for the staff meeting later that morning." Not waiting for a response, he glided out and down the hall.

As his footsteps faded, Susanna noticed for the first time her heart was working in overdrive. She hadn't faced an anxiety attack like this for some time, but thankfully she wasn't unprepared. She reached into her purse and unscrewed the cap of her bottle of Klonopin before downing one of the small pills. Opening her laptop, she logged into her email account and sent a brief message to Dave Slayden to ensure he was aware of this upcoming meeting. She hit the "send" button just as she had an epiphany. It would be best, she thought, if she called her husband and took advantage of his wisdom before his day began. She dialed his number on her cell before she was struck with another realization. Trent Fogarty had sneaked out without calling any of his clients.

2

He wasn't meant to wear a tie, thought Cameron Ballack. His tracheotomy tube interfered with a completely buttoned collar, and so his fake Windsor knot hung crookedly from his open neckline. Having left behind the spectators in the arena of conflict, Ballack tried to loosen his navy-and-white polka dot Stafford Executive model as best he could. It was one thing to have trouble with his ensemble from time to time; it was another to do so on the witness stand, and he was glad his time in the box was over.

He felt rather than heard the steps of his detective partner, Tori Vaughan, as she drew abreast of him. "Summers!" she snapped. "What an almighty insufferable broad! The moment I saw she was on the defense team I knew we were in for a day's worth of swatting flies."

Ballack whisked down the hallway in his wheelchair and found conference room number two, as Jackson Boesch had directed him. The assistant prosecuting attorney had prepared Ballack as well as possible for the interrogation that afternoon. Ballack chafed at some of the coaching, but that was due to the nature of the trial, not the prosecution. He knew Boesch was one of the best lawyers around for this event, which was rapidly turning into a circus. Over one year ago, the Ballack-Vaughan duo catapulted themselves to local prominence as they solved the St. Basil's Seminary triple murder case in Defiance. Now they were embroiled in *the* trial, the microscopic scrutiny of which was putting the spotlight on Ballack once more. The news storyline was enhanced by the reality of his continuing personal connection to this attempt at justice. One of the murder victims was seminary student Dieter Witten, whose devotion to graduate labors was matched only by his philandering ways. In the process of identifying the murderer, Ballack had not only saved a school but also earned a girlfriend. The element of intrigue was that he was dating none other than Dana Witten, Dieter's twentysomething widow. Her marriage had been marked by emotional distance and tragedy, but she and Ballack had been steering a decent course that balanced caution and intimacy. Lately though, the imposing reality of this trial had reawakened Dana's sadness, and Ballack found himself wondering how the future verdict might change anything.

He entered the conference room and maneuvered himself to the table while Tori sat down. "You thought it was a shambles in there?" he asked his partner.

"I thought you did fine," Tori replied, "and remember, we do the best we can under any circumstances. You had a steeper mountain to climb than I did."

"You can be honest, Tor," Ballack grumbled. "That was a disaster. Summers knows her job is to throw crap all over the courtroom and hope some of it sticks to the wall and the jury thinks its gold. My gosh, it's hard to believe that we have charges of three murders and two attempted murders and we might get nothing."

"The defense has the advantage," said a weary Jackson Boesch as he entered the room. "We know that going in to every trial. We have to prove; they don't have to disprove."

"Where's Dana?" Ballack asked with trepidation.

Boesch cracked his knuckles after he laid his briefcase on the table. "She said she might be along in a bit."

"I sense there's more you want to say than what you've uttered already about the trial today," replied Ballack.

"I do, but let me get my thoughts together." Boesch looked through his briefcase, shuffling papers at a low rate of speed.

Ballack sat back in his wheelchair and closed his eyes. He began replaying the cross-examination in his mind, remembering every detail.

He was on the floor with a portable microphone in front of him, given that the disabled access into the witness box was non-existent. Defense attorney Sarah Summers had approached him, coming within a couple of yards of his wheelchair. She leafed through several pages of notes while she fixed him with a calculating look, peering through her glasses and then smoothing her ponytail with a quick swish of her right hand. A slight smile formed at the corner of her mouth, one that Ballack did not return. He had no patience for the legal cat-and-mouse game of defense attorneys like Summers, who was known for taking difficult cases guaranteed to generate a tidal wave of press coverage. Boesch had mentioned the day before that Summers was "one of the all-time top fluff weavers" for her ability to obfuscate the prosecution's case. For his part, Ballack wanted this trial executed with efficiency and justice dispensed swiftly.

There were questions both innocuous and punchy, and Ballack spent much of his time answering with brevity and tact, barely meeting Summers' pusillanimous look while staring down the accused just yards away. He only needed to suction his trach once as the testimony wore down his lungs a bit, but in due time, he felt he was in a comfortable rhythm even under duress. That was until Summers unloaded the final shot in her verbal chamber, batting her eyelashes at Ballack briefly. "One last thing, Detective. You are saying my client murdered three people and tried to murder you and your partner. Correct?"

"I am testifying to that, yes," said Ballack, somewhat worried that he couldn't see where this was going.

"The prosecution maintains that the final murder victim was Dieter Witten, correct?"

"Yes," replied Ballack, his concern growing exponentially, his face blank.

"Mr. Witten was married, and he was having an affair, correct? You had mentioned that, and it has been brought up in testimony."

"That's right."

"Mr. Witten's wife's name is ..." Summers pretended to peer through the sheaves of papers in her hands. "Dana. Correct, Detective?"

"Yes," said Ballack in a flat tone, now seeing the corner into which she'd painted him.

"And are you presently in a relationship with Dana Witten?"

Murmurs and quick intakes of breath shot through the room a split second before Boesch roared, "Your Honor, objection! Relevance?"

The question hung in the air like a ballet dancer in *Swan Lake*. Ballack swore that each person in the courtroom craned his neck to hear Judge Bartholomew Kaufman's fiat declaration. He saw Tori by the back door, the veins in her neck sticking out with the tension she was enduring. He looked at the jury holding their collective breath. And he saw Dana, a row behind the prosecutor's bench, her chin resting warily between her balled fists, as if dreading the whole case would collapse like a rotted tree.

"Overruled," Kaufman intoned. "Detective Ballack will answer the question."

"Your Honor ..." protested Boesch.

"I note your objection, Counselor, but the balance of this line of questioning leads me to overrule you this time. Detective Ballack, we will hear your answer."

Ballack saw Dana's eyes go hollow. Whether it was due to fear of losing the trial or fear of what Ballack would profess, he couldn't say. Boesch sat down uneasily in his chair and tossed his new Cartier pen down on the table. The silence grew thick, almost viscous, and the longer it lasted the more Ballack realized it hurt the prosecution's case.

"Yes," he said before the murmurs and shocked gasps burst forth again.

"I'm sorry, Detective. Could you repeat that for the court?" said Summers, who did a lousy job of suppressing her beaming grin.

"I said yes. We've been dating some. I said yes." He allowed the gasps to wash over him and he vaguely heard Summers declare she had no need for further questions. He engaged his power wheelchair and glided toward the courtroom doors. But as he passed Dana he willed himself to glance toward her, just as he noticed her cross her legs and turn toward her left, aiming her back toward him.

"Seriously, Jackson," Ballack asked, willingly himself back to the present. "What do you think?"

Boesch shifted back on his heels and drew himself up to his full height. "That'll be difficult to say. I think we could possibly get four of the five counts. Both the attempted on trying to snuff out you two, and we can probably hope for the murders of Father Jonathan and Dieter to hold up. At least I was saying that yesterday morning when I woke up. Not as confident now."

"That's reassuring," grumbled Tori.

"Look," Ballack sighed, "in truth I don't care if her attempted charge for trying to nail me doesn't hold up. Tori may or may not feel the same. But what I do want is for the murder charges to stick. She confessed to those and now she's trying to hide behind a plea of mental anguish because of family trauma. If those charges don't get a guilty verdict, I'll start wishing I could handle a gun."

"You can't even if you want to, Detective," Tori said bluntly with a hint of a snarl in it. "Maybe we ought to change the subject."

"A change of anything would be nice," said a resolute feminine voice behind them. Ballack turned in his wheelchair and saw Dana for the first time since she had turned her back to him in court. She managed a weak smile, and then looking at Ballack, she dropped her

14

eyes. Ballack groaned inwardly. The clouds of anguish behind those lustrous irises were roiling again, and he had not a clue why.

"You sure appeared out of nowhere," he said to her, taken once again by Dana's simple, graceful presence and quiet beauty. She was wearing a white blouse that complemented her navy blue skirt that just touched the tops of her kneecaps. She wore white sandals on her bare feet and she smoothly removed her sunglasses from atop her head, which she shook to loosen her light brown hair.

"Dana," Boesch said in a measured tone, "before this turns into a mass gathering, I think we need to start talking about what to expect in closing arguments."

"Just a minute," Dana ordered in a curt tone. "I need to talk to my boyfriend."

The room went completely silent, so silent that Ballack could hear his heart thump against his sternum.

"Listen, Dana …" Boesch began.

"That's everyone. You too, Tori," Dana said firmly. "Sorry for being so snippy."

Tori pulled herself out of her chair and walked past Ballack on the way to the door. "Nothing like appreciation," she whispered so that only her partner could hear it.

When it was just the two of them together, Dana closed the door. Ballack, taking stock of their surroundings, cast a glance at the faux wood blinds, then at the table in the center of the room. He faced Dana, not sure what to expect.

She sat down in front of him, and not for the first time, he could sense the heavy waters of exhaustion spill over her soul. She was as beautiful as ever, but something over the past few weeks had aged Dana Witten. It was more than the grueling testimony, the unsuspecting questions, the media crush, or the verdict's uncertainty. Her spirit might not have crashed, thought Ballack, but it certainly had downshifted at tremendous force.

"I'm sorry about what you had to go through up there," she finally said, weakly. "My time on the stand was bad enough, but I think Summers didn't hit me as hard since I'm a woman."

"It's what happens in that room, Dana," Ballack replied carefully. "That's how the game is set up. But I don't think you came in here to talk to me about that."

"I know I haven't been myself lately with this trial, and all ..."

"Dana, I can take a little bit of distance," replied Ballack, "but my issue is that when I finished my testimony, I was staring at your shoulder blades. Do you care to explain why you turned your back to me?"

She flinched, measuring her words before saying, "Because I didn't know what to think, whether to be angry with you or with myself."

"Because I got hit with the relationship question on the stand?"

"I said I didn't know what to think. At first I thought it took you an eternity to answer the question ..."

"Kind of hard for me to get in a word edgewise. Boesch did raise an objection first, you know."

16

"Could you let me finish, Cameron?" she flashed. Her weariness was turning into frustration with him. It was an area they had not entered before. The times they had been able to spend together had been too precious to be laden with anxiety and acerbity. He was experiencing something different here, a Dana he wasn't accustomed to seeing.

She set herself and then continued. "This trial has hurt me, more than you know. I knew it would bring up a lot of emotions. I know and you know that Dieter wasn't the ideal husband. This hasn't been about getting him back. It's about getting what's deserved. It's all I feel can be salvaged from this."

Ballack agreed but this wasn't enlightening him any further. "I realize that, sweetie, but you aren't exactly covering new ground. We talked about this last month." That dinner date at the Cheesecake Factory was still fresh in his mind. Not for the conversation, or even the food, but rather because the storm heads had begun to appear behind her eyes. And now those clouds seemed nearly impregnable.

Dana looked trapped, as if she wanted to reveal something but quickly thought better of it. "These days have dredged up a lot of pain for me. Terrible memories. Brutal memories. Things that went way back in our marriage. Even … even before our marriage. And I've needed to come to grips with them for some time, and this trial has made that learning curve pretty steep."

"So this has nothing to do with my testimony?" he asked.

"To tell you the truth, I know how that would have looked to the jury," she replied. "But anyone might have hesitated, and I was

17

wrong to react to you the way I did. I am sorry, Cameron. It's just …
just …" She stopped, searching for the right nomenclature. Her hands,
clasped together, were shaking slightly.

"Dana?" Ballack ventured.

She looked at him, a tear making its way down her cheek. "I
love you, Cameron."

"Yes," he said. "But …"

"What do you mean?"

Jaw clenched, Ballack composed his thoughts before going on.
"Dana, I love you, too. You know that. You've known that for a while.
But I think it's moments like these when you forget I'm a detective."

"What are you talking about?"

"I know when someone has tried to be as truthful as possible
without revealing everything. I know when someone's showing me
only a few cards and is hiding others. And I know when you're
dancing around and not telling me the whole story."

Dana's eyes sparked with frustration, and she would have
responded had Ballack not preempted her by raising his hand. "My
point is," he continued, "there's been something gnawing at your soul
for some time. And the way that has played out is this: You've grown
comfortable enough with me without entrusting yourself to me. Do
you really think that I'm so out to lunch I can't see it? This isn't about
losing a husband, Dana! Of course, it's about garbage that took place
both when you were married and beyond that! But don't think I don't
see it for what it is. This is about something deep in your bones that
weighs you down! And I know something is there, but you won't tell

me. And I am tired of driving this relationship with the parking brake on!"

His words cut deeply, he saw. Dana flinched as if beaten with Singapore canes. He knew part of the shock came with the bluntness of his words. She cowered from their sheer force.

"I don't …" she began. "I don't have to listen to this."

Ballack shook his head. "Then we've come a long way from this verdict, Dana, whatever it might be. We're left with facing up to what can work or what we know won't. But if you feel like you don't have to listen to me, I think you've made your decision."

"Cameron, you know that's unfair," Dana began, pleading, but at that moment Jackson Boesch opened the door with a perturbed look on his face.

"Dana," he said. "Seriously, you and I need to meet with your family."

She sighed heavily, reaching for his hand and squeezing it lightly. "I'm sorry again," she whispered. "I'll call you, okay? And I'll let you know when the verdict is happening."

"Okay," Ballack replied, putting his wheelchair in gear. "In the meantime, I need to find Tori."

3

Wednesday brought warm temperatures and very little morning breeze. Susanna Delcliffe turned into the parking lot at Six North Cafe, situated just less than two miles west of Dayspring Counseling Center. The establishment sat just beyond the intersection of Clayton and Schoettler Roads, sharing space with a Pulaski Bank and Novak Jewelers. Six North had opened a mere ten months before in an attempt to capitalize on coffee drinking mavens in West County who desired something other than the usual Starbucks. The honeymoon showed no signs of wearing off, as the place was crowded with a chatty mix of suburban professionals and soccer moms.

Susanna opened the front door and headed straight toward the counter, deeply concerned about that morning's conference. Yet she was even more troubled facing it on an empty stomach, so she placed her order of machiatto paired with a blueberry scone. As she waited, she resisted the urge to sweep the interior of the café with her eyes, as she had no desire to hasten a first look. On the other hand, she hadn't see Dave Slayden with a discreet glance. It wasn't like him to be anything but ten minutes early, and since she was three minutes late, this did not bode well for her. A college-aged associate behind the counter called her order number, and she took the plate from him, inhaling the buttery and sweet smell with relish. Turning to find a table, she felt someone tap her shoulder from behind and nearly dropped her plate at the sound of a familiar voice.

"You made it," chuckled Fogarty. "Great. We're back over here."

Susanna turned and faced him. Fogarty was wearing a smile as badly as an oversized pair of sweatpants as he pointed toward the front corner. "Over there," he continued. "We got here about fifteen minutes ago. You might not have seen us tucked away there. You seemed to be preoccupied on your entry."

"I would guess so," muttered Susanna. "Did you and Dave already order?"

"I did, but Dave isn't here. We felt we had who we needed, so Dave allowed us to carry on."

"What do you mean, Trent?" she asked, clearly dreading where she saw this going. "You never told me about Dave not being here. He was my explicit suggestion and we agreed on this! So when you say 'we,' who do you mean?" Her heels clacked on the floor as they turned into the corner nook.

"Susanna! Good morning!" exclaimed the voice of pastor Paul Merriwether. For the second time in a minute, she almost dropped her plate.

Merriwether slid from behind the table and offered his hand to her. Dazed and outraged, she took it lightly in hers, shaking it once before struggling to her seat. This most certainly wasn't in the plans and Susanna knew the odds were more stacked against her than ever. She looked over her shoulder to the nearest exit, but—as if reading her mind—Fogarty sat down next to her and barred any path to the outside. He crossed his legs and smiled at her again, as if daring her to fight against this human siege.

She tore her eyes away from her fellow counselor, only to find herself looking at Merriwether. While she had misgivings about Fogarty's character and leadership, she deplored the Dayspring senior pastor outright. Merriwether sat down, decked in his pastoral finery—a mint green button-down shirt and navy slacks with loafers. He was in his mid-fifties, owl-featured and thatch-haired, and on Sunday mornings he exuded an image that walked the tightrope between kindly father and best friend. His sermons began with biblical texts and contemporary quotations, with a video sprinkled in for good measure on the big screen—what Susanna privately mocked as the "SpiritTron." It seemed that no matter where he began in any sermon, he ended up beating the phrase "relevance to our relationships" into the ground like it was a croquet peg. The five hundred member strong Dayspring congregation talked up his messages as if they were on a par with a Churchill speech during wartime. Susanna never publically ventured her opinion to others, having only heard Merriwether preach a select few times. She and Phil were members at First Evangelical Free Church on Carman Road, but occasionally they would attend Dayspring. Discussion of ministerial performance was not a common activity for them, but Susanna couldn't stop a nagging sensation that Merriwether just didn't impress her. It wasn't she, but Phil, who put it into words after they had gone to Fogarty's ordination service a few years before. Merriwether had not preached, but Warren Hobbs had done so in his role as associate pastor. Hobbs had stumbled through an insipid twenty minutes of monologue, and it was Phil who turned to Susanna when they stopped in at a Steak 'n Shake that night.

"You see how he does it, don't you?" he asked.

"What do you mean?"

He couldn't avoid snickering. "You're the counselor and I notice the vibe instead. I'm talking about Merriwether. The reason why he looks so good. It's not that he's a sharp tack. He's not even that brilliant, for heaven's sake. But he looks good by comparison. You have Warren, you take Trent, even that youth pastor … Chris what's-his-name. None of them can communicate their way out of a paper bag. None of them even look comfortable on that stage. It's like they stepped into shoes filled with tobacco juice. It's painful. And yet, I'd bet that when the time comes, they don't promote you to director. It'll be Trent." That quiet diatribe pulsated in her heart as she calculated the brutal chances before her.

Merriwether began. "Susanna, I believe you know that Trent asked for this meeting so that we could clear the air and help everyone come to an agreement about the direction of the center." He took a sip of his coffee and held up his palm as if to restrain Susanna from the slightest possibility of responding. "I believe we all would admit that no one's record here is spotless. Trent admits that he has not been up front with you about all the matters he has faced while making the transition to director. I probably have not been helpful because I haven't stepped into these matters as quickly as I should. But we need to hash out the concerns that are before us today and take the proper action steps to ensure a healthy environment for all the counselors on staff."

"You felt you could do that without Dave Slayden here, when I requested him, when I confirmed he'd be here?" Susanna blurted. She stopped for a moment, worried her anger would start to run off the tracks. "This was something Trent and I agreed on. Now it looks like someone's reneging on the deal."

Merriwether looked at Fogarty, then back to Susanna as a sour look crossed his eyes. "Reneging is not the word here, Susanna," he said, patting the table area in front of her, almost condescendingly. "Dave himself said he wasn't able to come and he felt he was confident the three of us could handle this."

"He said that?"

Susanna's query was sharp, and Merriwether drew back considerably. Fogarty himself picked up his coffee cup and sipped nervously, his own eyes darting to and fro.

"I come here under one assumption," continued Susanna boldly, "That is, I would not be subjected to a conversation without an elder whom I implicitly trust. Dave Slayden is that elder. Now, not only is he not here, but you've also given me different reasons why he isn't here. Either he said he felt the three of us were okay," she said looking at Fogarty, "or he was told he wasn't needed." Here she looked at Merriwether and spoke with a lilted growl.

Before either man could respond, she said plainly, "Bottom line: One of you is lying. I think I have a right to know which one."

Fogarty spoke first. "The issue of who is saying what is not the crux of the issue, Susanna. We are here to discuss some concerns about Dayspring's counseling program, and quite frankly those concerns largely center around you."

Susanna blanched. "What?!"

Merriwether broke in. "We wanted to meet with you today to let you know that for the past several years, we've had a commitment to try and make this vocational union work. What I mean by that is this: You and Trent are to work as a leadership team, he as director and you supporting his leadership with your supplemental direction. All of us at the church truly believe that both of you are immensely talented counselors, and we trust you believe that, too. Either of you would make a great director, even though there can only be one director of the center."

Which you determined should be a man, you misogynistic bigot, Susanna thought as Merriwether paused and sipped his coffee before resuming.

"Furthermore, even if you might disagree with our bylaws, we have had it in place that the director should be a member of Dayspring Church. That means when Perry Scholten left for Chattanooga five years ago, we had five people on staff that fit that bill. While the church membership issue was not the primary matter in our decision, it was one of them."

"Which you never told me," interrupted Susanna, setting her coffee mug down harder than she intended, "until the board of elders was getting ready to vote on us."

"I hope you would realize that was an oversight," put in the suddenly macho Fogarty.

"You're a member of the board, Trent, by being an assistant pastor at the church," she responded. "If you knew, why did you sit on that information? The bottom line is that there was careful consideration, I don't mind having lost out as long as the process was fair. It wasn't. You could at least have been up front about that."

"And it's equally disturbing to us," uttered Merriwether, "that in the four years since what we viewed as a careful, prayerful decision, you have done everything to justify it."

Susanna could not believe what she was hearing. "Excuse me, Paul?" She glared viciously at the senior pastor.

"I want to take the points one by one," he began. "First, several of your clients have mentioned over the past two years that you have become more and more distraught during sessions and that you have griped about unfair treatment. While we have been happy with your work at Dayspring over the past fifteen years, your recent actions are rather confusing."

"Actions during which sessions with which clients?"

Merriwether said nothing, looking around the area and avoiding her eyes.

"Paul, listen," she seethed. "If these are matters that came up with clients, I need to know so I can reconcile these misunderstandings, because I certainly never did this with anyone."

"I'm sorry, Susanna," he replied. "That's not possible with matters of this type of confidentiality."

"Confidentiality? They're my clients! If they shared this with you, it wasn't during a confidential session. Or maybe you're making this all up because there's nothing there!"

Merriwether was clearly shaken by her rage but he went on. "Secondly, there is the matter of what appears to be you trying to take clients away from Trent and suggesting they'd be better seeing you."

Susanna could not believe how this was playing out. "Taking clients from Trent? Good Lord, you cannot be serious! I saw his clients only because they'd come in and find he had run off for some reason and hadn't called them to cancel! What were we supposed to do, turn them away? In retrospect, maybe I should have. Then again, if I went that route, you'd be criticizing me for that move!"

"Susanna!" Fogarty snapped at her, but she wheeled toward him, eyes on fire.

"What, Trent? Are you feeling bold now because Paul has your back? You skip out on your appointments to play golf, and then when I meet your clients' needs and help them, I get blamed for it? Why don't you just admit this was a long-term set-up?"

It was a mistake, and she knew it immediately. It was one thing to know they were ganging up on her. It was another to express that out loud. She felt the helpless sensation of a key trump card withering away from the deck.

Sensing the tide had shifted permanently in his favor, Merriwether leaned in for the coup de grace. "And, quite frankly, there's the matter of your other interests. You publish in a lot of journals and magazines. You put out a lot of material on the Internet.

27

But some of it is … well, for the lack of a better word, it's a little punchy. Criticism of other counselors around the nation is especially noticeable. It's not that we disagree with your conclusions, Susanna. But when you take others to task in public venues, it reflects on the center, which in turn …"

"You're doing this because you feel I'm an embarrassment to your little kingdom?" All sense of caution was long gone. She was going to unload all her guns.

"Before you finish my next sentence, your time spent publishing takes away from valuable time you could have spent mentoring our capable but very young staff. They are licensed but still in need of training. If there is one thing that is a common complaint from them, it is that you've grown distant and haven't been there for them. And from our vantage point, we don't think this will get any better."

"Which people on the staff are you talking about?"

"Susanna, can we just stop the childish …"

"No! You listen to me, Paul," Her voice was so menacing that people from the surrounding tables discreetly listened in, wide-eyed. "You are not going to play this game and create a crisis that doesn't exist. I know for a fact you're lying; just have the guts to say it yourself!"

Both of the men leaned back in their chairs, eying one another for some veiled go-ahead. Merriwether spoke, and when he did, his voice was cagey, yet disturbingly gentle given the rancor of their gathering.

"As I said, from our vantage point, this won't get any better. Given the weight of what you have against you, we think you need to consider what your future in counseling will look like. Because it seems it is best if we part ways with you."

Susanna gave a nasty smirk, closed her eyes, and opened them after a deep breath. "So that's the game for the two of you. A nice sprinkle of revisionist history to benefit you while I was the one who kept the center together. Not just me, but a lot of us picked up your slack, Trent, when you were out golfing. Well, I'm sure you had this wrapped up for a long time, but even I know the bylaws better than you imagine. I happen to know that any dismissal from any staff position at Dayspring requires a vote from the board of elders. And if the person in question requests a personal appeal before the board, you have to grant it! And you can be sure I'll be there! Trust me, I'm not going to go quietly!"

She knew her point had sunk in, for their faces were ashen as she got up and stormed out, leaving her coffee and bagel behind. As she blew through the doors, she furiously dialed a number on her cell phone and made her way to her white Xterra.

Fogarty turned to his boss and spread his hands wide. "Now what?"

With a steely look on his face, Merriwether leaned across the table and scooped Susanna Delcliffe's bagel in his greedy fingers, bringing it to his lips. He chewed for several seconds before nodding, as if given a revelation from above.

"Time to get on the horn with others, Trent. You know what she's like. She'll be there Monday evening with both barrels loaded. We've got to make sure she can't do any damage."

Fogarty watched Merriwether nibble away at what was left of the bagel. He still wasn't convinced they were home free. "And if we can't make sure?" he asked.

Paul Merriwether's expression was icy and his voice was equally frosty. "Then we'll have to neutralize the danger."

4

Blissfully ignorant of the verbal donnybrook that was taking place just across the highway, the other counselors were gathering in the ground floor conference room at Dayspring Counseling Center. Tastefully decorated with minimal furniture expense, the structure doubled as a break room for those in need of a quick bite to eat. A large Formica table sat in the center of the room with nine chairs scattered around it. A sizable picture window looked over the church parking lot and playground. Three leather recliners were positioned on the side of the room opposite the window. A French-door refrigerator with a bottom-level freezer stood in one corner, near the sink counter that held a microwave and an array of newly bought canned sodas. Six counselors buzzed around the room in various levels of activity, all having come through the door which stood below a framed document bearing the center's justification for existence: *"Our mission is to provide healing, hope, and holiness to all who seek help, and to empower them to grow in relationship to God and to others."*

Katie Fish stood by the counter, cutting up a Granny Smith apple with surgical care and precision. Peggy Kimball, the oldest member of the staff, was opening her granola bar and chatting with Katie, largely about the developmental milestones of Peggy's one-year old grandson. Darci Cooper sat near one end of the table on her cell phone, imploring her husband to confirm their dinner reservations for that evening. Audrey Sneller moved around and sat down next to her. She was Dayspring's resident expert on art and narrative therapy, and even though she was the youngest member of the staff, she was already its primary go-to person for children. Smiling, she greeted Katie and Peggy with a wave as the two older ladies approached the table and fell into conversation with them.

In the meantime, one of the two figures in the recliners by the north wall stretched and tossed a copy of the *St. Louis Post-Dispatch* onto a coffee table. He leaned over to tighten the knot in his left shoe, and upon straightening up, he shook his fine, flowing black hair. His face was strong and angular, his eyes so brown that most people claimed they were black. It was both his appearance and mysterious temperament that earned him the nickname "the Gypsy."

But this morning, Seg Mulgakov seemed oblivious to labels such as those. He whacked his comrade playfully on the knee. Ethan Warrick looked up in response to his colleague's maneuver and raised his eyes questioningly.

"So," said Mulgakov quietly, "Where are they?"

Warrick craned his neck and ran his fingers through his dirty blond hair. "Trent and Susanna? Probably not back from breakfast at their version of the United Nations. They usually don't run this late. Maybe lost track of the time."

"You think there's any truth …" Mulgakov replied, dropping his voice when he saw Darci and Audrey cast a glance back toward them, "… you don't think something's going down regarding this place, do you?"

"Regarding what? They've had breakfast before, Seg. You think they're actually not having breakfast?" Warrick said with a wink.

"You're sickening," winced Mulgakov. "I know they've had breakfast before. But it's never been on a staff meeting day. We have clients to see in a couple hours, and I'd like to prepare a bit for mine. It's like Trent to lose track of time, but Susanna is pretty regimented."

Warrick dismissed any cloud of worry with a wave of his hand. "If that's the case, I'm sure they'd cancel the meeting if they were grossly late, or they'll shorten it if they are somewhat delayed. It's nothing to be worried about, Seg. They'll arrive soon."

A knock on the door by the sink counter caught everyone's attention, and Warrick smiled when he saw the source of the rapping sound.

"Speaking of arriving soon, my breakfast is here."

He crossed the room in several quick bounds and opened the door wide. In stepped a politely smiling young lady who was dressed in blue jeans, a blue v-neck windbreaker over a white crew neck shirt, and a pair of gray Lands End snow trekkers. She stood a shade less than five feet, four inches, and her brown hair was pony-tailed and threaded through a St. Louis Cardinals baseball cap. Her eyes warily looked around the group, as if she was concerned they might be analyzing her psyche.

"Hi, Jill. You made it," said Warrick, taking a Chick-Fil-A bag from her and giving her a peck on the cheek. "Thanks for picking it up, babe."

"Be glad I wasn't later. Traffic coming out Manchester was horrendous," she said. "I need to head out. Getting in my workout before going to Children's."

"I thought you didn't have to work this morning," Warrick replied.

Jill looked at him blankly. "I thought I told you that. My shift today is from one to nine-thirty. That's why we couldn't go out tonight. Just call me later and we'll figure something out for this weekend, I guess."

Darci Cooper came forward and held out her hand. "I'm sorry. I haven't met you before. I'm Darci, the latest edition on the staff. What's your position at Children's? I was there previously in the psychology department until four months ago."

Jill shook her hand, "Sure. I'm surprised Ethan hasn't mentioned me. I was about to say I know all the other counselors, but you looked unfamiliar. My name's Jill Ballack. I seem to remember seeing you around the hospital before, but I was in a different area. I'm in Child Life. Play therapy, visiting kids in the ICU, creative arts, helping them and their parents emotionally prepare for major surgery. A little bit of everything, and just my cup of tea."

"Well, it's a critical area," Cooper replied with admiration. "Glad to meet you."

"You too," Jill replied, then turning to her boyfriend, said, "Gotta go. Remember to call me later."

"Yes, dear," Warrick winked, watching her make her way to and out the door.

"How long have you two been dating, Ethan?" The question was Katie Fish's.

Warrick looked up at the ceiling, as if the tiles could coalesce the exact answer for him. "About two years now. Quite serious, if you ask me. Thinking of popping the question in a few days."

"Wow," exclaimed Peggy Kimball. "That's come out of nowhere."

"Are you confident in the return?" Mulgakov asked.

"If I wasn't, I sure wouldn't be asking, chum." Warrick confidently laughed.

As if on cue, the counselors sat around the table together as the chime alerted them someone had entered the front door. Warrick opened his bag to find two chicken biscuits, a packet of mayonnaise, and a serving of Polynesian sauce. He also pulled out two tubs of half-and-half and three packs of sugar. He doctored his coffee as the steps overhead thundered ominously. Seg Mulgakov, Darci Cooper, and Katie Fish looked up in confusion.

"Whoever that is, they are not in the most pleasant of moods," remarked Katie.

The normally reserved Audrey Sneller leaned toward Warrick. "She's a sweet girl, Ethan. You guys make a great couple. Interesting last name, Ballack. Is she Polish?"

Warrick shook his head vigorously as he bit into his chicken biscuit, the mayonnaise bulging out one side and spilling to the table. "It's a German name, actually. You might know of her brother. Police detective. In a wheelchair no less. Remember the murder at the Cathedral Basilica last fall? He was the lead detective on that case. Not secondary. Lead detective. How do you like that?"

Kimball looked skeptical. "How was he able to get on the force? Doesn't seem like the type of route one would take to get there."

"You'll have to ask him yourself, Peg. I've only met him a few times. He lives with their folks and the house is rigged for his needs. Has a great man cave in the basement."

Mulgakov rolled his eyes as the forceful steps upstairs drew closer to the west stairwell. "Whoever he is, he could come in handy for us if things get brutal around here."

The others looked at him dazedly for the remark. "What are you talking about, Seg?" implored Warrick.

He never got the chance to reply. The incensed footfalls were a vicious cascade down the stairs, and they belonged to none other than Susanna Delcliffe. The assistant director swept around the table, slapped a cluster of files at her place, and sat down, scooting her chair toward the table's edge in a graceless fashion. He eyes were puffy and red, her breathing unsteady. The ladies dropped their eyes shamefully, worried by what could have precipitated this. Mulgakov and Warrick exchanged glances, the Bulgarian raising his eyebrows knowingly and drumming his fingers on his leg.

It was when Susanna Delcliffe cleared her throat that Audrey Sneller, of all people, ventured into the breach. "Are we going to wait for Trent to arrive?" she inquired shakily.

The assistant director tapped her papers on the table's surface, then raised her flashing eyes to everyone. Her voice was low, flat, and soulless. "Trent feels it's more important to be elsewhere than here.

36

And we are at eight-thirty. It's time to get started. I'm leading this meeting. Let's begin."

5

Clicking the "save" button, Ballack pumped his fist with relief that his last report of the morning was filed. The post-breakfast office work at the St. Charles Police Detective Bureau was a pleasant alternative to incessant handwringing over an impending verdict. Ballack continued to hope for the best, a clean sweep on all the charges. He knew, though, that a guilty declaration on all five was as likely as John the Baptist avoiding water. He checked the time on his cell phone as they waited a mercilessly long time. Tori tapped her foot, and Ballack noticed her face work itself into a diminutive scowl. Getting any banter going this morning had been noticeably problematic. More was going on with them than the results of this trial.

Hoping a few words might get her to drop her guard, Ballack offered, "Maybe by the end of this, Dana will get her bearings. I have to say it's been like dealing with a completely different person."

At first Ballack didn't think his comment would crowbar anything from his partner until Tori said, "Maybe when this all is over, everyone will be different. Both those who have a stake in this and those who don't."

"Why should the latter group be of concern to us?" asked Ballack.

Tori shook her head. "I was just thinking about Paula."

"Why her?"

"She's been in a nasty mood off and on for a while," Tori began, clearly upset over the behavior of her ninth-grade daughter, "and then when she's not biting my head off, she looks like she's about to cry her eyes out. Can't say I blame her for the confusion. It's not like I've been home enough to be a mom, and even then, she's probably found better company in her friends."

"Is she still dating what's-his-name?" asked Ballack, his voice noticeably gentler.

Tori's jaw tightened and she nodded her head. "Going to the prom with him." She looked as she might say more, but Ballack's cell phone announced an incoming call.

"Hang on," he said with renewed vigor. "It's Boesch. Maybe they've got a decision upcoming." He pressed the device to his ear. "Good morning, Counselor. Are you calling to inform me that the jury has reached a decision?"

"Reached?" Boesch practically shouted into the phone. "Where the devil have you been? They just announced it and now I'm dealing with the fallout! Where were you?!"

Ballack's blood ran cold, his mind scrambling to comprehend what was happening. "What do you mean, Jackson? They just declared the verdict? Dana was supposed to call me and tell me when it was imminent!"

"And did she?"

"I've had my cell on at full volume and been checking every few minutes, Counselor. I swear ... scout's honor."

"God in heaven," muttered Boesch on the other end, "what a disaster this has been!"

"What's going on?" whispered Tori to Ballack, who put up a finger.

"Jackson, seriously," Ballack begged. "What were the results?"

"I can tell you, but you're not going to like ..."

"JUST TELL ME!" Ballack screamed.

Boesch paused before continuing. "The first charge of first-degree murder, they found not guilty."

"Good heavens," Ballack snapped sarcastically. "Nothing like confessing and then withdrawing it later. What a time to be alive. Next?"

"The second charge of murder, the one in the library. The jury called that guilty as charged."

"That's better, but it's not the one we're thinking about, Jackson. What about Dieter? What'd they say?"

Boesch hesitated, long enough where Ballack knew. "Come on, Counselor," he groaned. "It was second-degree, unlike the first two. What is it?"

"Not guilty," replied Boesch after an extended pause. "That's where the roof caved in. Dana fell to the floor and wailed like a baby. It was so horrifying. Kaufman even ordered her to get up as if she was being a nuisance."

And I wasn't there, thought Ballack. *Why didn't she call to let me know they'd reached a verdict?* He steeled himself. "And the attempted murder charges?"

"Guilty of trying to murder Tori," said Boesch. "Not guilty of trying to knock you off."

With all the force he could muster, Ballack blew the air out of his mouth, sending a small trickle of blood cascading over his chin. He wiped it savagely, and then he realized the truth. He had bitten his own tongue in anger at some point when Boesch had been speaking.

"I'm sorry, Detective. We got two of the five, but the two big ones we couldn't grab. Summers did her job, and we didn't convince the jury. That's all."

Ballack signaled the results to Tori, to which she slammed her fist down on the desk and stormed off toward the bathroom.

It pained Ballack to speak again, but the question had to be asked. "Do you think it had anything to do with my testimony?"

"Detective, you know how I feel about that."

"I didn't ask you what you *felt*! I asked 'what do you think'?" Ballack growled, and the acerbic nature of his voice was enough to make him wonder if Boesch would simply hang up.

But the attorney was completely professional. "No, it didn't. And that's God's honest truth. I told Dana the same thing when she calmed down enough to listen. And I told her parents likewise. Even her father said, 'No, you're absolutely right. Cameron was sterling in the box. Nothing more he could've done.'"

"That seems completely beyond the point now, but thanks anyway." The buzz of his cell phone alerted him to an incoming call. "Someone's trying to break in on us. Thanks for everything, Counselor."

"No sweat, Detective. I'll be seeing you."

Ballack pressed the answer button. "Hello?"

A halting, hesitant voice answered his. "Hi, Cameron. I'm sorry I didn't call you."

"Boesch just called me and told me everything, Dana."

Again the aggrieved pause. "I guessed he might do that."

"I'm sorry, Dana," Ballack uttered, groping for words that would keep his frustration at bay. "I hoped it would be different. It's not justice, and I'm so sorry."

That only sent Dana into another crying spell. After half a minute, she said, "I'm sorry I didn't call you."

"You said that before."

She said nothing in return.

"Is there a reason you didn't want me there?" Ballack continued, an icier edge to his voice.

"I needed you there, Cameron."

"And yet you didn't call to let me know they reached a verdict. We could've been there in twenty minutes."

"I needed you there, Cameron," Dana moaned, "and yet, to be honest, I didn't *want* you there."

Ballack shut his eyes, pushing back against the wall of emotion. Whoever this person happened to be, she wasn't the same Dana he had first met and loved.

"And yet," he said, "you want to call me and let me know you didn't want me there."

"Cameron, please don't make this worse …"

"I'm not trying to, Dana! But I should've been there."

"Yes, you're right," Dana choked. "And I can't be sorry enough. But I'm too sad to dwell on that right now."

Ballack desperately searched for a proper, diplomatic reply but his efforts failed him. "No, I guess you can't, honey. As you wish. I'll talk to you later." And he hung up the phone.

Tori emerged from the bathroom as the sudden clang of an unknown number caused Ballack to lurch. He answered his phone again, dreading what could go wrong now. "Ballack here."

"Cameron?"

The stiff anger within Ballack vaporized as he recognized the smooth intonations of Dana's father. "Mr. Powers, I'm sorry. It's been a hell of a day, but I know it's nothing like what your family, and I know Dana, has had to endure."

"That's what I called to let you know, Cameron," Sam Powers said reassuringly. "I'm just glad you answered your phone."

"Dana called me, sir, and before that Jackson did."

"Yes, I felt I should apologize for my daughter, young man. It was a horrible scene, but it's one for which you should've been here and Dana should have given you advance warning. I asked her why and she was considerably evasive, and I'm sure my extreme disappointment in how she handled it didn't help."

"You don't have to apologize for her, sir," Ballack replied, his voice and his pulse slowing down. "There's nothing to forgive. I'm just so sorry. I feel awful. We did everything right, everything we could. I'm sorry it wasn't enough."

"And I'll tell you there's nothing to forgive there, either. You did the most impressive, commendable job possible given those conditions." He waited, then said in a wavering cadence, "I'm very proud of you, son."

"Thank you, sir," Ballack muttered, overwhelmed by the familial moniker. "And thank you for calling. I'll be in touch. Good bye."

Tori approached him, her eyes red from crying and her few traces of makeup smeared. "I can't remember the last time I wanted to get absolutely beyond drunk. Well, where to, partner?"

Ballack turned from the desk and they headed toward the doors and Ballack poured on the steam with his wheelchair. "Anywhere but here, Tor. Anywhere but here."

6

The pastoral staff offices at Dayspring Community Church were abuzz Friday morning at ten thirty. The coffee pot in the copy room had just pumped out a full supply of Starbucks Gold Coast Blend, at Paul Merriwether's insistence. Anne Fortner, the administrative assistant, left her desk to pour Merriwether a fresh cup of java. Warren Hobbs and Chris Malone let out simultaneous laughs as they ducked into Hobbs' office to discuss a youth skit for Saturday night's service. None of the other office staff had arrived as of yet.

The vacuum of human presence in the office atrium might have seemed inconsequential at the time, but Susanna Delcliffe picked precisely that moment to enter from the hallway of the church and dash past Fortner's desk. Before anyone could discern her incursion, Susanna swept into the back corner office of the senior pastor and strode right up to his desk.

"What in the world is the meaning of this?" barked Merriwether, clearly intending to make others aware. "I'm surprised by your bluster, Susanna, but …"

"But what?" interrupted Susanna. "You didn't think I was serious about my place at the center? You just divined that with the odds stacked against me, I'd just roll over like some wildebeest? None of the above, Paul. I've come here for another reason."

Anne Fortner appeared behind Susanna in the doorway. A questioning look from her was all Merriwether could see. Susanna had come so close she was blocking his line of vision. Slowly but firmly,

45

he waved Anne to back away and she did so. He rested his elbows on his desk and threaded his fingers together.

"With all due respect, Susanna. We've discussed your role here. You know what has been decided. Now if you want to leave well enough alone, we could talk about some other options you have outside of Dayspring. But we made the decision that ..."

"Paul," she interjected again. "There was no 'we'. A meeting in a bagel shop is no 'we' as far as this place goes. I told you that you should have known the board of elders has to vote on this. I know that meeting goes down Monday evening, and I fully intend to be there. This ..." She pulled several white sheets of paper out of a file folder. "This is a copy of a letter my husband and I co-wrote over the last few days while we talked it out long-distance. We made one copy for you, Paul, but we also made copies for every elder on the board, as well as Trent. We are giving these to each of them and I intend to speak forth my case at the elder meeting Monday night."

"Susanna," Merriwether said in a huff, getting up to close the door as he saw Hobbs and Malone looking toward his office, "You need to slow down. We've set the agenda for Monday night. We're having a presentation on this matter before a final vote. Your presence is not part of that."

"Tell that to Dave Slayden."

"What?!"

"Dave added me to the agenda. I get to speak to the board."

Merriwether felt ready to spit fire as a result of this coup d'état, but just before she could spin away and head out, he gathered himself and gave a measured response.

"Okay Susanna, you want time, you have it. But Slayden can't dictate how much time you get. So here it is. You get a grand total of fifteen minutes, counting question and answer time. No more."

Susanna rolled her eyes in mockery. "You think I'd expect anything less, Paul? I'll take fifteen minutes. It'll take me less time than that to make my case. See you Monday." And with a turn of her heel, she was gone.

7

With a pounding heart, Susanna Delcliffe walked into the conference room of Dayspring Community Church the following Monday. Watching her were nine men, dressed in clothes ranging from flannel-and-denim to business casual. These were the ones to whom she would lay bare the facts. They would receive her epistle of logic, clarity, and trumpeting wisdom. That much, she knew, was in her control. But as soon as she looked at the group, her heart went numb. Nine men was not the full amount. Trent Fogarty, thankfully, wasn't there. But neither was one very critical member of this group.

"What's going on?" she asked, looking directly into the shifty eyes of Paul Merriwether. "Where is Dave Slayden?"

"Dave is not able to make it tonight, Susanna," the pastor replied smoothly. "But I don't think you need to worry. You asked for this time, for a hearing of the situation you believe has developed at the counseling center. It is also a time for us to raise concerns amongst ourselves regarding what we should do."

Before Susanna could retort, Merriwether gestured around the entire table. "As you can see, I decided to give each of the elders a copy of your letter. We read it so we could have a sense of the context and be prepared for your discussion."

"You gave them a copy of the letter?" Susanna gasped.

"Yes, I thought it would redeem the time and give you more time for what you truly wanted to say."

"Did I ask you to do so?" Her voice was increasingly strident.

"Susanna," came the calm voice of Robert Finch, the church's bookkeeper. "Can we ask you if you believe all these things are true?"

She felt the ground give way beneath her. Through gritted teeth, she said, "Why else would I write it?"

Several of the elders looked around before dropping their eyes before Merriwether took control of the floor. "While we appreciate your willingness to discuss this matter with us ..."

"Which I thought I was doing now, Paul!" snapped Susanna.

"We find it difficult to have this conversation when you are being so argumentative ..."

"Paul, it's either a conversation or it's not!"

"Okay," said Merriwether in a conciliatory tone, lowering his palms to the table as if he could lower the thermostat on this burgeoning quarrel. The elders to a man looked his way, and Susanna knew that she had already lost them. Merriwether continued with his crowning blow. "And here ..." he said, lifting several sheaves of paper from his briefcase that lay on the floor at his side, "we have what I've alluded to but what the elders agree is fairly hard evidence. In my hand I have several notations and emails from clients and even fellow staff members at Dayspring Counseling Center that speak to an increasingly authoritarian tone in meetings and counseling sessions. People like Trent, Seg, and even Audrey have raised compassionate but firm warnings about what they believe to be a very stubborn course on your part. We have heard a number of these stories and, while you do raise a helpful perspective of your own, we must consider that we have reached a point of no return."

Knowing all was lost, Susanna decided to play one final trump card before exiting this place and the job she loved so much. With a savage smile, she stood to go when she turned around and asked, "Paul, how do the elders hear a number of those stories?"

Silence. No one moved.

Triumphantly, Susanna spoke one last time. "I realize now that I can't continue on in a place dedicated to the glorification of ego rather than the healing of souls. But while you're holding forth this so-called evidence, I'd like to know if you made copies of those for all the elders, too."

Silence again.

"I didn't think so," she spat, pointing at Merriwether while looking around the table. "Remember this, gentlemen, if he does this, how can you trust his integrity on anything else? And if this is a lie, you can bet there's more filth about Paul that can be brought to light. All you have to do is be willing to open your eyes."

And she was gone. The elders remained silent, and while they did so, Paul Merriwether placed the papers—which happened to be a history assignment for his eighth-grade son—in his briefcase before the others could take a peek.

8

One of the blessings of an inevitable dismissal—if one can call it a blessing—is the sense of calm that can pervade once the watershed moment is accepted. While Susanna Delcliffe certainly felt a wave of rage at Paul Merriwether, she was already considering her next move. While this economy might not be the ideal arena for a move to private practice, she couldn't imagine a more thrilling venture. Not working for anyone, but simply having the sole passion of shepherding holistic change was enough gas in her tank for now. She and Phil could sit down once he got back from his sales run in Tennessee later this week. They would consider how much of their savings they might set aside for such a path. The process would hardly be filled with mirth. She wasn't certain he'd be overly enthusiastic about this new direction, not at first anyway. After all, she had been silently mulling it for a few months before broaching the possibility with her husband. But Phil was a patient thinker who was willing to adapt for her good. If he saw it could work, he'd find the way where it would work.

For now, it was time to eat, for she hadn't had a morsel since a late breakfast that morning. She drove across Highway 141 and turned into Lamp and Lantern Village, making a beeline for the McDonald's. She rocketed into the drive-through lane and ordered a McChicken sandwich, a small fries, and the biggest chocolate shake on the menu. Pulling over in the parking lot after getting the food, she spent ten minutes plowing through the meal as if she hadn't eaten in days.

After she sucked out the last bit of chocolate shake, Susanna pulled out her cell phone. In a strange, buoyant mood, she dialed Phil's cell phone, hoping he might be free to hear her tale of hardship and new hope. Her face soured when she heard his voice mail engage. *Probably out for a beer and closing another deal,* she thought, shaking her head. No one handled the art of these like her husband.

"Phil," she said, "Give me a call back tonight if you can, or tomorrow morning if that's better. Everything blew up tonight and it's going to be okay. I have something to bounce off you …"

She trailed off, remembering one more thing she had to do before she told him the grand vision. "Actually, I need to go back to Dayspring and get something. Then we can talk. Call me. I love you. Bye."

It had nearly slipped her mind to go back to her office and print off her entire primary client list. Once she had that, she could spend the entire next day beating Trent Fogarty to the punch and calling her clients, informing them of a potential move to private practice and asking if they wanted to remain with her. It made perfect sense, she thought. Why reinvent the wheel when you can bring the spokes with you? Besides, she normally stayed late on Monday nights to prepare for the Tuesdays she normally went in late. This was hardly out of the routine to be there now.

Yet there was another reason for her return to the office. She had to find that one document, the trump card that—if Paul Merriwether knew it was there—could be devastating to his ministry.

Not that Susanna truly would use it, but idle threats had gone much further before.

Her confidence began to trickle away, however, when she saw the center's interior light on when she pulled into the lot. *Odd,* she thought, bewildered, *no one should be on the campus this time of night.* The counseling offices were normally barren, and the elder board meeting had apparently broken up for the night. Desolation should be the hallmark of this structure at such a late hour.

She entered on the main level, turning left down the hallway, when she saw a bright light spilling into it from her office. Her anger over this trespassing more than overcame any apprehension she felt, and she burst into the room to confront the obtruder. A solitary figure was stooped over her computer at her desk, its back to the door.

"What are you doing here in my office?" she demanded. The interloper slowly turned and faced her, a dark green acrylic mask covering everything from the neck up. Nonplussed, Susanna took two steps closer.

"I'm sorry," came the crisp reply, "I'm so sorry to do this, but it's the only way."

Confused, Susanna was about to turn and run toward the reception desk security alarm when she noticed the blinds had been drawn shut. And with that distraction, she moved too slowly to prevent the attacker's move. Unexpectedly strong arms clamped around her rib cage, squeezing with the power of a python. She tried to breathe and failed miserably, and her panic only served to cut more oxygen from her brain. She felt a rib snap, then another, and then finally her abdomen gave way like dry kindling wood. Heaving for gulps of air that would never come, she collapsed to the floor and lay prone and gagging. And in those final moments, her entire being was shattered with several brutal punches to her back. She felt a weight begin to grow within her and began spitting blood. Her body began to twitch violently and then slowly lurched into silence as her killer quietly swept any damning evidence from the room before extinguishing the light and tiptoeing down the hallway toward the parking lot outside.

9

Karissa Emerson gathered both her purse and her packed lunch from her passenger seat and emerged from her green Ford Fiesta on a temperate yet breezy Tuesday morning. She noticed Susanna Delcliffe's car in its usual place, evidence of her penchant to arrive before the rest of the staff. Tossing her hair, Karissa began covering the few yards to the front door, a routine she had been accustomed to over her ten years as administrative assistant for Dayspring Counseling Center. Until less than a year ago, when she had finally married at the age of fifty-two, the staff of Dayspring had been Karissa's family by default. Introverted by nature, she found it difficult to forge relationships outside of work. Her time at Dayspring Community Church was marked by frustration, mainly due to feeling like an outlier in the single adults group due to her age. Orphaned at age eighteen, when her parents died in a horrific accident on westbound Interstate 44, she never believed she would find the love and intimacy she desired. But Mike had changed all that, giving her a life outside the counseling world. So while she enjoyed her job, she was equally thankful it no longer was the whole of her identity.

But upon reaching the front door, a sense of foreboding invaded her spirit. As she pushed it, she expected the door to swing open. Susanna always left it unlocked and silenced the alarm as a favor to her. This time, however, the door didn't budge.

"Strange," Karissa said, a quizzical look clouding her visage. She fished her keys from her purse, fumbled with the lock, and slipped inside. She deftly punched the alarm code and made her way to her desk in the waiting area. It wasn't, she thought, like Susanna to do that. She placed her purse on the desk and turned down the hallway to her left. Perhaps Susanna was experiencing a resurge of consternation and this was her response. As her de facto confidant, Karissa knew of Susanna's occasional need for her anxiety medication. Given the tension pulsating through the office over the past few months, something like this was certainly forgivable.

She intended to head down to the conference room on the ground floor and place her lunch in the refrigerator, but a quick stop by Susanna's office couldn't hurt. Beginning her journey down the hallway, she called out "Susanna? You here? The door was locked."

No response. Foreboding turned to dread. Karissa's pace quickened as she approached the assistant director's office. The lights were off and it was not like Susanna to work in the dark. Nobody there. Odd. Perhaps she was downstairs. It was when she went to continue her downward journey that her eye caught something on the floor. A shoe. Not just any shoe. A black Walking Cradle sandal purchased last year at Seliga Shoes on Brentwood Boulevard. And the sandal was attached to a human foot.

Pulled by a force she couldn't resist, she fell both screaming and choking into the room, falling with a crash next to the body of Susanna Delcliffe. The eyes stared across the floor at the comfortable sofa. A small mixture of saliva and blood had dried near the mouth. Everything else looked in order throughout the room. But not this. Karissa wept, trying to find her voice as her insides repulsed at the sight. She crawled down the hallway to the bathroom and promptly threw up in the sink. She collapsed to the tile floor and tore off her jacket, turning back to the sink and emitting another deluge of vomit.

Instinctively, she turned to the bathroom door and pressed her foot against it, barring any unseen lurker from barging in. Hands shaking, it took her nearly a minute to open her cell phone and call the church. She knew it was no guarantee anyone would be in just yet, but she had to try. She was relieved when Paul Merriwether answered on the first ring.

"Dayspring Community Church."

"Pastor Paul? It's Karissa. I'm … I'm over here. I need you to come over quickly!"

"Karissa? What's wrong? What's going on?" Merriwether, she could tell, had gone into full blown "comfort mode."

"It's Susanna. I just arrived here and the door was locked. I was headed down the hallway and found her on the floor of her office! She's dead, Pastor Paul! Dead! Please, please, can you come over?"

"Oh, dear God," he muttered. "Oh, Karissa, what a shock. Yes, I'm coming. One moment. First, where are you in the building?"

"I'm in the bathroom. I'm scared. Did something happen to her?"

"Okay, I know this has been a terrible shock and you may feel like you're in danger but if you can, leave the bathroom and lock the front door. Stay nearby and don't let anyone in until I arrive. I'm going to call Trent and let him know and we can both be there with you."

"Shouldn't we call the police first?" she asked through tears.

"We are, Karissa," said Merriwether in his soothing voice, "but this is potentially an extremely delicate situation. We probably don't want a bunch of cop cars flooding the parking lot. That would only invite a media circus."

"But we still need to report it."

"And we are. But we need to use discretion. Listen, I know someone on the force. Something called the Special Investigative Division or a name like that. This is a situation they can work through with some care. I'll call them and they can begin the investigation. Don't worry. I'll handle this."

"Thank you, Pastor Paul," she replied in a choking voice. Her tears had forged rivulets in her facial makeup.

"Just wait for me," he said kindly, "And you did fine. It's only going to be faith and prayer that will get us through this tragedy. Good bye." And he hung up.

PART TWO
A Shaken Landscape

(April 10)

10

In no time, the entire team headed toward the scene from their varied provenances. SID Commissioner Stu Krieger, upon hearing word that the murder had occurred on a church campus, had selected Cameron Ballack and Tori Vaughan to head up the investigation. Ballack, for his part, had demanded that Zane Hull and Missy Crabolli join the team, and Krieger had acquiesced to this with no delay. The four detectives had—after shaking off some initial growing pains—performed admirably the preceding autumn on their first case together. It was as Tori crossed the Missouri River on Interstate 64 eastbound that Ballack called Hull to brief him on the details.

"So what's this pot we're boiling today, C.B.?" Hull queried, using his nickname for Ballack.

"Dayspring Counseling Center on the southeast corner of Clayton and 141," replied Ballack. "It's in the foreground while Dayspring Community Church is in the rear, connected by a parking lot. We've got a member of the counseling staff found dead in her office this morning. Secretary found her and called the senior pastor at the church. Definitely suspicious death, but no one mentioned if it looked like she'd been killed. Hopefully, they haven't mucked up the scene at all."

"Never heard of Dayspring. What franchise are they?"

Ballack smiled at the use of the term *franchise*. "The denomination? Not sure. I think it's some sort of independent Protestant church with the white bread praise band, comfortable seating, video screens, and coffee bar in the lobby. Interestingly, my sister goes there, for what that's worth. Anyhow, Krieger said he was calling Marcus and Sheilah to get them free for this case."

"I just spoke with Marcus," said Hull. Marcus Broadnax was the medical examiner for their previous case, working in hand with forensic expert Sheilah Grimshaw. "He said they'd be there, but likely about thirty minutes or so after we arrive on site."

"Then we can get a preliminary view of the scene, talk to members of the staff who are present, and go from there," said Ballack. "Where are you two now?"

"Missy picked me up at my place and we just passed Lindbergh heading west. Traffic is a bit sluggish. Reports are coming in about a wreck at Mason taking things down a lane. You'll probably get there before we do."

"Take Ballas south to Clayton and go west," Ballack suggested. "That could be the better option. We'll see you when you arrive."

He hung up as Tori blazed around two cars at the Boone's Crossing exit and gunned it past seventy miles an hour. "Everyone's in place. Marcus and Sheilah, too."

"That's a relief," said Tori. "Why was he so interested in the church's affiliation?"

"I don't have a clue, Tor. Although you must admit, we seem to be going through quite the Roledex of world faiths with each passing case. St. Basil's? Orthodox. The Cathedral covered the

Catholic side of things. Now we've got Protestantism in our sights. Makes you wonder."

"Yeah," she chuckled. "Don't count out hitting a synagogue or mosque one day for a case like this."

Ballack smiled as he worked his portable suction to clear out his trach. To the west, the sun battled to work its way through streaked clouds as the Sprinter closed the distance on its journey into the shadow of death.

11

No more than two minutes after Ballack rolled down the van ramp, he was relieved to see Missy Crabolli negotiate her way across traffic and pull into the Dayspring parking lot. Zane Hull tumbled out of the passenger side and trotted over. A Saint Louis County policeman stood guard at the door of the center.

"Here we are again," Hull said in a chirpy voice that belied the cloud hanging over the scene. "Thanks again for the chance to join in."

"I don't think Cam would've taken it if you two weren't part of the deal," added Tori. "He's a tough negotiator."

"How are you doing, Missy?" asked Ballack as the four detectives came together in a tight circle. Although all of them got along fine now, Ballack remembered the rocky start he had with Crabolli last fall and was overcompensating now with friendliness and warmth from the beginning. For her part, Crabolli brought considerable insight to any case, even though her detective abilities could get lost behind her photogenic looks and silky blond hair.

"Ready to get started more than anything," she replied. "Let's head in."

The scene that awaited them upon their entry struck Ballack as that of a clubhouse in an apartment complex. Light blond beams of wood made up the walls and ceilings, and the many windows brought in an abundance of natural light. A desk sat straight ahead from the door entry. To the right was a spacious area of comfortable chairs and tables with neatly arranged stacks of books and magazines. A table near the oversized south-facing picture window supported a station of carafes for regular coffee, decaf, and hot water. Valets containing an array of tea bags and condiments sat on either side of the trifecta of carafes.

"Looks more like a ski lodge," muttered Tori, a split second before her attention turned toward a figure coming down the hallway. Ballack turned with her.

"Good morning, detectives," said a soft-featured man wearing an exhausted face. "I am Paul Merriwether, the pastor at Dayspring Community Church right across the lot here. I'm the one who called the Special Investigative Division when made aware of this tragedy."

Ballack wheeled the few feet between them and extended his hand. "Cameron Ballack, lead detective for this SID team. Good to meet you, Pastor, although the circumstances most certainly are less than ideal. With me are Tori Vaughan, Missy Crabolli, and Zane Hull. Our medical examiner and forensic investigator will be here in due time."

Merriwether swept his eyes over the team, betraying a worried look. "Four detectives? Is that the standard size for a case like this? When I asked for the SID, I was assured there would be discretion and minimal intrusion. As this counseling center is a major ministry of our church, we don't want this to be a public matter that scares away our clients."

Ballack had expected a reaction along these lines, and he made a special effort to control the frustration in his voice. "I think you'll find the prudence you're hoping for is found not in the size of the team but by their collective approach. I can personally vouch for everyone here that we won't be any more 'public' than is absolutely necessary. However, for the purposes of our investigation, we will need to shut this center down for today at least, probably tomorrow as well. I know this will inconvenience your counselors and their clients. But for the purposes of establishing the facts of this case, it's what we need to do."

The pastor looked as if he wanted to protest, then thought better of it. "Then you'll have our cooperation. But we must still deal with the matter of our counselors who have sessions scheduled for today. I have contacted them and asked them to delay their arrival for an hour, but even that means the first of them will be coming in within the next ten minutes. How are we to handle their arrivals?"

"Is this front door the only entry point?" asked Tori.

"No, there is a sliding door entry to the conference room downstairs, accessible from the ground level parking area adjoining the church."

"Then here's what we'll do," ordered Ballack. "Have everyone come in by that lower entry, remain in the conference room, and go nowhere else. We will brief them on our specific requirements after our preliminary sweep of the scene and the victim. But it is important they do exactly as they are told. Have any of them been informed what has happened?"

"I told most of them we had an issue with the security of the center, and thus to delay their coming in," said Merriwether. "The only one I mentioned Mrs. Delcliffe's death to directly was Trent Fogarty, the executive director here and a member of the pastoral staff at the church."

"Was that wise?" The question came flying out of Hull's mouth.

"He's the executive director," Merriwether replied bluntly. "Mrs. Delcliffe was our assistant director. I think it was a situation that warranted full disclosure to him."

"Not necessarily," said Ballack. "I know you could not have been prepared for this, but as a rule, let us handle the announcement to the remainder of the staff. In the meantime, let's post a large sign on the front door directing staff members to enter below and to remain in the conference room. Then lock the front door. We will take a look in Mrs. Delcliffe's office and then we will brief those gathered in the conference room. Before we do so, is the person who discovered the body still here?"

"Mrs. Emerson, yes. I was just with her in the business office. It's the first door there to the right. She's already downstairs."

"Make certain she stays there, but let her know that we will need to speak with her first thing after we take our preliminary look. Remember, all staff members go to the conference room. And no one goes out."

"Detective," said Merriwether. "You don't propose that I remain as well? I have a number of things I need to get to today, and I have a sermon to write for this weekend."

"No one includes you, Pastor," ordered Ballack. "I think your church will survive without you for a few hours. And as for your sermon, today is Tuesday. Something tells me you have plenty of time to play catch up."

12

Once assured they had the entire floor to themselves, Ballack turned to Crabolli. "Better text or call Marcus and tell him to let us know when they arrive. We can let them in the front."

The rest of the team put on soft slippers and gloves for the initial peek into Susanna Delcliffe's office. While the hallway had maintained the same look and décor as the waiting area, the individual offices and consultation rooms bore a marked difference. The walls of the inviting chamber were covered with a calming light blue eggshell paint job. Her two diplomas stood on the west wall. Ballack noted them both, a bachelor's degree in psychology from Iowa State University and a master of arts in counseling from Covenant Seminary. A solid blue love seat sat with its back toward the diplomas, forming a right angle with a larger cream fabric sofa that rested against the north wall. The counselor's computer station stood against the east end of the room, with copious file cabinets on either side. A window on the south wall looked outward toward the church. But the obviously arresting icon was the prone form of Susanna Delcliffe herself on the floor, head gazing leftward with glassy eyes. A pillow from the love seat had fallen near her hip. What also struck Ballack about the room were the drawn shades, making for a difficult light.

Hull snapped his gloves. "Okay, C.B. We're ready."

"Let's ask first what is readily apparent," said Ballack. "The wall hangings look intact and there doesn't seem to be any initial sign of breaking and entering. That we can see, anyway. That doesn't mean it wasn't murder. What do you see by the computer, Missy?"

Crabolli swept her hands over the workspace. "It's not warm. Obviously turned off some time ago. We wouldn't know what to look for in her file cabinets, if anything was missing, even if we did get into them."

"I have no doubt," laughed Ballack, "that you'd be resourceful enough to get in regardless." He had full recall of Crabolli's success in this area from their last case. "Tori, what do you see on the victim?"

"A pool of blood and saliva near the mouth," she reported, kneeling down by the body. "The rigor mortis seems to have set it really well. She's been dead since before midnight last night. And … well, I'll leave this for Sheilah, but there appears to be something lodged in her teeth. Zane, you see this?" She pointed toward the mouth.

Hull stooped and pulled out a rectangular magnifying glass.

"It's a thread. Red in color. Some sort of fabric. Makes you wonder how that got there …"

"Possibly fighting off her attacker?" Crabolli asked.

"No proof it was that," said Ballack. "But we do have to admit, outside of knowledge of her health, that it's a distinct possibility. It would be even more interesting if Marcus finds anything under her fingernails, like skin remnants."

"Um, Detective?" Crabolli cut in. "I'm looking at the workstation plain as day and I just checked the keyboard shelf. Funny thing, there's no keyboard."

"No keyboard?" Tori was practically incredulous.

"Not only that," continued Crabolli. "But it must not have been a wireless keyboard. There's the end of it extending out of the CPU, and it looks like someone cut it loose."

Hull's cell phone beeped and he pressed the talk button. "Hull … Yeah … You made good time … Must've taken Clayton like we did … Okay, we'll let you in."

He turned to Ballack. "They just arrived. I can let them in."

"Do that," said Ballack. "And Tori, if you'd go downstairs and see who has arrived in the last few minutes. I heard the alarm beep several times as if for an open door, so it has to be that reason. Tell them the rest of our team has arrived and we will be with them momentarily for some initial questions. The missing keyboard will be among them, but if they ask how we are investigating this, it's merely a suspicious death for now. Thankfully, I noticed that elevator across the hall. That means I won't have to go the long way around and down to cover the distance."

"Will do," said Tori, snapping the last of nearly thirty photographs of the scene. She put her camera away, but before she moved for the door she asked, "Do we want to nail down a nickname while we're all here?"

She and Ballack had a tradition of assigning a cognomen for their perpetrators in every investigation. Hull and Crabolli perked up the ears and rose to their feet.

"Ideas?" asked Ballack.

"I don't know any famous counselors," said Hull. "Only one I'm familiar with is when R. Lee Ermey played the screaming one on that Geico commercial a couple years back."

"If we're talking about psychology, we could do worse than Sigmund Freud," ventured Crabolli.

"Freud works," announced Ballack. "Now, Zane. Let Marcus and Sheilah in. Tori, talk to the rest downstairs. We'll huddle in the waiting area and let the experts get to work before we all go down."

13

"Slowest elevator ride I ever had," complained Ballack upon dismounting from his traverse to the ground floor. The hallway looked remarkably the same as the upstairs, but as he could see ahead, the conference room bore none of the semblance of the waiting room. A popcorn ceiling was directly overhead, bearing a nickel-plated chandelier that hung over a long meeting table. The space obviously doubled as a break room and lunch nook for the staff, many of whom seemed to have arrived. Paul Merriwether was speaking in hushed tones to a matronly lady in the southwest corner of the room. Most of the others were unmoving or ceremonially quiet. As if picking up an unspoken vibe, they began trickling toward the detectives. As they did so, Ballack noticed one individual in particular. His dirty blond hair was cut nicely, and his six foot two frame moved gracefully toward Ballack, who recognized him immediately.

"Well, Detective Ballack, what an honor, although the circumstances are especially tragic," said Ethan Warrick in as compassionate a tone as he could deliver. "This, um … this is indeed an interesting wrinkle."

"It is indeed," said the wary Ballack. "I knew you had been here, Ethan. I was under the impression this was a previous place of employment."

Warrick shook his head. "Still here, and finding it a rewarding place to be. Under most circumstances, of course."

"You know each other?" exclaimed a female counselor at the table, one who looked no older than twenty-five.

"Remember Jill, who dropped off my breakfast last week? This here is her famous brother, Detective Cameron Ballack, that I had told you about."

"Excuse me," interrupted Merriwether. "You are the brother of the girlfriend of a staff member here at Dayspring, and you are the lead detective for this case?"

Ballack felt the air go frosty around him. He cursed himself inwardly for not remembering Ethan was still working here. His immediate anger was in turn replaced by another concern, if this would be interpreted as such a complication that he'd be taken off the case. His initial sensation was *No, why should that matter?* For one thing, according to him, Ethan Warrick wasn't family. And, even though there had been talk of marriage, there was no guarantee he would become family. But that was beyond his ken now. He needed to get this session going.

"Pastor, that's not an issue for the time at hand," he replied. "We need to begin things as soon as possible here. Sometime later, perhaps it will be conducive to revisit your concern. For now, if everyone could have a seat, please."

Once everyone had done so, the other detectives took their places on different sides of the table. Ballack wheeled himself to the head of the table, looking down the length of it at Merriwether. Warrick sat next to the pastor, on whose other side sat a nervous man with an ornate wedding ring on his left hand and with hair that seemed more carved than styled. Merriwether introduced himself as the center's executive director, Trent Fogarty.

"If I could, I'll run through the rest of the introductions, Detective," said Merriwether as he seemed to be in a terrible rush. "Here with Trent on this side of the table are Peggy Kimball and Audrey Sneller. With Ethan on the other side are Darci Cooper and Seg Mulgakov, along with Karissa Emerson, the center's administrative assistant."

"And these are all the counselors on staff?" inquired Tori, leaning up against the sink counter.

"No, Trent had explained to me earlier that Katie Fish is not scheduled to be in today. Also another counselor, Dennis McDougal, is on vacation with his family in Florida. And …" Here, Merriwether paused before he let anything slip, then continued, "You will inform us of the other."

Ballack leaned back in his wheelchair and gathered himself for the announcement. "It is good to meet you this morning, but the situation before us is one of tragedy for this ministry. Susanna Delcliffe died here at this center last night. Mrs. Emerson discovered the body in her office this morning, and we are viewing it as a suspicious death. As of right now, the medical examiner is there determining time of death and the possible manner thereof. It will be some time before we can allow you all to utilize this facility again. Now that doesn't mean you can't keep your business running. If you can, say, manage some meeting space over at the church temporarily, we have no objection to it. We can even place signs outside here to that effect. We do not want to detain you any longer than necessary, but we will need to question each of you regarding this tragedy."

It was Trent Fogarty who raised protest, with his head cocked far to his right shoulder. "I don't want to push a panic button here, but why are we being questioned? You don't believe anyone here had anything to do with her death, do you?"

Ballack raised his eyebrows to Tori, who said, "We simply want to know several basic matters that we would ask in the scope of any investigation. How long you knew her, were you here last night, were there any recent events in her life of particular difficulty? And other questions, as needed."

When Tori finished, Ballack laid his hands on the table in front of him before fanning them outward. "We can't automatically assume it is even homicide, if that is your concern. Certainly, it has certain hallmarks of a suspicious death but I think we need to say no more about that. However, there is one thing we should figure out at first. When was the last time you were in this building, and when did you leave the building?"

It was Karissa Emerson who found her voice first. "I left yesterday at five and didn't return until this morning."

Fogarty chimed in. "I worked from eleven in the morning until nine last night, when I left and set the alarm. The center always closes at nine."

Peggy Kimball responded next. "I was done at four-thirty yesterday. Left for dinner with my daughter. Never came back until now."

Ballack looked at Seg Mulgakov, who said, "I wasn't here at all yesterday. It was a scheduled day off."

"I was here from nine until noon," said Audrey Sneller, "when Susanna was here. Then I had to go over to Covenant Seminary for a few hours, after which I was back from five until eight-thirty. I left before Trent did and didn't come back until this morning."

Ethan Warrick spoke next. "A short day for me. Ten until three. Had lunch with Susanna in the break room, but after I left the center, I didn't return."

"That leaves you," said Ballack to Darci Cooper.

Darci licked her ample lips before purring forth her answer. "I was here from the lunch hour until nine. I left the same time as Trent and can confirm he set the alarm."

Ballack scratched his left temple with his finger and cast a glance at Hull, who spoke from behind Darci. "You both saw the other leave the parking lot?"

Darci was shocked by the question, and Fogarty's head immediately tilted sideways again.

"Yes," he said. "We left at the same time."

But Hull, like all the detectives, had noticed that Darci had flinched—not merely at the question, but at Fogarty's response. It was Crabolli who jumped on it. "You *both* saw the other *physically leave* the parking lot?"

Fogarty nodded. The suddenly apprehensive Darci Cooper looked down at the table, silently tracing a line with her index finger, before looking up and meekly offering, "Yes."

Uh-huh. Sure, thought Ballack.

His cell phone beeped with a message from Marcus Broadnax, letting the team know things were clear for them to come upstairs.

"We need to return upstairs for the time being," he said firmly. "As you all are to remain here for a little while longer, perhaps you can inform your clients that you need to tweak their appointment times? I assume you'll want to do that before they start realizing they can't get in. In the meantime, we will also need to get fingerprints from each of you, as well."

"We can make those adjustments from the phones down here," said Fogarty.

"As a reminder," said Hull, "Make darn sure you tell them nothing of what has occurred here."

"But certainly they are going to want to know!" blurted Merriwether. "And it's not like we can lie to them!"

"Pastor, before you continue," Ballack replied sharply, "No one is asking or telling these people to lie. But we are not going to compromise the integrity and chances of our investigation! To the rest of you, if you are asked why you are postponing these appointments, then tell them it's due to an unforeseen facility issue."

"An unforeseen facility issue?" Merriwether shot back, shocked. "Are you serious, Detective?"

"Can you explain to me how that's a lie? It's an issue, it was unforeseen, and it's at a facility!" Ballack said. "We're wasting time. You all have work to do, and so do we." And with a nod to his colleagues, they turned toward the elevator down the hall.

14

Ballack rolled into the waiting area, pausing briefly to peek into Susanna Delcliffe's office. Sheilah Grimshaw and her team of forensic investigators were hard at work on the other side of the yellow police tape. The four detectives gathered around Marcus Broadnax, who stood near the coffee kiosk. Having been through a number of murder cases before, Ballack knew instinctively this was where the pursuit of justice took on an even more serious pace. Knowledge of the time and manner of death had a knack for establishing this. It was also during these moments that Ballack was grateful for being the exception rather than the rule within the Special Investigative Division. Normally on its crimes, the SID would have anywhere from ten to twenty experts in detection, forensics, and computer expertise on any one case. But in matters regarding sensitive religious areas which necessitated a hushed process, a squad needed to be meaner yet leaner. Thus, these operations required a mere four detectives, a medical examiner, and a forensics team. Ballack personally felt any more fingers in the pot would be a hindrance.

"Okay, here's what we know," said Broadnax, looking up from his iPad screen full of notes. Ballack noticed he rarely faltered in his delivery or his movements. Even when he moved around the body, he had the smooth, controlled speed of an outfielder. This was an apt analogy, for Broadnax had spent some time playing minor league ball in the Pittsburgh Pirates' organization.

"Sheilah and three of her associates are tearing that place apart and will give you some of the forensic details," he continued. "But as far as the time of death, the rectal temperature is telling us about nine-thirty last night, give or take an hour."

"That would have been just after Fogarty and Cooper left last night," said Tori.

"Or said they did," cautioned Ballack.

"Well, if they just missed it, that makes for some intrigue," Broadnax said, continuing his line of thought. "However, the big storyline is the method of death. Unless we get any medical records on this lady that reveal a major blood disorder, I think we have another murder on our hands."

"Marcus?" Tori said quietly. "Shhh." She lowered her palms toward the ground as if she could do the same with Broadnax's volume. She jerked her thumb toward the ground in the corner, motioning toward an air vent stuck in the ground. The message was obvious: *The vents can carry our sound.* She quickly flipped the notch to close off the vent. Crabolli crossed to the other end of the room to do the same there.

"My bad," confessed Broadnax. "Gather 'round. My point on the mode of murder is this. A quick observation showed no ligature wounds around the neck, nor any blunt force trauma to the head. No gunshots, no knife wound. It was when we checked her back that we found this."

He held up his iPad to show them his pictures, the first one from the list for today. It showed the smooth back of Susanna

81

Delcliffe, by all appearances well-toned and tanned. But the most arresting feature was a massive bruise in her lower back. Its bordering red splotch that surrounded it made this contusion even more grotesque.

"Okay, explain," whispered Hull. "What are we looking at?"

Broadnax whistled softly. "I won't know definitively until we get her on the table today, but I'd be willing to bet on my most intelligent guess. The victim seems to have been attacked by her assailant. That's not only borne out by this photo, but …" he switched to another picture on his iPad. "Here, this one. Notice the bruising here one each side of her rib cage."

"Punched?" asked Tori.

"Doesn't look like the trauma we had with the back bruise, but when I checked the lower ribs it was clear they were broken. Not just cracked. I mean, snapped like the bones were raw spaghetti noodles."

"Meaning that …" began Ballack.

"Whoever did this has a lot of strength. That much is clear. The back bruise, though, is what makes me think this is a calculating perpetrator. Like I said, I won't know for sure until I can do the autopsy. But the redness you see around the bruise tells me that she's got some internal bleeding into her abdominal cavity. She bled out from the inside of her lower back."

"Somebody punched her hard enough to cause that?" asked Crabolli.

"You can," replied Broadnax, taking a sip of coffee he had pilfered from the kiosk. "If you know what you're doing. And I'd bet the farm that this person knew what he—and given the impact, I'd lean strongly toward a male perpetrator—was doing. A punch in that area targets both the renal artery and the renal plexus. Let's take the artery first."

He took out a large college-ruled notebook and sketched out a figure, explaining as he went. "The renal artery arises from the abdominal aorta and connects to the kidney. Hence, renal. From where this spot is, I would bet that the punch—or rather, several sustained punches—severed the artery and caused the blood spillage into the abdominal cavity."

No one spoke, so Broadnax continued. "The renal plexus can be more of a wild card, but even more delicate and susceptible to damage. Think of it as the communication line from the kidney to the spinal cord. It's a conglomeration of filaments, sort of like fibers from the solar plexus, other ganglia …"

"Gang-what?" asked Hull.

"Masses of nerve cells," explained Tori, who relished the chance to remind others she had a nursing background.

"Exactly," Broadnax said. "And the aortic plexus. Basically a cluster of nerves around the aorta. Now if the renal plexus is snapped fairly significantly, the kidney can't communicate with the central nervous system. The victim would likely twitch violently with the onset of death that's already coming with the severing of the renal artery. But the damage to the renal plexus could cause paralysis to surrounding areas, such as the diaphragm. Bottom line is, you're dealing with a pretty strong person to pull this off. Possibly could chop soft wood with his bare hands. And has a solid knowledge of human anatomy."

"Could anyone know this from Wikipedia?" Crabolli inquired.

Broadnax shrugged. "Potentially. But these strikes looked pretty targeted. Specifically executed. It tells me they're at least well-read in this area."

"And you'll be able to tell this when?" asked Ballack.

"Once I get her on the table this afternoon," reminded Broadnax. "But like I said, I think what I described are pretty good odds."

15

"Okay," said Ballack after Broadnax had packed up and left, "We have some time before Sheilah and her crew are done. First thing we need to do is get a batting order. Missy, take Karissa Emerson. She's the secretary who saw the body first. I'll take Paul Merriwether myself."

"We'll need to call Susanna Delcliffe's family," reminded Tori.

"Missy, find out that information from Mrs. Emerson and make the call," Ballack redirected. "However, let's pursue Fogarty and Warrick concurrently with all that. Zane, you take the director. Tori, I want you shadowing Warrick."

"Is that because you know him and Tori doesn't?" asked Crabolli.

"I don't truly know him well, and I'll say it again: He's not family," Ballack hissed, tired of revisiting the issue. "Then split up Darci Cooper and Peggy Kimball, and finally we'll see Audrey Sneller and Seg Mulgakov. In that order. Whoever gets done first gets the next in the lineup. Usually, there's wisdom in doing a two-on-one, but we have a lot of folks here. Be concise and efficient, but cover all the bases. Reiterate when they were last here, how long they knew Mrs. Delcliffe, any personal or professional issues with her, any idea if she was in danger."

"You thinking inside job or outside work, C.B.?" Hull asked.

"I don't know. We won't get a good sense of that until we gauge them. From what Broadnax is saying—if he's right—then Freud could be a pretty strong thoroughbred. There's no evidence yet presented that the alarm went off—it was set, remember. So it looks like an inside job on the surface, but of course we seek an open mind. I'll have a word with Sheilah on the way back down and tell her to get with us before they leave."

Sheilah Grimshaw was in no rush, yet she and her team had already covered the office rather painstakingly when Ballack stopped to speak with her. She was glad to have found some fingerprints, but given their delicate look she knew it couldn't fit Broadnax's estimation of the murderer.

"And besides," said Grimshaw, whose dazzling smile obscured the harsh nature of her vocation. "We went ahead and got the victim's prints, and the ones on the door were an exact match. Nothing else has turned up. However, we did notice the red fabric in the victim's teeth. Are you planning on asking for the clothes they were wearing last night?"

"And if we do," Ballack replied while rolling his eyes, "and if the murderer is among them, how certain can you be that he or she will just hand over a shirt with a teeth runner in the collar?"

"I see your point, but it's something. And the thread could be from a sweater, a shirt, a stocking cap, or anything else. We noted the missing keyboard, by the way. If you ask me, I'd say the murderer was at the computer station when surprised by the victim. The attack was swift and brutal. I'm assuming that since the shades were drawn when you were here, that was the way it had been along. I dusted the cut site on the keyboard wire, but I doubt anything will turn up from that. If so, I'll email you the compiled list of everything."

"That would be helpful. Thank you."

Grimshaw looked down the hall both ways. "Where's the rest of the team?"

"They went downstairs to start the interviews, and I should probably head down as well. Thanks for everything, Sheilah. I assume you'll wait until the body is removed."

She nodded. "Sad she was attacked here. You'd expect to feel safe in an environment like this."

"We thought the same about the Cathedral last autumn, Sheilah," deadpanned Ballack. "I think the world is running out of secure harbors, much to our chagrin."

16

Ballack steered Paul Merriwether into the theater room on the ground floor. The other detectives were busy with their subjects in other rooms but had somehow overlooked this gem. Graced with dark blue—almost black—carpet and comfortable, overstuffed sofas and chairs, the theater boasted a sixty-five inch Sony Bravia flat screen television screen mounted on the wall. The entire space could comfortably fit seven people. Merriwether selected a recliner nearest the door and cautiously lowered himself into the seat.

Ballack seldom sensed a greater feeling of guilt from a subject. He knew that said nothing of whether or not this man—pastor of what was said to be the most friendly and innovative church in the area— was truly Freud. Yet there was a secondary form of guilt, and it could just as easily be exploited. It lay within the man or woman who knew they had not shed innocent blood, but their actions had made this tragedy possible. Why Ballack smelled this out, he couldn't say, but he resolved to discern why.

"How long have you been the pastor here at Dayspring?" he began, thinking a question regarding Merriwether's normal world might put him more at ease.

The pastor stretched and then folded his hands. "I came here about seventeen years ago. The church had experienced a rocky beginning. The first pastor built it up, but once attendance shot past one hundred fifty, he left to start another church in Kansas City. Evidently, he was like that, just a good starter but wouldn't see things through. The church was down to eighty when they called me. We made a number of changes my first year. Went from a traditional worship format toward the one we have today—what some call uber-contemporary. Took out all the hymnals and had all song lyrics projected on the wall, and now we have what we call the Shepherd's Screen, the big video monitor, for that purpose. Also pushed the welcoming and assimilation ministry with small groups, and part of that is reflected in our visitors' center and the Holy Grounds coffee shop."

Ballack did a double take. "Holy Grounds?"

Merriwether nodded with a beaming smile.

"Just making sure," said Ballack, weary of getting the pastor's resume. "The counseling center is related to the church, but in which way?"

"A good question," said Merriwether, leaning forward and turning his palms up. "The center's budget is independent of the church, but we do provide it with some minimal funding every year. This funding covers the cost of our church members who get free sessions if they use Dayspring's counseling services. However, the church's board of elders is the overseeing agency for the center. We oversee any hiring, firing, and promotions, when they occur. And because the center is an official ministry of the church, all the staff members' checks are made out by the church."

Ballack feigned a solemn look at his laptop screen before asking, "Were you here at the center any time last night?"

The cagey eyes grew slightly narrower. "I was on campus, but that was at the church."

"Time?"

"From six-thirty until nine-fifteen."

It was time for Ballack's eyes to narrow. "And why were you there?"

"Board of elders meeting."

"And you left the church at nine-fifteen. Did you come over here at all?"

"I did not. I left the church, called my wife that I was coming home, and was home in five minutes."

Switching gears, Ballack asked, "How long was Susanna Delcliffe here on staff at Dayspring?"

"Fifteen years. She came to us highly recommended on all counts. She was especially strong in mentoring younger counselors and in writing for various publications. She was a very solid assistant director. We'll miss her terribly."

Merriwether had rambled through his answer unconvincingly. "Fifteen years is a long time to serve in one place," Ballack noted. "And you said she was only an assistant director. Why not full blown top dog?"

"Trent Fogarty has been our executive director for the past four years and has served admirably."

"And how many years has he been on staff?"

A pause. "Almost seven total."

Ballack looked up, his suspicions confirmed. "Susanna Delcliffe was on staff for twice as long as Fogarty. At the time of Fogarty's promotion, that meant she'd have been here eleven years and his time was three. Why was he made executive director instead of her?"

And here was the first stab of fear. Ballack saw it conclusively in Merriwether's eyes and could sense the pastor going through a catalog of excuses and buck-passing.

"Well, several things," said Merriwether when he found his voice. "For one, Trent Fogarty is a member of this church, whereas Susanna was not."

Ballack gave a forceful and quizzical look. "So?"

"It's in the center's bylaws that the executive director needs to be a member of the church or a pastor on staff."

His cynicism building, Ballack asked, "And was Susanna aware of that particular bylaw in question?"

"That's neither here nor there, Detective …"

"Pastor," Ballack said tersely, "I determine what is here and what is there. Was she clear on this matter?"

"We made her aware."

"So she knew she couldn't become executive director. Did she want to?"

"Detective …"

"Pastor," said Ballack, his impatience rising, "I think once we speak with her husband, we'll likely find out for ourselves. It would help you tremendously if you laid out the full skinny for now."

Merriwether blew a shot of air through his nose and leaned back in the chair. "For some time, there had been developing problems in the counseling center. Susanna was a good mentor and writer, but her gifts were becoming better suited for outside the center's walls. She had shown a remarkable propensity for taking on cases that should have been handled by Trent, and she would delegate clients to other counselors that would not be a good fit. We were concerned about how well she would continue to work with the rest of the staff, especially when there was leadership friction between she and Trent. We had several recent meetings to deal with these matters and they remained unresolved."

"Was one of these meetings last night?"

Stunned at Ballack's insight and pugnaciousness, Merriwether meekly offered "Yes."

"Was Susanna Delcliffe there at the meeting?"

A pause, then "Yes."

"Was Trent Fogarty?"

"No."

"And was the purpose of said meeting to relieve Susanna Delcliffe of her duties?"

"Now wait a second, Detective! I never said ..."

"Pastor, you didn't have to, and I'll save you the deceptive energy," snapped Ballack, who barely recognized his own voice. "My father is a clergyman. Just up the road at St. Luke's. One thing he's passed on to me is the ability to know when a preacher is hedging on the whole story. I know the code words, I know the tells, I know the body language when a preacher is lying to me. And if you tell me anything other than the plain fact that you guys were cutting Susanna Delcliffe loose, you are lying to me!"

Ballack's voice had turned into a savage growl. The events of the past week had swirled within him, and the vortex had just consumed this man of the cloth in front of him. But this was the pursuit of truth. Why should he apologize to Merriwether for that? It was a gamble, to be sure, but a reasonable one at that.

"Whatever we did last night had no bearing on Susanna's death, Detective."

"First of all," Ballack popped, "that sounds like an admission you did fire her. And secondly, we'll determine if it has a bearing or not. Because it seems like whether her job was at stake or not, she was in danger."

"We can never know that for sure," challenged the pastor.

"Actually, we can determine that," rejoined Ballack, "but after the fact. That's the bad news, sir. And the only good news is that you can finally return to your office."

Merriwether rose from the chair and turned the doorknob. "I assume not to mention any of this at the church just yet?"

"Only if you want to arouse our suspicions," said Ballack, who watched the pastor turn and briskly make for the sliding glass doors at the rear of the conference room.

17

Tori Vaughan was surprised to see her partner step into the conference room the same time as she did. Before going on to their next interviews, she pulled him aside into a computer nook just off the conference room. Ballack took a brief look around and guessed the area doubled as a business office.

"One thing before we go to round two," whispered Tori. "I just talked to Missy. She's taking Peggy Kimball for her second interview. Before she went in, she told me she got hold of Phil Delcliffe, Susanna's husband."

"And how's he doing?" asked Ballack.

"On his way home on the next available plane. He was in Nashville on a medical supply sales trip. Missy said she caught him coming out of St. Thomas' Hospital there and gave him the bad news."

"Is he calling her when he lands here?"

"Affirmative. He's also given permission for an autopsy, so Missy gave him Marcus' number and told him to let Marcus know he was on his way. Chances are if we knock this out we can meet him at the morgue."

"Let's not assume, Tor. We might have other trails to chase, and we don't know when Marcus can get the body on the table. Just a second." Ballack looked off into the distance.

"What?" Tori had seen that look before.

"Normally, we can't subpoena records like Susanna Delcliffe's, right?"

"Normally."

"When either the counselor or the client is alive, right."

"Right," said Tori, recognizing where this was headed.

"Now that our counselor is dead, let's work on trying to subpoena her records, which will take some time, and we can expect some resistance. At the very least, let's look for clients that had any reason to sour on her."

"You think it was a client?"

"I think," said Ballack carefully, "it could well be anyone we meet along the way. In the meantime, let's get our next two. You want to shake down Mulgakov or Sneller?"

"I'd like to see what the man does when I'm staring him down. Besides, the lass seems more your type." Tori peeked her head into the conference room and signaled Seg Mulgakov to follow her.

When both had passed Ballack, he wheeled up to the table where Audrey Sneller sat, nervous as a high-strung kitten. Figuring she had enough upheaval for one morning, Ballack smiled. Eventually, she smiled back.

"Would you want to meet in the theater down here," he began, "or given that you've been through a great deal today, would you rather have a seat in the recliner over there and talk with me?"

Either she found his voice extraordinarily kind or she didn't want to go into a closed room on principle. Whatever the reason, Audrey Sneller nodded. "The recliner, please. Thank you for suggesting it."

After she had plopped in the chair, Ballack made sure his Dragon NaturallySpeaking software was in full gear and ready to transcribe their conversation into written form as it happened, but kept one eye on her. Audrey was far and away the youngest member of the staff, a normally gregarious spirit at five feet four inches tall. Her blond hair fell just past her shoulders, and she was wearing a gold top with her navy slacks. Ballack noticed she was barefoot, having left her shoes behind at the conference table, and when she spoke he detected an enchanting Southern accent.

"Miss Sneller—it is Miss, is it?" Ballack began.

"It is … correct," she responded.

"Once again, I'm Cameron Ballack, and I am the lead SID detective for this investigation. I am asking you these questions simply for the sake of information. I know these can be difficult moments for you, and I don't want you to feel like we have to do this immediately. But the first hours after a death can be the most critical to solve the case, so if you think you can handle a few questions, that would be helpful."

"Thank you, Detective Ballack," drawled Audrey through a sniffle. "I can try."

"Can you tell me something of how you came here to Dayspring? I understand it was relatively recently."

"I've been here less than two years. I was licensed fifteen months ago. I am somewhat new to this area. I grew up in Tennessee. High school in Murphysboro, near Nashville. I went to college at UTC—the University of Tennessee at Chattanooga, and majored in psychology there. I came up here four years ago for the two-year Master of Arts in Counseling program at Covenant Seminary."

"So you graduated in two thousand ten. Did you start here immediately?"

"I interned here. In fact, Susanna was my mentor and she was instrumental in getting me on staff." She lowered her eyes and began to cry. "Everything ... everything I am as a counselor I owe to her. I can't believe she's dead!"

Ballack felt sorry for her, but condolences needed to wait. "What was Mrs. Delcliffe like as a counselor and leader?"

Gathering herself, Audrey searched for the right words. "High expectations, but even-handed. She wanted you to exhibit professionalism and compassion. She had a way of being approachable so you'd want to tell her your life story, but she had a plan for how to proceed from the very beginning."

"Well loved?" asked Ballack.

"Well respected," said Audrey after some thought. "She had so many professional interests and her writing was taking off. Her opinion on paper was much sought after, and so sometimes she'd be presenting some research or doing a book review."

"So people who were well read in the counseling field would be knowledgeable regarding her opinions?"

"I would guess."

Ballack decided to try something new. "Have there been any counselors who left the center since you've arrived? Anyone who has moved on? Anyone who might have had an issue with Mrs. Delcliffe."

Audrey looked slightly worried at the implication in Ballack's question, but she pulled herself together for the answer. "Just one, actually. Jena O'Connor. Darci Cooper is her replacement. She left just last year. There were times when she and Susanna didn't see eye to eye, but truth is there might have been some fallout over when neither became executive director some time back. I try to stay out of office politics, but you don't need good ears around here."

"So where did Jena O'Connor end up?" asked the increasingly intrigued Ballack.

"She went into private practice. I think she and Susanna would still talk, still get together for lunch on occasion. Jena's practice is in Maryland Heights, on McKelvey Road just north of Dorsett. I'm sure she could tell you more. Karissa would know the address. She's still forwarding mail on to her."

"Was Mrs. Delcliffe disappointed that she never got a shot at executive director?" Ballack's question came out of nowhere.

"I … well, we never spoke of it directly, but in my opinion Susanna would have been a great one. It's just that …" Audrey tailed off and looked around. "Detective, if I share something with you, can you promise not to share it with the rest of the staff?"

Ballack quickly rubbed his forehead and looked her dead in the eye. "I can do so, insofar as it makes no impact on the success of the investigation. If I will have to share or verify what you tell me so that we might make a break in this case, I will do so. That may not be what you wanted to hear, but I need to be honest with you."

Audrey nodded and looked down at her feet. "I'm just worried that something might have happened to her. She was in a bad mood last week after a meeting with Trent Fogarty. That could have been nothing, but she followed it up over the next few days by asking Karissa to compile her entire client lists, even from a few years back. She said she needed some past due accounts settled or else. Plus, there was one day she went over to the church in a really ugly mood."

"Do you remember the exact dates on any of these events, Miss Sneller?"

"The meeting with Trent would have been Wednesday last week. They were late to our staff meeting and we always meet every other Wednesday. I'm afraid I can't remember the other dates."

But Ballack already had enough to go on as he asked one final question. "One more thing, Audrey. Do you think anyone would have wanted to harm Mrs. Delcliffe? A client? A member of the church?" He paused for effect. "Someone she knew well?"

It was clear the interview was getting to Audrey Sneller, who shook her head violently, splashing tears over her legs. "No! No! She was a wonderful person. I can't imagine anyone wanting to hurt her. Why would anyone try?"

Ballack engaged his wheelchair power and shut his laptop. Before excusing himself to leave, he leaned in for one final word. "That, Miss Sneller, is the question that most often gets stood on its own head, sad to say. And even sadder, I have to proceed on the assumption that someone wanted to harm her."

18

When Ballack finally got upstairs, he was relieved to discover his other team members had completed their interviews and were waiting on the next directive. He was also surprised to find another had joined them. Lieutenant Scotty Bosco was speaking with Zane Hull when Ballack motored up to them.

"Chief, to what do we owe this honor?" he asked, wondering why he was arriving well after the fact.

"Seeing where you were on all this," said Bosco. "Sorry I wasn't here earlier. Stu let me know about it. I was out in Lake St. Louis and came in at my first available opportunity. There was an intruder at Green Tree Elementary School, so the whole place was on lockdown for ninety minutes and we had to make an arrest. I couldn't well leave my primary objective. Stu understood."

"Who was the intruder?" asked Tori.

"Parent whose ex filed a restraining order against him. The guy was trying to make off with their second-grade daughter by checking her out through the office. He freaked out when the secretary flagged him on the computer, so it was a chase through the whole school until we cornered him in a bathroom."

Ballack stood a few paces away. Lieutenant Bosco was the reason for his rise in the police ranks. Years ago, Bosco had taken a chance on Ballack due in large part to the recommendation of a professor at Missouri Baptist University who had taught both men. Ballack was grateful for Bosco's leadership and advice, but as they had already started this case under Ballack's generalship, he found himself wishing his superior might busy himself elsewhere.

Bosco turned to Ballack and asked, "So where are we?"

"Well," answered Ballack. "Here we finished up with interviews of the whole staff, including the senior pastor of the church. None of them know how the victim bought it, but it's clear we have a murder. Crushed ribs, maybe from a bear hug assault, plus a nasty bruise on her back with a massive edema at the site. Now that it's late morning, we're going to the next phase."

"Which is?"

"Missy will talk to Karissa Emerson and see if she'll hand over a list of past clients with dates and times, but no session notes, of appointments. We may need to subpoena records later. Zane, call ahead to Katie Fish, who is the one staff member available who wasn't in today. You and Missy see her. On the way, comb through the list of clients and see if any jump out as having reason to feel negatively about Susanna Delcliffe. I'm not saying Freud will necessarily be among them, but we have to scope out everything. Tori and I are going to stop in on Jena O'Connor, who left here last year. And for that, we'll need some information from the front desk."

"You've contacted the victim's family?" asked Bosco.

"Missy did," said Hull. "Husband is on the way back from Tennessee on the first flight he gets. We'll connect with him when he lands. I think he wants to see his wife's body. By then Marcus might be working on it at the morgue."

"I can meet him at the airport, if need be," said Bosco.

Ballack turned quickly. "Then I say let's get at it."

19

The intercom on Paul Merriwether's desk buzzed, startling the
pastor and causing him to knock several sheets of paper to the carpeted
floor. He pulled himself together and punched the button. "Yes,
Anne?"

"I'm sorry, sir," came the pleasant, irritation-defying voice of
his administrative assistant, "but Ethan Warrick and Seg Mulgakov
just came in and they were wanting to chat with you. Are you busy?"

Am I busy, Merriwether thought dryly. Then, before a sarcastic
word could erupt from his lungs, he restrained himself. "No, not
tremendously. You can send them in." He retrieved the papers from
the floor, saving himself the embarrassment of others seeing any sort
of mess.

Ethan Warrick and Seg Mulgakov slowly made their way to the
two seats in front of Merriwether's desk. Neither spoke immediately,
as if the death of Susanna Delcliffe had cast an irrepressible pall over
the life of the Dayspring campus. Merriwether, for his part, sensed
within a modicum of suspicion. There was something about these two
men that caused him to feel like he was being watched. What was most
unsettling was the silence that hovered in the room for moments after
all three were seated.

Impatient, Merriwether broke the solemn hush. "Well, I
assume you both are here for a reason."

Both Warrick and Mulgakov glanced at each other before
Warrick took the lead. "I don't think there's any doubt we're pretty

spooked. A colleague shows up dead in her office, so I don't think it can be expected that life goes on. Our first question is, why is the Special Investigative Division involved?"

"I'm sorry," began Merriwether, "for not addressing that initially. When Karissa found Susanna's body, she asked if we should call the police. I agreed, but given the nature of our ministry here—not to mention the critical nature of the counseling center—I felt it best that this be handled as much under the radar as possible. When I spoke to Commander Krieger, I was assured they had a team set up specifically for these circumstances. Usually the SID will have more detectives on a case, but their contingent that deals with religiously-based crimes is small by nature. This discretion is helpful because it won't cause this to go public too quickly."

Mulgakov frowned at this. "But we can't just hide the information. I'm sure Susanna's husband has been told. You can't strong-arm the media forever."

"And we're not," replied Merriwether evenly but firmly. "We'll have a press release ready to go and we'll try to coordinate everything with the investigating team."

Warrick tugged at the hem of his corduroy slacks before fixing his eyes on the pastor. "This doesn't have anything to do with Susanna being at the elders' meeting last night, does it?"

Merriwether hid an incredulous look before the two counselors could see it. "What in the world are you talking about?"

"Come on, Paul. You seriously don't think that when our esteemed directors are going at it behind closed doors that the walls are sufficiently insulated, do you?"

"Susanna Delcliffe was at the elders' meeting last night, that's true. But I fail to follow your reasoning."

"Were you guys cutting her loose?"

So there it is, thought Merriwether.

"That was the word," said Mulgakov with an even darker look in his black eyes.

"Whether or not we were coming to terms with her employment is one thing," said Merriwether. "But I think it is presumptive for any of us to connect those dots together."

"So what was the result after the meeting? Trent never told us."

"Why would he?"

"He said," replied Warrick, "that he would be at the meeting. He was there, wasn't he?"

"Are you sure he said he'd be there?"

"He said so himself."

"When?"

"Told us yesterday that was his plan," said Mulgakov in a tiresome voice.

"Yesterday?"

"That's right."

Merriwether scooted back in his plush office chair. "Then there must be some confusion." He broke off, hopeful that confusion was all it was and dreading what this potentially could mean. "He wasn't there last night. Last minute decision on his part. Did he tell you otherwise today?"

"We haven't seen him since the cops swooped in," said Warrick flatly, "but this news definitely has us worried."

"It's bad enough Susanna died in the same place where we work every day, sir," continued Mulgakov, "but it would be much worse if something was going on where I couldn't trust what's going on behind the scenes."

Desperate to put this fire out, Merriwether held up his hands. "Men, I don't know what's going on, or why Trent told you something that ended up being completely off base. But trust me, I'm going to find out why."

20

The Dodge Sprinter swung westward down Dorsett Road west of Interstate 270. Tori had called ahead to ensure that Jena O'Connor would be at her office. Yes, the office manager had assured her, Mrs. O'Connor was there and if they could wait a few moments for her to finish up an appointment, they could have thirty minutes with her. Having this good fortune dovetail into their schedule put Tori in a good mood, but Ballack was relatively somber. The back-and-forth with Scotty Bosco—a boss he highly respected—had come out of nowhere and Ballack was second-guessing his highly critical response. Not even the phone call to Stu Krieger could assuage his frustrations.

Leaning back in his wheelchair, Ballack replayed the conversation in his mind. It had all the feeling of an Olympic boxing match that ended in a draw but that the referee had desperately wanted to lean in his favor. If Krieger had been annoyed by Ballack's inquisition, he hadn't shown it.

"Yes, I told Scotty about the case and where you guys were on it," said the commander. "But it was more of a need-to-know thing. What's your question about it?"

"Nothing," replied Ballack, feeling slightly edging having this talk with Bosco only a few feet away. "It's just that I—or we—hadn't been informed about other personnel joining a case where the team is kept small by necessity. But if we have something for him to do, then by all means let's get it done."

Krieger, by now used to Ballack's occasional rigorism, chuckled and said, "One thing you need to remember. Whatever I tell someone else about the case, you're still the lead investigator on it. You're completely right to check and make sure there wasn't something going against the book. Scotty has plenty across the river to keep him busy. The question is if you want him on the case with you. Or do you want to have him on as co-counselor?"

"That choice of words is ironic given we're dealing with a flood of psychotherapists ourselves."

"You make the call," encouraged Krieger. "He's SID, but you need to lay out the assignments."

And so that was how Ballack asked Scotty Bosco to rendezvous with the new widower Phil Delcliffe at Lambert Airport. Zane Hull hid his amusement of this situation by promising to call with news of their inquiry with Katie Fish. On the whole, thought Ballack, the confusion had dissipated well. Though he had to admit that Bosco's interjection was unusual, it wasn't going to strain their close relationship. Of course, the extra personnel matter was hardly what was eating him. Rather, it was the systematic weakening of his relationship with Dana that brought out his fresh irritation.

He had no time to reflect further, because they had parked in the lot at New Creations Counseling Clinic. The front glass door of the single-level dark brick structure identified Jena O'Connor as the clinic's director, and the same assistant with whom Tori spoke earlier directed them to a seat in the narthex. The waiting area was considerably more staid than Dayspring. The aura was more appropriate to a dental office, and noticeably lacking was the plethora of coffee and tea selections, although a table held a plate of cookies and some bottled water.

"Detectives Vaughan and Ballack?" came the voice of a medium-tall woman wearing black slacks and a red sleeveless top that clashed with her wavy blond hair. She bore a warm smile and a bold confidence that she could convince anyone of her way of thinking. It didn't hurt, thought Ballack, that she bordered on excessive attractiveness. It was all her could do to keep his focus when she leaned forward to shake his hand, for he noticed her neckline was deceptively low.

"Good morning, Mrs. O'Connor," he got out when he found his voice. "We have a few questions to ask about your time at Dayspring Counseling, specifically about your relationship with Susanna Delcliffe. Could we speak in your office?"

"Certainly," said O'Connor, leading the way and oblivious to any foreboding implied by the presence of two detectives. "And call me Jena, by the way. Can I get either of you anything? Water? Cookies? A soft drink?"

Both detectives kindly refused her offer and waited until she shut the door of her office to speak again.

"First of all, we do want to apologize for the generic nature of this request," continued Ballack. "The reason why we need to speak with you is because Susanna Delcliffe was found dead in her Dayspring office this morning. We have interviewed the staff there, and we are going to be questioning some additional people who have known her. You obviously enter that latter category as a former member of the Dayspring staff."

At the sound of the word *dead*, Jena O'Connor lifted her hand to her mouth and let out a gasp, while her eyes began to swim with tears. Whatever the history between her and Susanna Delcliffe, it seemed obvious she was distraught by the tragic report. Ballack gave a sidelong glance to Tori, whose upturned thumb against her right thigh gave him the signal she believed this sorrow to be sincere.

"Oh my dear God. Dear God!" gasped O'Connor. "How did this happen? Was she hurt? Was she attacked? Did someone break in?"

"As far as we can tell, the alarm wasn't disturbed, but that is just one detail among many. Our medical examiner can likely examine her body more fully at the morgue later today, but we won't know anything more concrete until then. However, it seems best to investigate this as a suspicious death."

"At the very least," sniffed O'Connor before another flood of tears slid from her eyes. "Have you all contacted Phil?"

"Her husband is returning from out of state as we speak," said Tori. "A member of our team will meet him at Lambert upon his arrival."

Ballack wanted to get back to why they came. "We can see this is very difficult news for you to digest, but would you be willing to tell us a bit of your professional relationship with Mrs. Delcliffe?"

"You can't be asking if I did this?" she responded in a shocked voice.

"If you want to cover that from the beginning, we could," said Ballack, raising his eyes slightly.

"I haven't gone by Dayspring since I left there last year," she began, "and as far as being near Susanna, I haven't seen her for three weeks."

"Just where you were last night through now will do fine," said a slightly antsy Tori Vaughan.

"Well, my husband and I had a date night last night. We went to a Chinese buffet on Page for an early dinner around four, then went bowling at Tropicana Lanes in Clayton. We then went to the Galleria to see a movie, went up to Ladue Road for some ice cream at Maggie Moo's, and then we got home around ten. In bed by ten-thirty. Ben— he's my husband—had to be at St. Mary's at seven this morning. He's an anesthesiologist there."

"Did you keep any receipts, just so we can confirm some or all of your story?" said Ballack. "Although I am impressed you were that specific."

"Got the movie ticket right here. We saw the seven o'clock showing of *The Hunger Games*." She reached into her purse and, after a few seconds of fiddling, produced the stub.

Ballack, satisfied for the time being, re-visited his original question about O'Connor's time at Dayspring.

"Well, that was an up-and-down affair," she said, arching back in her chair and revealing a slight portion of her well-toned belly. "Susanna was a dynamo and you could take her several ways. People who needed that energy appreciated her. Those who felt she splashed over the reservoir didn't care for her too much. My own time there ended non-ideally, mainly because there were times she was critical of my counseling method. But there was no doubt in my mind that she was outstanding at what she did, and she was a phenomenal mentor."

"She had criticism of your method? What do you mean by that?" Ballack asked.

"It had to do with my approach to clients. Susanna believes— or I guess we should use the past tense now—that the counselor sets the agenda and gives a clear plan for what therapy should look like from the initial session onward. You lay out the expectations for what interpersonal work and exercises the client will perform, what success will look like, and why you are headed in that direction. I come from a different approach that is more fluid and open, what Susanna called the 'tell-me-your-story' school of thought. Counseling exists for the client to express their life journey since the last session, and then the counselor reacts to the journey with suggestions or soliciting feedback for where the client wants to go from here. Some people find that approach maddening. Others find it liberating. Neither of us was going to change who we were, and it inevitably led to some escalating tensions."

"Was it a problem for you to have her as an assistant director?" asked Tori.

"Not as things went on and resolved of their own volition," O'Connor responded. "We go to Kirk of the Hills Presbyterian, so I know there's an us-versus-them approach from the members of the staff who attend Dayspring for church. So I sympathized with Susanna feeling there was a glass ceiling for her. In time, I was getting the itch to go into private practice myself and break free of the group. So when the chance came to purchase this property and start out on my own, I took it. It's not as high profile as Dayspring, but the daily pressure is a more manageable level. It's basically me and one other woman who works primarily with eating disorders and self-harm disorders. Susanna didn't like my moving on at all, at least not at first. It appeared I was frustrated with her and moving out was a way to avoid that. It wasn't true, but perception can be reality for many. But over the past year we've made a point of getting together for lunch every month and gradually burying whatever hatchet was there."

"What was she like as a boss, as a leader?" said Ballack.

O'Connor looked wistful. "Tough, but fair. Demanding, sometimes beyond what you felt you could produce. But there's no argument she had even higher standards for herself. Prolific writer in all the major counseling publications. Incredibly self-driven woman. And even if she disagreed with you, she'd always hear out your side of things. That's something you never get from Trent Fogarty."

The mention of the executive director's name piqued Ballack's interest. "I gather you're not too keen on Mr. Fogarty."

"All I can say about that," rejoined O'Connor, "is that skipping out on appointments, using your lunch breaks to yell at your wife over the phone, and caddying for Paul Merriwether really doesn't endear you to others."

"Did the other staff members feel the same way?" asked Tori, equally intrigued.

"Scuttlebutt is a powerful thing in a group context. I'd wager about half the counselors there would believe the same about Trent."

It was a powerful accusation, and one that would require a return to Dayspring for confirmation. "You said you got together with Mrs. Delcliffe regularly," said Ballack. "And the last time was three weeks ago. What was the nature of that? Were there things that came up that you would deem unusual?"

O'Connor closed her eyes in an attempt to resurrect the exact memory. "It was the twentieth of March. We had agreed to meet for lunch at Addie's Thai House. It's a little nook at Olive and Woods Mill Road. Susanna was unusually tremulous when she called to confirm our lunch, and I asked her what was going on. She muttered something about the usual office entanglements, but her tone seemed more troubled than normal."

"And you both spoke of this over lunch on the twentieth?" asked Tori.

"Things were coming to a head at Dayspring. Trent Fogarty was skipping out during the day, missing an unusually high number of appointments. Susanna was taking up a lot of the load, even coming in on some of her days off to oversee things, but it was turning into a boomerang. Fogarty and Paul Merriwether capitalized on this, and what any rational soul would have seen as Susanna holding the clinic together, those two were calling insubordination. They actually told her—and leaked to others—that she was trying to make Fogarty look bad."

Ballack looked out the window, gathering his own thoughts. He figured this might have been part of the story. Merriwether hadn't shared any of this with him, but why would he?

"So was she using you as a sounding board?" he asked. "Or was she asking what life was like on the other side as if she was hoping to make a potential leap into private practice herself?"

O'Connor looked surprised. "How did you know?"

"I live and breathe and know how to ask good questions," he replied, sensing that her next words would confirm Audrey Sneller's previous report. "What had she done to take steps in that direction?"

"It was what she was going to do. Obviously, if you are thinking of striking it out on your own, you want to get the clients loyal to you to move with you. She was asking me how I went about keeping my clientele when I moved out here. I advised her that in a situation like that, to request a compiled list, you'd need a good smoke screen to avoid suspicion. What some people would call a white lie."

"Like wanting the entire list to check on delinquent accounts and reasons like that?"

O'Connor straightened in her chair. "You really have me worried, Detective. So again, how did you know?"

"Same answer as before. And I think you've given us a good bit to move on. Here's my card, Mrs. O'Connor. If anything else comes to mind that seems relevant, no matter how small, don't wait around. Just call me."

Ballack discreetly looked away as Jena O'Connor leaned forward. The counselor took one look at his card and nodded. "Believe me, Detectives, I will. Because if someone has taken the life from Susanna's bones, I want to make sure that person pays dearly."

21

"Two-thirty, mate," said Tori once they pulled out onto McKelvey Road. "I wasn't aware we had blown through this much time already."

"Get back to 270 and hopefully the traffic won't be as bad," said Ballack. He dialed Hull's number and waited. "Well, at least we got a tenuous connection. It seems like Susanna Delcliffe was headed out, and she was in the process of taking clients with her. Now the question becomes this: Is her death an inside job, or is it something else?"

"What 'something else' could it be?" asked Tori.

"Well, it … hold on. Zane!" Ballack barked into the phone as he heard Hull's greeting. "Where are you?"

"Didn't get very far with Katie Fish. She had a sinus infection today and that affected how good of an interview she was going to be."

"So you got nowhere with her?"

"I didn't say that, C.B. To her credit she let us into her apartment, but it was hard for us to get a coherent ten minutes squeezed out of her when she was blowing green snot everywhere."

"Thanks, Z, for the image. At least I didn't have lunch yet."

Hull laughed. "So where are you and the queen headed?"

"First of all," Ballack remembered, "can you manage to look through Susanna Delcliffe's client list? Any of them look like things went bad, cut off any further visits, anything of note?"

"We're probably not going to know anything in depth unless we hit a grand slam and subpoena these records. We would be in for a dogfight if we try to hurry along the process. In fact, every legal advice website I've seen maintains that counselors should wait it out, give only the minimum, and so on. You've got to get the records over the counselor's dead body."

"The counselor in this case," Ballack reminded him, "*is* a dead body. But the law is still very specific on what happens when you're dealing with a therapist who's gone tango uniform. The client-counselor privilege stays in effect even after death. I looked it up. You're right. We might have a fight on our hands and we might have to wait it out have a chance."

Ballack heard Crabolli say something in the background before Hull continued. "So what's the next step? Where are you headed?"

"Let us stop by the church and see if any of the counselors are still there. It would be helpful if we could speak with Fogarty at the very least. Merriwether wasn't helpful at all, so if he's around this could be a wasted diversion. We'll be brief there and then head out to the morgue. Tori's waving her cell at me and telling me Marcus is already there."

"Got that," replied Hull. "Also, Missy just said that she heard from Scotty. He's connecting with Phil Delcliffe at the airport. Southwest Airlines flight 1082 nonstop from Music City, if you're interested. He should be in just shy of three o'clock. He wants to come direct to the morgue."

"That's rather chilling."

"Not to watch, but to see her one time before Marcus gets to work and to give permission on the impending autopsy anyhow. Can't say I blame him."

"Nor can I," Ballack mused aloud. "Well, you two head on and meet them there. Maybe interview the husband if he feels up to it. Every additional perspective helps."

"While we're there we can talk about her client list," reminded Hull. "Missy seemed to think there'd be a couple potential leads from that."

"When we cross that bridge, my friend. For now, just get to the morgue and hang tight. We'll see you soon enough once we climb out of purgatory."

22

Ballack was hoping to get at least one member of the Fogarty-Warrick-Mulgakov triad. Two would have been a downright bonus. But upon entering the office at Dayspring Community Church, he was thoroughly overjoyed to find each of them sitting in Fogarty's assistant pastor study. A brief inquiry at Anne Fortner's desk verified that Paul Merriwether was nowhere on the property, and breezing down the hallway, both Ballack and Tori strode right into Fogarty's abode.

Fogarty rose from behind his desk with an indignant look on his face. Warrick and Mulgakov were less annoyed but just as shocked. For his part, Ballack felt no guilt for interrupting their conclave. They were in comfortable enough environs. Mulgakov and Warrick were sitting on an overstuffed leather sofa that dominated an entire wall. Warrick sucked down the last of a bottle of Sobe before tossing it loudly into the trash can next to him. Mulgakov was working his way through a giant can of Arizona Green Tea, while Fogarty placed a granola bar on a napkin on his desk. Tori felt her cell phone buzz in her pocket and she fished it out to observe a message.

"May I ask what brings you here, Detective?" asked the visibly upset Fogarty.

"Working your way through the pawns you didn't get to this morning?" Warrick ventured.

Ballack ignored the bubbling antipathy and got directly to the point. "We're about to meet with Susanna Delcliffe's husband. He is due back in town at any moment. Our concern for the time being is figuring out the noteworthy details of last night. Mr. Fogarty ..."

"Reverend Fogarty," the director corrected him.

"Excuse me?"

"I am ordained to the pastoral ministry. It may seem like a small detail, but the title is important."

Ballack's glance hardened before replying, "Very well, Reverend Fogarty. What was the nature of last night's elder board meeting here at the church?"

Fogarty tipped his head to the side before responding. "I would think you'd remember that sliver of knowledge from this morning, Mr. Ballack. I wasn't ..."

"Detective," Ballack shot back, practically feeling Tori's smile behind him.

"Pardon?"

"I happen to be ordained to the investigative ministry. As someone has said, it may seem like a small detail, but the title is important."

The barb seemed to have a strangely relaxing effect on Warrick and Mulgakov, who hid their wide-eyed looks from Fogarty like seventh-grade schoolboys.

Fogarty recovered, remembering his previous point. "I wasn't at the meeting last night."

"No," said Ballack, "but surely as a member of the church's pastoral staff you'd have an idea what was going on. Maybe someone shared the results with you. Was there to be any discussion of Susanna Delcliffe' job situation by the board of elders?"

"That I was not privy to, Detective," said Fogarty, "and I think it would take only a quick check with Detective Hull to figure that out. He did interview me, after all."

"He did, that's true," smirked Ballack. "But we've already established that you claim not to have been at the meeting last night. But I think pastors in a church environment share any number of details about ecclesiastical intrigue. Did you have any knowledge of the agenda for last night's meeting?"

"None, Detective. I told you that already."

"Not even a line item?"

"No!" barked Fogarty, "And if this is all you came here about …"

"Not even a letter?" Tori's feminine voice carried a good deal of shock in the male-dominated quarters.

"A letter?" It was Mulgakov's voice registering surprise.

"Reverend Fogarty," said Tori, slowly enunciating every syllable of the word *Reverend*. "Did you receive a letter from Phil and Susanna Delcliffe regarding the way she claimed to have been treated? A letter that was addressed to you, Pastor Merriwether, and every elder on the board?"

Ballack knew little of this reactive soul before him, but he knew enough of suspects to understand when one felt caught in a web of circumstances. He could practically see the gears turning in Fogarty's head, searching desperately for an excuse of some nature.

"I'm waiting," Tori said with a hint of exasperation.

"Evidently, I was addressed in this letter," Fogarty finally replied. "Is that what you are saying?"

"What I am saying," Tori uttered, "is that one of our team members has just met with Phil Delcliffe at the airport upon his return. He just confirmed, according to our lieutenant's text message, that he co-wrote this letter, could produce it on his laptop computer, and could show us everyone to whom it was addressed."

Fogarty's head was listing to the side and his left hand began to jiggle. Ballack could feel guilt pouring out of him. Whether it was because of direct iniquity for murder or indirect remorse for complicity, one couldn't say. But the sensation was palpable.

"It seems clear," Ballack addressed all three of the men, "that there was enough emotional C4 around this place to cause a significant explosion. All we have to do, Reverend Fogarty, is to confirm the letter with Phil Delcliffe. And there is one more thing. We will be bringing a demand to subpoena Susanna's session notes and records as vital to our investigation."

"That you cannot do, Detective," growled Fogarty.

"He's right, Cameron," said the unctuous Warrick. "You can't slice and dice the therapist-patient relationship like that."

"First of all, Mr. Warrick, no matter what your relationship to my sister might be, for the course of this investigation, you will still refer to me as 'Detective.' Secondly, I realize the gravity and sanctity of the therapist-client relationship. However, you all need to realize there is one complicating issue: Yes, when the therapist is dead, the relationship with all clients is still in force. Yet you are wrong in saying we can't demand a subpoena of her records. You can dogfight us and refuse all you want, and even successfully bar us from her records through all the legal logorrhea you can muster. But you can't stop us from delivering a request. So a little humility, please. It's the least you can offer."

"I'd say you can expect a fight on this one," Fogarty said defensively.

"And I don't see how this helps your investigation," added Mulgakov.

"Unless you know what or who caused this death," replied Ballack, careful not to reveal too much of the details, "you aren't in position to see what helps or hurts. That's for us to decide. And since there seems to be little headway being made now, we'll decide the next move after we meet with Phil Delcliffe."

23

The St. Louis County medical examiner's office takes up a small portion of real estate just off Hanley Road near St. Louis Lambert International Airport. The Gantner Building was located in the inner-ring suburb of Berkeley, a long way indeed from the Chesterfield enclave where Dayspring was, both in distance and in socioeconomic status. Ballack rolled down the Sprinter's wheelchair ramp and winced at the sound of a Delta jet screaming overhead. Both he and Tori entered the functional, nondescript brick building, hoping to get more answers here than they received at Dayspring.

Ballack's mood had lifted when Crabolli called him with the news that the Chief Medical Examiner had expedited the autopsy. While some members of the police bureaucracy could frustrate him at times, Ballack had the highest respect for Dr. Marney Casson and for her work in improving the activity within the Gantner Building. A major renovation six years before had enhanced the function of the morgue operations. Modern stainless steel cabinetry, improved downdraft ventilation, spacious work surface, and a biological safety cabinet made this a virtual mecca for regional pathologists.

Both Ballack and Tori moved into the heart of the complex. Spotting Marcus Broadnax and a couple assistants through a sliver window, Ballack went off in search of Phil Delcliffe. Leaving Tori to oversee the autopsy, he found Missy Crabolli coming out of an office down the hallway. Scooting forward briskly, he waved her down.

"He's devastated," she said, wiping her eyes one after the other. "Scotty got him calm on the way over, but when he saw her body he lost it all over again. The poor guy wants to hit anything that moves and is showing a lot of restraint, if you ask me."

"Zane in with him now?"

"And making very little headway. Maybe you want to go in and see if you can change things up?"

"I'll give it a shot," said Ballack, and Crabolli held the door open for him.

The man sitting at the table upon Ballack's entry was hardly the sort he envisioned as the new widower. While Susanna was of slender build, Phil Delcliffe was a solid six feet four inches and had to weigh about two hundred sixty pounds. He wore a button-down oxford shirt with wide navy blue vertical stripes, matching blue slacks, and cordovan dress shoes. Ballack noticed a silver chain bracelet on his right wrist, as well as a Mont Blanc pen sticking out of his shirt pocket. It took a few seconds, but Phil Delcliffe finally lifted his head and acknowledged Ballack's arrival.

Hull handled the introductions and then announced he would step out for coffee. If he was upset over Ballack's intrusion, he didn't show it.

"Mr. Delcliffe," said Ballack when the door closed behind Hull, "I am Detective Cameron Ballack and I'm heading up this investigation for the SID. I see you've already met Lieutenant Bosco and Detectives Hull and Crabolli."

126

"I did," said Delcliffe. "They've been very kind ever since I got here."

Ballack endured a noticeable pause before continuing. "I realize this has been a very painful day for you, and I'm extremely sorry for your loss. I do have some questions I need to ask, but given the circumstances of the last few hours I would completely understand if you would want to put them off for a bit."

Delcliffe looked out the door window. "Detective, have you ever lost someone you loved?"

It was an odd question, but Ballack instinctively figured why Delcliffe posed it. "Actually yes, Mr. Delcliffe. When I was ten, my baby brother died. And then four years ago, the girl I was dating at the time committed suicide. It's not information I normally offer but it is part of who I am." He swallowed hard. "And you did ask. So it's only fair."

Delcliffe, still staring out the window, closed his eyes and nodded. "I could tell. Don't ask me how. It was a sense I got when you started speaking. Nothing against the others, but they don't have the earthiness you seem to have." He turned to Ballack. "I'm sorry for rambling. Just some things I noticed. Comes from being married to a counselor."

Ballack returned the nod. "Completely justified."

It was Delcliffe who asked the first question. "How did Susanna die? None of the others have ventured a reason."

Ballack knew that Broadnax was several minutes away from a final call, so he understood his teammates' reticence to divulge anything less than one hundred percent absolute. But he also believed Broadnax would not have put forth a theory unless he had a working hypothesis well beyond reasonable doubt.

"Nothing is written in stone yet," he said slowly, "but given the initial examination we have a decent theory. It's a strong probability she was attacked."

"Where?"

Ballack paused, looking down. "In her office. From what a preliminary examination showed, her ribs were broken and there was a bruise in the middle of her back. That is why the strong case is there for being attacked versus natural death."

When he looked back up at Delcliffe, the widower's eyes were red and moist. "It was someone at Dayspring, right?"

"We're not making any assumptions, Mr. Delcliffe. We obviously have interviewed everyone there on staff, but we are keeping our options open."

"Open?" Delcliffe slammed his fist down on the table. He was screaming. "What are you talking about? Who else would it have been?"

"Mr. Delcliffe," Ballack responded, extending an open palm in the mourner's direction. "That's exactly my point. We have to ask those questions …"

"Not that it seems to be doing you any good!"

Ballack stopped himself from barking back in return. The escalating rage was hardly helping.

"Mr. Delcliffe, I am not denying the possible or even the probable. What I am saying is that we want to find the person who did this, not just anyone with a pulse just to satisfy a search for personal satisfaction. I'm not denying you the right to feel the way you do! But if you can't slow down just a touch for me, I can't do my job, which is solving the matter of your wife's death."

Phil Delcliffe glared at him as if contemplating murder himself. The widower was a veritable volcano ready to blow. Then, just as suddenly, his emotions turned on a dime and he placed his head in his hands, sobbing terribly. The waterworks spilled on and on, Delcliffe weeping for at least three minutes. Finally, with a puddle of salty liquid on the table, he wiped his eyes and looked directly—albeit ashamedly—at Ballack.

"I'm sorry, Detective. I woke up this morning thinking I was a happily married man. Susanna and I have had a wonderful twenty years together. We never had children. We weren't able to. But we were happy. Now I'll never wake up to another day with her at all."

"And that tragedy," replied Ballack after a few moments of respectful silence, "makes our pursuit of justice all the more critical. And that is why I want to stay on track with you. Do you have any idea if someone would want to wish her harm? It could be someone at Dayspring that she mentioned. I don't know if legally she could have talked about certain clients who were especially difficult, but perhaps she told you."

Delcliffe looked thoughtful. "Her major complaints about Dayspring centered around two individuals. Trent Fogarty has been the biggest thorn in her side. She has had to pick up his slack and confront him over his incompetence and indifference. I'm sure you've probably met him, as well as that schemer Paul Merriwether."

"The Dayspring pastor?"

Delcliffe nodded. "The gods he worships are public relations, the adulation of his congregants, and the manipulation of his kingdom there. He's wired to have sycophants. He and Trent have been a potent double team against everything Susanna has worked to become. Their normal modus operandi is to wait for her to speak out and then accuse her of fomenting rebellion. Things finally came to a head last week when I was out of town. Trent and Paul wanted Susanna to meet them over breakfast near the church to talk over their differences. Six North Café was the place. She told them that was fine as long as she had someone else there she trusted to hang with their conversation."

"Someone," said Ballack, "to verify everything that was said."

"Correct."

"That was very wise."

"I would say so. She wanted Dave Slayden, likely the only elder on the church board whom she trusted for a situation like this. Of course, when she showed up for the meeting, Slayden wasn't there. Evidently, Merriwether and Fogarty had told him he wasn't needed."

"They said that to her?"

"They didn't need to. The whole talk was one in which they quickly moved from a let's-work-things-out mentality to one of 'we're pushing you out the door.' That's when she got on the phone with me soon after. When I came home for Easter weekend, we put together a letter of protest and recommendation for change. It was really a note to throw out to the whole board to make sure they knew what went on while Susanna crashed and burned. But we wanted to go out with the moral high ground."

"Do you have that letter?" asked Ballack.

"I can produce it for you, Detective."

"Thank you, sir. And did she have any other contact with them before today?"

"Yes," said Delcliffe. "She attended the board meeting last night and presented the letter to everyone. Neither Fogarty nor Slayden were there, interestingly enough. She texted me that."

"If we can check that message, if you still have it, that would be helpful as well. Now, Fogarty said he was at the counseling center for his appointments, according to our group discussion with the entire staff."

"And you believe that?"

"I have to take everything with a grain of salt, Mr. Delcliffe. Did Susanna call you after the meeting?"

"She went out to eat, called me, and got my voice mail. I still have it, if you would like to listen."

"Yes, I would. Thank you."

It took little time for Delcliffe to get to the message. Ballack listened to it twice.

"What did she mean," asked the detective, "that everything would be okay and that she had something to bounce off you?"

Delcliffe folded his hands. "She had wondered out loud about leaving Dayspring and going into private practice. It was something I guess she wanted to talk about when I got home. Things would be tight, but I think it would have been a good fit. She would at least have been happy. One of her former colleagues had a private practice and seems to be hanging in there, and so Susanna felt she could do the same."

"Jena O'Connor, correct?"

"You've obviously been judicious in figuring out who to speak with, Detective."

"Had you two been talking about her going into private practice for some time? Was this a new thing? Was Dayspring that bad of a situation?"

"I'll take those in reverse. Yes, it was. No, it wasn't a new thing. She has been talking out loud about this for a couple years with me. Let's face it, she'd never be executive director there. We don't attend Dayspring for church. We go to First Evangelical Free, so according to the center's—and church's—bylaws, she'd never be the big cheese. And she was a woman."

"They'd never have a woman as executive director there?"

"You've been there. You don't think the sexism is thick at Dayspring?"

"It was hard for us to get a sense in under three hours, but you seem to think it is. If I might, were there any clients who might have not liked her advice, who might have suffered interpersonal issues and wrongly blamed their failures on her, and who might be a threat to her safety?"

"You couldn't check at the center?"

Ballack smiled. "We'll see how it goes on getting the records."

Delcliffe returned the grin. "You might not need it, Detective." He leaned in. "Susanna has her own personal notes on our computer at home. It would take nothing to get into those files."

"They aren't protected by the therapist-client privilege?" Ballack asked, quickly calculating the potential storm that could come from a move like this.

"I wouldn't think so. They aren't official session notations. Susanna would journal some things and reflections on some of her experiences, especially with her most trying cases. So these aren't clinical documents. I never looked at them myself, but I know the file name and would be able to access it."

"You would be doing this?"

"Problem?"

"No," said Ballack. "As long as you are voluntarily mentioning this and acknowledge that and hand it over of your own free will, it shouldn't be a problem."

"Volunteer? I'll do anything I can to help you. Just give me this evening to nail them down."

Ballack held up a finger. He was pleased with this progress but wanted to chase one more ball he was certain needed pursuit. "I understand your wife was a prodigious writer. She wrote a number of articles and book reviews in counseling publications. Is there a possibility someone might have taken offense to something she wrote?"

"What do you mean, Detective?"

"I mean, could someone have felt she had criticized them for something? Could a person have felt she was unfair to them in a book review, or in an article about a certain method of counseling? I'm not saying she did this intentionally. But was she ever the recipient of professional hostility because of a perceived slight or critique?"

Delcliffe closed his eyes, thinking hard. "I can't think of a specific person who did, Detective. Susanna wrote a lot and spoke at a number of conferences, and I'm sure there were opportunities for people to see a difference between how she did things and how they did things. Now that you mention it, that was one complaint coming from Fogarty, that Susanna had pissed off several people in the field, that she had hurt some feelings. Strangely though, he could never identify a specific case."

"Funny how that happens among Christian organizations," noted Ballack. "It's one of my father's chief complaints. People cutting people's legs off with a pure bluff."

"It's why she got more and more miserable at Dayspring," recalled Delcliffe. "But here's where I can't follow you on this point. If she was attacked by someone in her office, that speaks more to an inside job than anything else. Technically, an enraged client could get into the center, but that would be a very risky attempt. And the last category is even less of a chance. Someone in the larger counseling arena who has a bone to pick with her likely isn't going to come to St.

Louis from Atlanta or Phoenix or Baltimore to stalk her and corner her in her office. It doesn't make sense to me."

Ballack was expecting this reaction. "I realize that, and it's why I am loathe to put the primary suspicion on a former client or angry fellow counselor. But I think in concentric circles to keep all the possibilities before me. Then I narrow down the probabilities."

It was then that Tori knocked quickly on the door before pushing it slowly open.

"I don't mean to break this up," she said quietly. "But Marcus wants to see us."

24

"Call it a lucky guess," said Marcus Broadnax when the entire team gathered around him, "but I was right. The trauma to the back area seems to be so great we had to surmise the bruise was from several calculated blows. We checked inside and it was an almighty train wreck. The renal artery exploded and she bled into the abdominal cavity. Plus the damage to the renal plexus was extensive. The diaphragm had been paralyzed by the trauma. That's why she couldn't breathe."

"So why crush the ribs if all that's needed is to cause the damage around the kidneys?" asked Hull.

"Most likely to immobilize her, to render her helpless and be easy prey for the follow-up," said Ballack, his photographic memory pulling together a vivid picture of the dead counselor's office from that morning. "The question is, was she attacked from the front or the rear. Maybe it was a sneak attack. Or perhaps she saw Freud there in the office ahead of time and he attacked her face-to-face. Squeezed her in a bear hug, crushed the rib cage, and then she's set up for the finishing blow."

"If it's someone doing a frontal attack, the likelihood is it's someone she knew," said Crabolli, "Like a counselor on staff."

"Or someone from the church," chimed in Tori.

"You snapperheads can mumble about the positioning and what not," said Broadnax wearily. "I just deal with the medical side."

"Time of death confirmed?" asked Ballack.

"I'd say in between nine-thirty and nine forty-five," Broadnax looked around at the team. "And if there are no more questions, I have to get back in there."

Ballack looked at Scotty Bosco. "You okay, Chief?"

"I am," Bosco replied. "If you could, keep me in the loop and email me the daily report. I have to go back across the river. The suspect from the school lockdown this morning finally got his lawyer to come in, so interrogation is about to begin."

"Good luck with that," said Tori, clearly vexed by the activity of the day.

When Bosco walked through the outer doors, Ballack turned to the others. "Now we have some homework to do before shutting down for the evening. Phil Delcliffe said that Susanna had journaled about some of her experiences at Dayspring with some difficult clients. Those matters are on their computer at home and are separate from the therapeutic files at Dayspring itself. He said he could go back to the house and procure them given time."

"Is that a risk worth taking?" said an amazed Crabolli. "Can we even use those?"

"I know some might think that's privileged information," responded Ballack, "but the truth is these are informal recollections, not medical records or official therapeutic documentation. In my view, it's a separate issue. And her husband is voluntary making these available. And you might find some more honest statements in these papers than what's on her stuff at Dayspring. Zane and Missy, since you've already got the client appointment logs, follow Phil Delcliffe to his home and collect what he finds on his computer."

"You got it, C.B.," said Hull.

"Be grateful but discreet," reminded Ballack. "The man is trying to be of help, but when he walks through the doors of his home there may be a flood of emotions and he might get knocked off stride."

"We'll be patient," assured Crabolli.

"What about us, Cam?" asked Tori.

"We're going to swing past Trent Fogarty's house and ask him some questions. A number just arose when I was speaking with Delcliffe just now."

"Like what?"

"I'll brief you on the way, Tor. Let's be off."

"Okay. Hold on, hold on," said Hull, hands up in the air. "What about after that? Are we meeting somewhere afterward to debrief?"

It was an excellent, and necessary, question. The time had gotten away from them and the shadows outside had lengthened considerably.

"Tell you what," said Ballack after some thought, "Why don't we do something different? We've hit information overload so far and tomorrow will be just as big a tidal wave. After you deal with Delcliffe, email me your findings and I'll include them in my report. But let's get an early night tonight and an early start tomorrow. Depending on where our first interviews are, we can target a central location where we can meet for breakfast and debrief after we've had some time to let our brains recharge."

"No objection here," said Crabolli, and both Tori and Hull agreed.

"We're out of here," remarked Hull, who headed toward the hallway room to get Phil Delcliffe.

Ballack turned around to head out to the Sprinter with Tori when his cell phone went off. He looked at the number and his heart instantly lurched. Grinding his teeth, he punched the call button. "Hi, Dana."

He heard her breathing on the other end before her quavering words came through the line. "Hi, Cameron. I hope this isn't a bad time."

His pulse began to lower as he steeled himself. "Not at the moment. I'm in between interviews and we have a drive before the next one. But I'm listening."

"I won't keep you long."

"You can if you want to," Ballack said in an attempt at reassuring humor.

"I'd like to. Problem is I'm headed to St. John's for my support group tonight. But I was wondering if I could come by and see you tomorrow night at your place. I haven't spoken to you since the trial and that's unfair for me to put you through."

Ballack remained silent, unsure where he was headed. Dana had been a regular fixture, as she called herself, at a bereavement recovery group since the beginning of the school year. While Ballack hadn't protested her entry into the group, her verbal celibacy about it frustrated him.

"It's okay," he heard himself saying, "Just let me know when you're on your way." He waited, unsure if he should put his soul over the line but decided to risk it. "I've missed you."

He swore he caught a loud sniff, nearly a cry, from her, but she quickly pulled herself together and said, "Miss you too, Cameron. I'll call you tomorrow when I'm on my way in."

Ballack mouthed a silent rejoinder to her audible goodbye. He scooted up the ramp before Tori closed the van door behind him. He looked at the sun desperately trying to peek through the dusky clouds, wondering if this was a harbinger of what was to come.

25

According to the staff directory, the Fogarty residence would be just south of Dayspring off Highway 141. Tori overshot the turn on Dutch Mill Road at first before finally getting a chance to re-route herself at John F. Kennedy High School. Then she forgot the right turn she should have made heading south needed to be a left turn across the highway now that she was going north. Instead, they spent five minutes scrambling around the wrong neighborhood before Ballack pointed out rather stoically that they needed to be in the subdivision across the highway. She was angry for her double mistake. He was frustrated that he had been so distracted by Dana's pensiveness that he never noticed Tori's transportational sins. Plus, he had jammed in a quick phone call to Zane Hull on the matter of his earlier interrogation of Fogarty, and thus he was able to concentrate little on Tori's struggles. They finally parked in front of the Fogarty residence, where Trent stood on the front porch drinking a soda and wearing a morose look.

Tori began unlatching Ballack's wheelchair. "You could have given me a little more help on the directions, sport."

Her clipped tone roiled Ballack somewhat, but he kept his temper in check. "I wasn't able to give full attention to your getting lost because I was on the phone. I get it. I also let whatever's going on with Dana affect my mood, okay? Sorry. But we got here just the same. Plus, it's not like you haven't been somewhat melancholy about whatever Paula seems to be going through."

"She's my daughter," Tori grunted, clearly worried. "I should care."

"And I shouldn't about Dana? Come on, Tor. Let's at least pull it together. Neither Paula nor Dana is a suspect, and a suspect should be our focus now. Like this suspect coming toward the car." He nodded toward Fogarty just as Tori straightened up and then flipped the switch for the side ramp.

As the ramp lowered torpidly to the ground, Ballack studied his partner. It was clear she was bringing considerable energy to this case, but the lines of torment were etched on his face. This was vexing enough, but what was even more difficult was the fact Tori wasn't discussing it much. Then again, thought Ballack, her daughter might not be shooting straight with her at all.

Trent Fogarty came up to them and extended his hand, any trace of earlier antagonism now gone. "Good evening, detectives. May I ask why the late visit?"

"Sorry to pester you at this late hour," said Ballack. "There have been a couple matters that have come up since we left the center. Given that these were issues we didn't have a chance to address to you, we were hoping to have a few spare moments now to do so. Is this a good time?"

"I'm the only adult here," Fogarty replied, an odd reply indeed. "What I mean is, my wife is out with some friends. Our kids are doing homework in their rooms. I guess I could speak with you for a bit. Will it have to be out here?" He gestured at Ballack's wheelchair.

"As long as you have an accessible entry where we can place the needed ramps," said Tori, "then we can do it indoors. But if you are trying to shield your children from particulars of the investigation, I'd suggest meeting outside."

"We have a brick patio out back," suggested Fogarty, looking at the portable ramp to which Tori pointed. "I can light some tiki torches and I think your ramp will be fine for the lip onto the landing."

"As long as I can get back there," said Ballack, who began to follow the director around the back of the house, but quickly circled back as Tori got the portable ramp from the van.

"Tor," he whispered. "when we get back there, let's check the windows. I don't want them being open on this sixty-degree night and having the kids catch snippets they don't need to hear."

"It'll be the first thing I check," replied Tori.

The swing around the house was brief, and Fogarty directed them to take their places around an Amazon teak patio table, which was accented by matching chairs. Ballack decided not to open his laptop in the tricky light, instead opting to recall the conversation in his steel-trap memory and typing it later in his final report. Tori scanned the back windows and gave an imperceptible nod to signal her satisfaction they were closed. Ballack lowered his palm to remind her to keep their voices low regardless.

"You said you had some follow-up questions for me, Detectives?" asked Fogarty as he tried to pull together some bravado.

"It's what happens when we have a chat with Phil Delcliffe," said Ballack.

The color drained from Fogarty's face, leaving it ghostly bloodless in the darkness. Something about Phil Delcliffe's name caused the director to come unglued. His head literally flopped to the side and his excuses faded away in a wave of stutters and stammers.

"Mr. Fogarty, I fail to see how your case is made stronger by your little trickle of guilty gasps," said Ballack. "Our team member who interviewed you this morning put you through as much of the wringer as he could. But one little question stood out. He asked if there were any conversations or events in which you might have been involved, either with Mrs. Delcliffe or not, where her job status was a primary target."

Fogarty shifted uneasily in his chair, looking to the windows of his house as if he could mentally command one of his children to come out and save him with a question about biology homework. He gazed at the far edge of the house, seemingly wishing his wife might return at any moment. His head never rose very far from his right shoulder.

"We spoke with Phil Delcliffe soon after he got back into town this afternoon from Nashville," continued Ballack. "He told us several details about last week that you never mentioned to Detective Hull. You said nothing about your little pow-wow at Six North Café last Wednesday."

"Pow-wow?" parried Fogarty.

"Yeah. Evidently, you, Paul Merriwether, Susanna, and a certain well-trusted Dave Slayden—who was told by someone at the last minute he wouldn't be needed—were to meet and try to clear the air about significant issues that were there. Instead, according to Mr.

Delcliffe, it turned into an accusation of everything she had been doing wrong and ways she was undermining your authority."

"He said that?" replied a clearly worried Fogarty.

"Is he lying?" said Tori.

"I'm sure that we can verify if she had a receipt from that morning," said Ballack. "And even if she doesn't or you or Paul Merriwether don't, we can have other ways of finding out."

"We'll check at Six North sometime tomorrow," mumbled Tori.

"Look, we've had many meetings about the relationships on staff and the peacemaking we have to do at times," pleaded Fogarty. "It can be hard to pinpoint one needle in that haystack."

"A needle in a haystack?" snapped Ballack. "This is something that purportedly happened six days ago! You can't remember if you had coffee and a bagel just down the road from your office?"

Fogarty looked down into his lap.

"Tell you what. Forget that," said Ballack. "You were sent a letter by Susanna Delcliffe—co-written with her husband—that protested what she felt was going on at Dayspring. There was also a reasonable prescription for change and moving forward within the letter, according to Mr. Delcliffe. It's only a matter of time until we are given this letter and see the precise contents therein. My question to you is, were you given a copy of this letter? Were you one of the addressees?"

Fogarty hedged again. "Not to my knowledge."

"Not to your knowledge?"

145

"That's right. Why would that be important anyway?"

"Mr. Fogarty, do you realize what was going on last night at Dayspring Community Church?"

"I believe an elder board meeting was taking place."

"Rather odd, don't you think. The day after Easter Sunday, and there's a meeting of such momentous decision-making importance?"

"I don't question the schedule, Detective."

"No doubt about that. Are you aware this letter was being distributed to the elders and would be dealt with at the meeting? And that Susanna Delcliffe herself was there?"

"I wasn't at the meeting."

"Yes," said Ballack forcefully. "You told us that before. Phil Delcliffe also let us know that Susanna had mentioned that to him in a text message. And there was the other morsel of interest—that her favorite elder and best confidant Dave Slayden was not there, either."

"Do you normally go to the elder board meetings?" asked Tori.

"Yes," replied Fogarty, "since I'm an assistant pastor at the church, I am technically what they call a teaching elder and so I am on the board."

"Yet you weren't there last night?"

"No, you remember that I had appointments until the center closed."

"You had appointments until closing last night on a night when Susanna Delcliffe's job was on the line a few hundred yards away," said Ballack, his anger rising. "She leaves the meeting, comes back to the center, and then this morning is found dead by Mrs. Emerson in her office. She is stubbornly determined to justify herself, to show that others and not she are the problem, and she ends up dead. Mr. Fogarty, this is not painting a good picture, and perhaps you should be realizing that before it's too late."

"I had nothing to do with her killing!" Fogarty snarled.

"Really?" Ballack replied. "None of us have told you about what the manner of death was. Why is it you are assuming a kill?"

Fogarty was wide-eyed now. His head swiveled into a straightened position. He shrieked, "God help me, Detective! You were practically making that case yourself when you said 'suspicious death' earlier today! I have no idea what happened to Susanna. I might not have been the kindest soul in the universe toward her, or she toward me. But I didn't kill her! I had left the center before she could have even come there. And I'm not going to sit here and watch you move heaven and earth to put me at the center of that guilty storm!"

At that moment, the back door opened and a girl of about fifteen years of age peeked out. Her blond hair was cut somewhat short but pulled back into a small ponytail. She wore cutoffs and a North Face T-shirt and looked worriedly out on the patio proceedings.

"Daddy, what's going on out here?" she asked, looking at Ballack and Tori with anxious eyes. "Is everything okay?"

Fogarty waved his daughter back in the house. "Everything's okay, Lydia. These people were coming by to ask me a few questions, and now …" He turned to the detectives, "… they were just leaving."

Tori turned away from Lydia, her eyes wet and her lips trembling, and she took two deep breaths.

Fogarty glared at them. "That's it for tonight. When you get me that upset in front of my family, it's time for you to go. This is over."

Ballack turned on his wheelchair to move out, but not before a parting word. "When you're a suspect, Mr. Fogarty, you certainly don't have enough leverage to say it's over. Be assured, you'll see us again."

It was when they approached the Sprinter that Ballack's cell phone rang. It was Hull calling to report progress.

"Tell me some good news," Ballack muttered.

"We've got some possibilities. It took several minutes before the husband even got to the computer. He walked in and started crying immediately for ten minutes. Collapsed at the dining room table."

"That's completely natural. What did you find when you found it?"

"Several clients that look like they could have a bone to pick with her. Some in arrears with their accounts for some time, some not."

"Where are these people located?"

"We have home and work addresses for all of them, thanks to the center's log. The work addresses are pocketed from 170 westward. One's in Maplewood, one's at St. Luke's, others are in Kirkwood, and so on."

"That's our target tomorrow morning, then. How are you guys tonight? I expect you're worn out."

"I can crunch some more data myself," said Hull. "But Missy has a nasty headache that has no sign of slowing down. Has all the feel of a migraine, so she needs to get to her Maxalt, which she left at home."

"Of course," Ballack rolled his eyes. "Send me the info in an email and I'll incorporate it in my Krieger report. The question is, then, where to meet tomorrow morning to debrief and plan out the day. If our lineup is primarily from Chesterfield in, and we're coming from St. Charles, you from McKnight, and Missy … where's she coming from?"

"She's got a place in Overland, just off Page Avenue."

Ballack shifted through his encyclopedic knowledge of the general area, narrowing things down to a spot or two where they could eat breakfast the next morning. "I got it. It would be good for location for all of us, not an extensive trip for either of you, and excellent food. It'll be an easy fit for us, and if the weather's nice, we can eat outside."

"What did you have in mind, C.B.?" asked Hull.

Ballack told him. Hull smiled.

"That is a good location," he said, "and a good choice no matter where we'd be. What time?"

"Try seven-thirty."

"Seven-three-oh. See you there."

26

Six ladies raised their heads after the final "Amen." No one spoke for a long time in the semi-dark room. There was no sound except for the quiet hum of the video projector. The dominating image in the room was the picture that emanated from it, an airbrushed photograph of a vineyard at mid-morning, with the faces of hope-seeking women clustered strategically at the bottom of the image.

One female remained with her head bowed, breathing calmly and wiping away a final tear from her cheek. Finally, she looked up at her friends, common pilgrims on this road of difficulty. Without a word, as if in silent acknowledgement of the task set before her, she slowly got to her feet and nodded.

"I'm ready," she said.

The group leader, a woman forty years old with short brown hair, stepped forward and hugged her.

"We're proud of you, you know," she said. "For your vulnerability, your honesty, and your sense of peace. Whatever happens will be for the best."

"You're certain about this?" asked another.

Dana Witten released herself from her present embrace. "I've been carrying this for too long, and I've done enough damage with my lack of honesty. Wherever this goes from here, I need to look in his eyes and tell him."

PART THREE
A Shattered Dream

(April 11)

27

A sunny morning in the enclave of Kirkwood is made delightfully complete with a slight breeze and a stop at Kaldi's Coffeehouse near the square. The interior of Kaldi's has what locals term "properly funky ambiance" where one can enjoy light-hearted conversation, catch a quick bite to eat, or take advantage of the free Wi-Fi to catch up on some work. But on a morning like this, many choose to sit out on the expansive patio facing City Hall, munching on breakfast, watching the passersby within sight of the historic Amtrak station across Kirkwood Road. The station itself is an iconic location that had seen busier days. The first train that arrived in Kirkwood was for an auction sale of town lots, and it became the first planned suburb west of the Mississippi River. The present station was built in 1893, a classic display of Richardsonian Romanesque architecture. However, the passage of time has seen a reduction in arrivals and departures, with only a few of each per day. Nonetheless, a dedicated squad of volunteers keeps the station running, and the crowd that would arrive at Kaldi's later this morning would enjoy the exodus of the nine-forty-four train westward toward Kansas City.

Trains were the least of Ballack's concern this morning as he and Tori made their way into Kaldi's to place their orders. They waved at Hull and Crabolli who had already arrived and were waiting on their orders.

"In or out?" asked Tori.

"It's a nice day," said Crabolli, "so I have no objection to the patio."

And so it was that ten minutes later, the four of them were huddled around a table overlooking the railroad tracks with their respective breakfast selections. Crabolli chose a roasted apple egg white sandwich with brie, while Hull felt the need for the sausage and cheese variety. Tori decided on the Kaldi's Scramble of eggs, sausage, roasted red peppers, spinach, basil, and provolone. Ballack rebelled against protein and tore into a Belgian waffle covered in butter, syrup, and sliced bananas. All of them were downing copious amounts of coffee, except for the outlier Ballack, who was sipping both ice water and a chocolate mint frappe.

"Alright," said Ballack, looking up from a forkful of waffle dripping with sugary fluid, "Let's talk about how yesterday went. Go around and give me everything on your interviews at Dayspring first now that we've had time to reflect on them. I put the basics of what you emailed me in my report last night, but it would be helpful if we went around and verbalized our impressions."

Crabolli went first. "Nothing special from Peggy Kimball. She reiterated she was out at half past four, as she said during our group session. She's been at Dayspring for twelve years, so she's known Delcliffe the whole time. Said she liked her tremendously and never had an argument with her."

"Find that hard to believe," grunted Hull.

"It's what she said. Took thirty minutes to get through the interview because she broke down crying several times. The biggest

154

thing was he shock for her. She couldn't imagine anyone wanting to harm Delcliffe, nor did she ever imagine her in danger. I think Kimball thinks they're all under threat now."

"Which should be reduced a bit since we've shut down the center for the time being," reminded Ballack. "What about Karissa Emerson?"

"Now that was an interesting take, C.B.," Crabolli replied, looking at her notes. "She's out of there every day at five. Given her slight frame, we can't see her as a suspect. She said that Delcliffe always treated her well. Very professional, especially compared to Trent Fogarty."

"She said that out loud?" said a somewhat shocked Tori.

"Yeah, I was amazed, too. Anyway, this is her tenth year at Dayspring, and she said it's definitely been the strangest. Before, the staff used to get together for the occasional luncheon and even had a Christmas party every year, but this year they put the kibosh on it."

"Did she have any clue someone would want to do Delcliffe any harm?" asked Ballack, wanting to move the conversation past Christmas parties.

"Not overtly, but she noticed Delcliffe seemed more and more skittish recently. Lots of tension, especially when Merriwether and Fogarty were around, which—she told me—in and of itself means nothing. But she also confirmed what you've mentioned, that Delcliffe was getting her backlist of clients and made Emerson promise not to divulge that she was doing so. Still, it took little prying from me to get that out of her."

"Okay, that's two down. What about you, Zane?"

"I had Darci Cooper and Trent Fogarty, and that was fun playing their reports off against each other. Fogarty maintained they both had seen one another leave the night before, but Cooper was hedging big time. She later admitted she had pulled out and saw that Fogarty had turned his lights on and backed out of his spot. But ..."

"She never saw him leave the area," said Tori.

"No, she didn't, although she maintained that it would be a decent assumption he did. Sounds like she was protecting her boss."

"For what reason? Could you tell?" asked Ballack.

"She gave nothing away. She did say she's happily married, almost as a defense against if I suspected there was something going down between the two of them."

"Any problems between her and Delcliffe?"

"Seemed to be normal growing pains," Hull said while taking another bite of his sandwich. "Cooper had come over from Children's Hospital in the psych department there. She had squeezed in some counseling classes over at Covenant Seminary before coming on at Dayspring. She wasn't used to Delcliffe's style or method, but she said her leadership was hardly dictatorial. In her words, she said, and I quote, 'At least Susanna was on site, unlike Trent Fogarty.' I thought that was a stunning admission of his deficiencies by an employee."

"That seems to be a recurring theme lately," remarked Ballack. "Any sense from her that Susanna was in danger?"

"None, but then again, she admitted to not being especially watchful about office politics or how Delcliffe felt about what was going on."

"And Fogarty?"

"Can't figure him out, C.B., and for the life of me I can't see why he's Merriwether's golden boy. He's not even originally from around here. Came here six years ago from a clinic outside of Chicago. He's not even in the usual network of folks here who did their training at Covenant. His degree is from North Park College and Seminary. After two to three years here, he was elevated to director. I think he believes he's a more effective therapist than some of his colleagues think he is. Somewhat open but very cagey about any specific issues between he and Delcliffe. In fact, like I told you, he never mentioned what the husband had said regarding their breakfast meeting."

"That's likely not the only detail he's been avoiding," replied Ballack. "If you caught my report from last night, you know about how uncorked he got with Tori and I."

"That leads to me," said Tori. "I'll take mine in reverse. Seg Mulgakov—short for Sergei—he was an interesting character. Originally from Bulgaria, he grew up outside of Sofia, wherever that is."

"The capital," said Ballack.

"You would know that," grumbled Tori, perpetually amazed at her partner's grasp of a universe of random facts. "He came over here in 1994 on an exchange program with St. Charles High School outside of Chicago. Actually came over a few months before the school year because of the World Cup."

"Why did that make a difference?" asked Hull.

"He was a soccer player," said Tori.

"The World Cup was held in America that year," said Ballack as an aside. "He probably came over to follow Bulgaria's team because they qualified for the tournament. Good year to do it, also. They got all the way to fourth place, though I'm not happy how they got to the semifinals."

"Beat Germany, didn't they?" teased Tori.

"Shut up and go on," barked Ballack, consoling himself with another bite of waffle. "What's the rest of his story?"

"Went to Bucknell for college, played soccer there, graduated with a degree in sociology. Had a conversion experience at Bucknell when he got involved with an organization called InterVarsity. Said that his faith changed him and he wanted to go into counseling. Went to a place called Gordon-Conwell near Boston, and he got a master's degree with an emphasis in counseling there. After that, it was five years in Pittsburgh at a clinic there. Came to St. Louis six years ago. Thirty-six and still single. Hard to believe."

"If I'm not mistaken, he said yesterday was his day off," said Ballack. "Did he mention coming in for any reason at all?"

"He said when he gets a day off, he stays out the whole day."

"Relationship with Delcliffe?"

"Seemed fine. In fact, out of all of the males we talked to, he was the most devastated by her death. Also claimed he couldn't imagine why someone would want her dead."

"Not that he had that much competition on the male sadness ratio," groused Ballack. "What about Ethan Warrick? I know plenty of details through Jill, but let's hear it from you."

"Graduate of the University of Wisconsin. Psych major. Counseling degree from Denver Seminary. Fourth year at Dayspring. According to him, his parents were wiped out in a chance drive-by shooting in Madison when he was in college. Devastated him. No family to speak of outside of himself. For all that's happened to him, he seems remarkably sure of himself. Confidence bordering on cockiness, if you ask me. As far as Delcliffe's death, he was deeply concerned for her husband, but he seemed more concerned for the future of the center."

"Interesting how the three male counselors are all from the same general area," Crabolli said suddenly. "Two from Chicago, one from Madison, Wisconsin. How far apart are those places?"

"I'd ballpark about one hundred fifty miles," said Hull, who was a native of Milwaukee.

"That sounds about right," opined Ballack. "No more than two-and-a-half hours drive time. The cluster of their locales is of interest, but it could mean nothing. Especially if one of them is being less than forthright."

"You think one of them is lying about their background?" asked Crabolli.

"Not necessarily lying," said Ballack, "but perhaps omitting critical truths. Now on to my cases."

He gave all the necessary details on his talks with Paul Merriwether and Audrey Sneller, needing to repeat nothing. He made it obvious Merriwether was a person of interest, but Ballack didn't want to poison the well.

"Even given how nervous Fogarty was yesterday afternoon and last night with us," he continued, "we need to consider there could be some level of collaboration somewhere, if Fogarty is Freud. And that's 'if.' It's pretty clear he doesn't seem like the type who is a proactive leader or strategic murderer."

"What's the lineup to replace Susanna Delcliffe as assistant director?" asked Hull. "Could this be part of a plot to grab her spot?"

"I don't know," Tori thought out loud. "If someone is that ambitious, would they commit murder to become *assistant* director? Murder is pretty total. And that's assuming it's an inside job."

"Well, I see what Zane is saying," interjected Ballack. "And while I think we should check out these possibly disaffected former clients today, the inside job theory fits best. Why would anyone else— outside of the staff and Merriwether—even have access to get in at that hour? It would take knowledge of the alarm code and other matters. To your credit, Zane, ambition and hierarchical lust can be a powerful motive. Maybe someone felt she was in the way. However, it's difficult to see why that person would be satisfied with an assistant position. It would be like a special teams coach for a football team knocking off or leaking damaging information about the offensive coordinator, in the hopes that he could stop working with kickers and punters and be the top assistant on the team. It's possible. I'm not convinced it's probable."

"But are we generally agreed that Freud is a male?" pressed Hull, wanting to have common ground on at least one thing. "Given what Marcus said about the method of death, it's ludicrous to believe a female did that. No offense, but you have shattered ribs and a punch of that magnitude. It adds up to a male."

"No offense taken," said Tori, "and no doubt on my end. The question is which male."

"And all the smoldering ex-clients you two came up with are males," noted Ballack to Hull and Crabolli. "Take us through them, if you would."

"We have Michael Talbridge. Divorced father of two kids. According to Delcliffe's personal notes on the home computer ..."

"I hope you're right about using these, Cameron," sniped Tori, rubbing her forehead, "because if not, do you realize how many confidentiality laws we've broken?"

"Then in the process of interrogation, we'll ask them what they went to her for!" Ballack gasped. "And the husband gave these to us, remember?"

"Does that make it right?"

"It's not wrong!"

"It means we're rushing in where angels fear to tread!"

"They aren't official counseling documents, Tori," reminded Hull. "It would be the same as if we ran across her diary about life itself."

"Can we move on, please?" Ballack snapped, sucking down the last of his frappe.

"Anyhow," said Crabolli, looking nervously around the table as if checking the relative safety of reading more. "Talbridge was dealing with a significant pornography addiction but he thought he had a chance at romancing Delcliffe. These are her estimations. She was more confrontational than he liked, again she's quoting him. He pushed back. His marriage ended badly. Work address is St. Luke's Hospital. He's a radiologist who works primarily in mammography."

"A porn addict who spends his time nonstop around women's bodies," complained Tori, shaking her head. "Oh, this just keeps getting better and better."

Ballack elicited a pained smile. "No kidding. The depths of irony."

"Next is Victor James. Victim of child abuse when he was younger. Affected his work relationships. Difficulty holding down a job. On and off client. Delcliffe notes a lot of screaming from him during their sessions."

"God help us," muttered Tori, "this is so much private information. We are in so much trouble if there's a misstep."

"Where's he?" asked Ballack, ignoring his partner.

"Here in Kirkwood. South of the park. Zane and I can take him. Another thing is that Dave Slayden, whom Susanna's husband said respected her a lot, is also on the client list and in her personal notations. Nothing glaring or specific as far as problems—maybe just some situational challenges—but if he was close to them it wouldn't hurt to chat. He's here in Kirkwood also, up on Wilcox just southeast of the high school."

"Take him also," said Ballack. "Who else?"

"One more. David Stump. Workaholic. Neglect blew apart his marriage but he was willing to go to counseling there. Member of Dayspring Church, too. At least, he was at the time of their counseling sessions. Runs a business in Maplewood on Manchester just east of Big Bend."

"We'll take Stump and Talbridge," announced Ballack. "You two hit Slayden and James. Also, see if you can run down Darci Cooper since she was the last one there with Fogarty the other night. After we meet with Talbridge at St. Luke's—if he's in today—we'll check in with you."

"You got it, C.B.," said Hull, grabbing his trash for disposal. "Until then."

28

Tori lowered the Sprinter's ramp in the parking garage. Ballack thought her actions since their argument over breakfast seemed wooden and halting. Obviously, there was something about her daughter still troubling her. Ballack opened his mouth to ask her, hoping a gentle question would provide an interlude to a more peaceful morning together. But just as he began to speak, his cell phone rang. He went to turn it off, but when he saw his sister's number show up on the caller ID, he hit the talk button instead.

"This had better be good," he said.

"I'm not so concerned about what's good as much as what's good for my sanity," Jill said rather loudly against some significant background noise.

"Where are you calling from," Ballack laughed. "Linkin Park concert?"

"Yeah, right. At nine in the morning. I'm in the parking garage at Children's. Listen, Ethan and I went to a movie and then to Chick-Fil-A last night and all he could talk about was the case at Dayspring. You're not pissing in their pond, are you, big brother?"

"What in the bluest of blue devils is Ethan talking about the investigation for?" Ballack yelled. He looked at Tori, who shook her head angrily while mouthing the words, *"I told him to keep his mouth shut."*

"He wouldn't stop talking about it, Cam," his sister continued. "It got so annoying I finally told him to talk about something else, which he was either unwilling or incapable of doing. He started in on questioning why you were on the case when he was on the staff. I said it's not like he was family."

"You're right, little sister."

"Stop it. Anyhow, he got irked about the family remark and it led nowhere good. We had to cut it short but it's clear he was upset by what I said. I'm just passing that on to you, not that's it's a big nugget of insight. But in case you meet with some resistance from him over the course of your investigation, you'll have some context."

Ballack set himself in the passenger seating area and Tori began strapping his wheelchair down. "What do you mean," he said wonderingly, "about that. 'Over the course of the investigation'? Does he have a long-range smoldering temper?"

Jill hesitated, as if gauging the safety of involving him any further into her next step. "No, he's really sweet. It's about the family thing. We've talked about the idea of getting married for some time and he's gradually brought it up more and more with increasing regularity. And—long story short—while it excited me at first and intrigued me for a season, I've really done a one-eighty on him lately."

"You're wanting him to put on the brakes?" Ballack asked as Tori sat in the driver's seat, started the engine, and hit the button to raise the ramp.

"More than that," replied Jill. "Listen, don't tell Mom and Dad this. I want to let them know after the fact. But I don't want it to continue with Ethan. This is beyond taking a break. I'm done. It's over."

"Just like that?" Ballack could barely disguise his joy over this good fortune for the case.

"Yeah, just like that. I'll probably tell him tomorrow night. I need to move on. Yes, I want to get married one day, and one day my prince will come. But it's not today, and it's not Ethan. It's nothing glaringly horrible. I just don't want it."

"Wow, Jill. What a shock. I didn't know you had it in you to lower the boom like that."

"I didn't know," Jill said, "that your opinion of me was that strong."

Ballack ruefully considered the secrecy of his brotherly affection. Perhaps the reality of his difficulties with Dana caused his own concern for Jill to burn that much more brightly. "Just stay strong and be honest. I'll be careful myself."

"Of course you will, big brother. I've got to go now. Love you."

Ballack shut his phone and turned to Tori. "Flashpoint on the horizon. Jill's dropping the bomb on Ethan."

Tori smiled slightly as she worked her way through morning traffic northward toward Manchester Road. "You're right. He's not family. Good call. Just wish Paula would exhibit some discernment herself."

29

Failing to discover a parking spot out front of Great American Graphics, Tori found a clear zone in the lot behind the neighbor chain of stores on Manchester Road, a few blocks east of Maplewood-Richmond Heights High School. The sun had peeked behind some clouds as Ballack took the lead in rolling around toward the front entrance facing Manchester. As they approached the door, a strong yet pleasant odor bisected their nostrils.

"Does he keep a truckload of cinnamon bongs in the office?" asked Tori.

Ballack chuckled. "It has nothing to do with him at all. Penzey's Spices is two doors down. I have a mind to go in and get some Fox Point seasoning myself. Have you ever had that on scrambled eggs?"

"Can't say I have."

"You're missing a slice of heaven."

They entered a door on the northeast corner of the building, noting the plaque that identified the space as belonging to Great American Graphics, LLC. A tall strawberry blonde with wavy hair that cascaded past her shoulder blades rose to meet them from behind a faux pine desk. Her breath was minty fresh, her perfume slightly alluring, and her button-down blouse was strategically missing a button. Ballack wondered privately if this leggy vixen was part of the workaholism that contributed to the Stumps' shattered marriage.

"Hello, welcome to Great American Graphics. My name is Rachel. How can I help you?"

Ballack's badge was out before she could project another word. "Detectives Ballack and Vaughan. We're with a team from the Special Investigative Division of Metro St. Louis. Is there a chance that Mr. David Stump is up and about today?"

Rachel's visage clouded over. "Is everything okay? He's not in trouble, is he?"

Tori was quickly to pounce on the comment. "Interesting questions, to be sure. We just have a couple questions to ask him. It's not related to the company, if that's what you're getting at."

Rachel relaxed and turned to her desk phone, briskly tapping a few strokes. The speakerphone engaged and they heard a slightly exhausted "Yes?"

"I'm sorry to bug you, David, but there are two detectives here up front wanting to speak with you. They said it was just a couple of items. Should I send them back?"

A pause, then "I'll come up."

Two minutes later, a solidly built, yet lithe, man strode into the waiting area. His blue oxford shirt and khaki slacks projected a professional aura on his trim frame. His brown hair had a few flecks of gray, but he seemed to be a handsome and easily confident soul.

"Detectives, hello. I'm David Stump. Could I see your identification?"

Once satisfied they were who they claimed to be, he waved Ballack and Tori back to his office in the rear of the building. A bevy of computers and printing presses flanked the spacious work area, and an overabundance of windows let in an extraordinary amount of natural light. He ushered them to his corner office, sat down, and cast a suspicious look at both of them. The majority of his skepticism, it seemed, was directed at Ballack.

"So, Detectives Ballack and Vaughan—how can I help you? Is my company under some kind of secretive threat?"

"Actually no, Mr. Stump," began Ballack. "What we're about to share with you is something we're asking you to keep private. Did you formerly attend counseling sessions under a Mrs. Susanna Delcliffe?"

Stump was floored by the question. "Um, yes," he slowly ventured. "When my wife and I were still together, we sought out counseling during some fairly difficult stretches. We were members at Dayspring Community Church, and if members went to the center for counseling, they didn't have to pay the fee."

"Free advice. Can't beat that," remarked Tori.

"It is a big carrot they hold out there to have their people keep up appearances, if you ask me" replied Stump, still wary. "How did you know we saw Susanna?"

"Attendance logs of clients," assured Ballack. "Relax. We didn't get the information from any private records at Dayspring." He swallowed on the misleading truth. "How long did you go to Susanna for counseling?"

Stump leaned back in his chair. "Let's see. We began going there in September of 2009 and stopped in January of last year, so roughly sixteen months of every other week."

"Why did you stop?" asked Ballack, recording everything carefully.

"It wasn't working out. My ex-wife has a knack for telling believable tales about me not caring about her, and Susanna bought it hook, line, and sinker. I lost patience and believed that if we were going to rebuild the marriage, it wasn't a house worth patching up again."

"That's it? Any sharp disagreements with Mrs. Delcliffe?"

"Yeah. About one every session. It usually followed when she'd blame me for wrecking my marriage."

"Were you?"

"How is that any of your business?"

"Hey, you knew Delcliffe," said Ballack calmly. "A counselor. Maybe she saw through things."

"Through what?"

"Well, you said your 'ex.' Using the powers of logic, I would guess that means the divorce went through."

"Just recently. And I repeat," Stump implored, his face reddening, "what business is it of yours?"

"It seems you don't hold Mrs. Delcliffe in the highest regard."

"I don't give a rat's behind about her. And my earlier question stands. Why is my past at Dayspring your concern?"

"Precisely because Mrs. Delcliffe was found dead in her office yesterday morning, the victim of a brutal assault. And we're on the case. You just happen to be on our list."

"Why? As a suspect?" Stump's anger had cooled to a noticeable fear.

"Let's say a person of interest, but that can go either way depending."

"So given that the fee slate was non-existent, there would be nothing regarding a bad payment record with Dayspring?" asked Tori.

"None," said Stump, his anger returning. "But I didn't do it, whenever it occurred."

"Oh really," said Ballack. "You have an alibi."

"My alibi is right out there on the floor," he replied. He stood up and went to the door. "Rick? Could you round up Vance and Rachel and come back here for a second?"

"Three people are your alibi?" asked Tori.

"That's correct, and you'll see this done with not a trace of leading the witness," Stump said with a look of fierce pride.

Rachel approached the door with a smile toward her boss that Ballack swore could be a come-hither look. The graphics technician whom Stump had addressed as Rick—a short red-headed young man with smoothly manicured nails—arrived next with an older black man in a navy polo shirt and white slacks.

"I'm sorry to pull you off the floor like this," Stump began, "but these detectives are trying to solve a case and are wanting to account for my whereabouts the other night. Did you have a time range in mind, Detective Ballack?"

Ignoring the challenging tone in his voice, Ballack looked at the threesome in the doorway. "I'd say a range from eight o'clock until eleven on Monday night."

Vance was the first to speak. "That's easy. We were all with David here. Closed down at six and he took us all out to eat over at the Post just a few doors west of here."

"How long were you all there?" asked Tori.

"There till about ten," continued Vance. "Took us some time to get seated and the food was a bit slow, but we stayed for four hours. Watched the Cardinals play the Reds on the big screen."

"Had a few beers," said Rachel with a badly hidden smile.

"I took the entire company out for dinner and drinks Monday night," explained Stump, trying to drive the attention away from Rachel's entendre. "The numbers were great for the first quarter of the year. We have twelve employees overall and eight could make it. The four of us make half the bunch there, but hopefully their word will suffice."

"Just so we have a clear understanding of when you left," reminded Ballack.

"That would be ten o'clock," piped up Rick. "I did happen to look at my watch when we were leaving."

"Is that good enough, Detectives?" Stump asked. "I'd like to get my people back on the floor."

Ballack and Tori both nodded their assent and soon it was just the three of them in the office. Stump's eyes trailed Rachel as she returned to her desk and then his attention turned back to them.

"Look, I hope that's good enough. And for the record, I didn't like Susanna Delcliffe, but in retrospect she was just doing her job. After a bit, I just didn't want to hang around. My ex-wife has full custody of the kids. I just grew beyond marriage, that's all. But that doesn't mean I'm glad she's dead. We have a few positive memories of our time at Dayspring. I can't imagine this is going to be a good thing for the church or the counseling center."

"Nor can I," said Ballack, already gathering his things and thinking about the next step. "Thanks for your time nonetheless." He turned to go, reminding himself that an expected dead end was no less palatable.

30

Stunned, Zane Hull leaned closer in. Sitting across from he and Missy Crabolli in the comfort of the breeze-caressed gazebo, Dave Slayden had just laid a bomb in their laps. The kindly gentleman of sixty-one years took off his glasses, wiped them slowly, and placed them back on his head. Hull looked at his notes, unable to process the story fully.

"You'd better be on the level with us, sir," said Crabolli. "You're saying that Fogarty and Merriwether were all but determined to get rid of her?"

Slayden took a sip of iced tea and looked directly at her. "And kept me out of it. They demanded I go along with it or resign as elder. And during the whole time this went on, all this unfolded. And now I've lost a dear friend over it, for which I will never forgive myself."

Hull wasn't interested in Slayden's remorse. He stepped out of the gazebo and dialed Ballack's number before they made another move.

31

"I'll take Big Bend north since 40 West is our fastest bet to reach St. Luke's," said Tori as she headed west on Manchester Road.

Ballack's phone rang. "Yeah?"

"C.B., it's Zane."

"The caller ID never lies. What do you have?"

"Okay, Slayden just spilled a few things. He said he's been strong-armed by both Fogarty and Merriwether—mainly the pastor—to remain silent about Susanna Delcliffe and her plight. Basically, if Slayden had gone to bat for her, as he was planning to, he would have been shamed right off his pedestal. Kicked right off the elder board at Dayspring."

"You've got to give me more than this," said Ballack. "That's a rather unspectacular dare. Most people I know would jump at the chance to remove themselves from the front lines of the church. What's the back story? What was Merriwether's leverage?"

Hull told him. Ballack lifted his eyebrows.

"That is low, Zane," he said. "Okay, we've got something there. We're on our way to St. Luke's to speak with Michael Talbridge."

"How did David Stump turn out?" Hull wanted to know.

"Airtight alibi, unless all involved were lying seamlessly on the spur of the moment. You heading on to your next one?"

"Almost there."

"We might stop in on someone else at St. Luke's, just to get the shape of the threat toward Slayden. Later."

Ballack immediately began dialing another number as Tori approached Highway 40 and signaled her to move into the left-hand lane.

"Who are you calling now?" she asked.

"Seeing if Dad is available after our Talbridge query for an early lunch," he replied, "and to be our guide through the mind of Paul Merriwether."

32

Tori rolled the Sprinter into the east parking garage at St. Luke's Hospital. The sprawling complex, which had seen its share of upgrades and new construction, was an impressive facility overlooking the juncture of Conway Road and Highway 141. Episcopalians who sought to provide the best in medical care for area settlers founded it in 1866. Local Presbyterians joined the mission in 1948. While St. Luke's had not been in his medical orbit for his specific needs, Ballack knew of its well-deserved reputation. It ranked in the top one percent of hospitals in the nation for clinic excellence. Physicians and staff tended to go above and beyond the professional call of duty. And, claimed Ballack's father, it was so clean you could eat off the bathroom floor.

"So number one, do you know where we're going?" asked Tori. "And number two, are we sure Talbridge is here?"

"In reverse," replied Ballack. "I have no clue, but we've got a chance. If not here, he could be at one of the other clinics. I think there's one out at Boone's Crossing and I'm sure there are a couple others—one's at Winghaven. And as to finding the mammography clinic here, Dad said all we have to do is walk through the doors here off the parking garage and we're there."

The Breast Care Center couldn't have been easier to find. After they entered the East Medical Building through the garage doors, they found the office on the left at the end of the hallway before a dogleg right. There were a smattering of women in the waiting room, and not a few of them wore curious looks when Ballack scooted up to the receptionist area.

The lady at the window greeted them with a smile. "Can I help you?"

"Yes, although in truth I don't need an appointment," winked Ballack, chastising himself immediately for his poor attempt at humor. He and Tori showed their SID badges. "I'm Cameron Ballack and this is my partner Tori Vaughan. We are hoping that Michael Talbridge would be in today and could spare a few moments of his time to have a chat with us."

The receptionist, a friendly-faced brunette with a freshly cut bob, looked slightly worried. Tori spoke up. "It's not an issue of him being in trouble." She grimaced inside at her half-truth, not knowing for sure what Talbridge knew. "We're on an investigation about another matter that has nothing to do with St. Luke's or this office. But he could be helpful to us and it's imperative we see him if he is here."

"He is," said the receptionist. "I can see if he is free. If not, I am sure he's helping with a patient screening. Can you give me a few moments?"

Both detectives nodded their agreement. They didn't have long to wait, as a nurse opened the door after thirty seconds. "Mister Ballack? Miss Vaughan? Right this way. We have a room where you can wait."

It happened to be a conference room, likely one where staff meetings were held and major decisions were hammered out with families affected by the sobering news of breast cancer. Ballack had

Tori set his portable suction machine on the table, and he promptly turned it on to suction out his trach tube. The pollen count must be worse today than normal, he thought.

"This is a formidable place," Tori finally said after a sustained silence. "I'd hate to have the day come where someone looks me in the eye and says 'It came back positive.' I don't know how I'd react."

"Does breast cancer run in your family?" asked Ballack kindly.

Tori shook her head.

Ballack looked at a picture on the wall. "Both of my great-grandmothers had it. Mastectomies came of it, of course. For their age at the time, they combated it fairly well, from what I know."

Tori nodded, then looked down, pulling her cell phone from her belt clip. "Good night! Someone's tried calling, and I haven't noticed."

"Who is it?"

"Don't know. I never remembered to turn the volume up. It's not Scotty or Stu, or even Paula. I don't recognize this number, although something tells me I should."

She never got the chance to call the number back, for at that instant a slender thirty-something man with black, curly hair entered the room. He wore white scrubs with a navy blue shirt underneath that matched the Crocs on his feet. The nervous aura he brought into the room with him betrayed his trepidation at sitting down with two detectives.

"Michael Talbridge?" asked Tori.

"That's right," he said, as if it took extreme effort to push the words from within himself. "And you are?"

"Tori Vaughan," she said, shaking his hand. He looked at Ballack, who held up an open palm in greeting.

"I'm Cameron Ballack, Mr. Talbridge. Together, we're members of the Special Investigation Division of Metro St. Louis. Relax," he said, noticing that Talbridge was as twitchy as a rabbit chased by coyotes. "Sit down. We just have a few questions for you and are hoping you can give us some honest answers."

"Why would I give any other kind?" Talbridge smiled.

Ballack's look grew more intense, remembering that—if Crabolli and Hull were correct—they were dealing with a porn addict, a breed that neither he nor Tori trusted at all. He raised his eyebrows toward his partner, signaling her to begin.

"These questions might seem a bit odd, but they are important, as we've said," Tori began. "Did you ever seek counseling services at Dayspring Counseling Center just down the road?"

Talbridge looked as if what little wind he possessed had been sucked from him. He looked at Ballack like he was some inquisitional savior, seeking a way out from an invisible noose.

Ballack tilted his head slightly leftward, gave a brief grin, and spread his arms, palms up. "I'm afraid we need an answer. Better now than later."

Like a frightened child, Talbridge locked his fingers together as if steeling himself for a season of protective prayer. He peered at

Ballack. "This is about Susanna Delcliffe, isn't it? She hasn't said anything to you about me, has she?"

It was a response neither of them expected. They hadn't been given the same reaction from David Stump, although that might have been due to his single-minded focus on work, financial celebration with his crew, and trying to get his secretary into bed. Talbridge was either clairvoyant about their presence or extremely paranoid.

"It is," replied Ballack. "But no she hasn't. There's a reason for that. She's dead. Found in her office yesterday morning."

Talbridge's voice gave a hint of irritation. "Was she … murdered? Is that why you're here? Am I a suspect or something?"

Tori intervened. "Not yet. But the original question is still hanging out there. You seem to be admitting you were a client of Dayspring Counseling Center? Specifically, was Susanna Delcliffe your therapist?"

Talbridge looked at Tori. "I did. She was my counselor. Briefly. It was during my second marriage."

"Second marriage? What happened in your first?"

Again the pained lacuna. "I got married during college. After my sophomore year. It didn't work out. Then again, round two wasn't any more successful."

"Were you seeing Mrs. Delcliffe because of marital issues?"

"Yes."

"What were those issues," said Ballack, "if you don't mind me asking?"

Talbridge shifted, annoyance transformed into anger. "And why is that so important?"

"A counselor is dead. According to the scheduling data, you are a former client," said Ballack in a firm tone. "And according to the same data—not the private sessional records, mind you—we discovered that you abruptly stopped seeing Mrs. Delcliffe three months ago. Your account was in arrears. You've admitted to having a marriage that has fractured. You did use the past tense—'was during my second marriage,' if we heard you correctly. I think if you want to be both helpful and above the fray, you'll give us exact answers."

Talbridge looked at both detectives as if weighing his options. Ballack knew there was only so much they could squeeze out of him, and he knew that Talbridge understood that as well, being a medical professional. The only chance they had was for him to offer the darkest parts of his soul voluntarily.

"If I tell you the whole story," Talbridge began, "you won't arrest me for anything else, or mention it to the doctors here in the office?"

"Unless you admit to something that is a clear felony where we'd have no choice but to do so," replied Ballack.

"Well, here's the thing. Both of my marriages have imploded because of me. I can talk a woman into bed with no problem. But staying with them beyond the night is problematic. The compounding issue with Ellie, my first wife, is that she was just as promiscuous as I was. Or rather, as I still am. But she wanted out. That was twelve years back. I met Andrea five years ago and we got hitched in four months. One of those things where I was selectively true about my past—I told her about my sleeping around, but I neglected to mention I had a fairly significant stash of porn. Collector's items, actually. Some might be considered antiques by today's standards. Issues going back to the seventies. But of course, now that's more passé and the Internet is where the action is. Anyhow, Andrea started going to Dayspring to church when a friend invited her, and she suggested I go with her. Never did. I have no use for God, to be honest. She did want to go for counseling and I agreed, just to get her off my back."

"The counseling didn't help?" asked Tori, who also wondered how much of his story Talbridge would reveal.

"She didn't care for me too much. No matter how honest I was about dabbling in pornography."

"If you're collecting *Playboy* and *Hustler* from forty years back," Ballack said tersely, "you've got more going on than a dabble. That's a full-blown, bizarre addiction."

Before Talbridge could offer a defense, Ballack decided to go for the kill, caution be damned. "The point is this, Mr. Talbridge: If your mind is fried on porn, and if you've got promiscuity layered on that sandwich as well, eventually you're going to lose control around those people with whom you can least afford to do so. I can follow that wiring diagram as well as any detective and I think you know where I'm going."

Talbridge was silent. Ballack continued. "You agree to go to counseling in order to get your wife off your back, in your words. You have no desire to cut down on pornography or sleeping around. You abruptly stop going to counseling even though you weren't interested in the marriage. One couldn't have put the puzzle together more easily, Mr. Talbridge. You weren't trying to score points going to counseling. You were trying to score with the counselor."

The cords in Talbridge's neck quivered with rage and confusion, but his hesitation had given himself away, and he compounded his guilt with a tepid protest. "Detec … now come on …"

"Mr. Talbridge, you come on. You're dealing with two cops who have seen and heard plenty and know how the equation plays out. Look, possession of soft-core porn is no crime. I don't see the attraction, but that's not a crime. Being attracted to your counselor— again, I'm not seeing the plus side—that's not prison-worthy. But I'm painting by numbers here and you've given me enough to put together a fairly clear motive. You wanted to bed Susanna Delcliffe and she stoned you! And then you stopped your sessions given that you couldn't have her."

"Bet that stuck in your craw, didn't it?" asked Tori, playing the game just as smoothly. "You knew Dayspring. You had to know the hours there. Someone like you who stalks people would know the ins and outs of a facility to get access! All you needed was for her to be there."

"Oh for the love of God!" shouted Talbridge. "It's not true! It's not true!"

"What?" asked Ballack. "The porn part? The coming on-to-Susanna-Delcliffe part? Or the breaking in and killing part?"

"Listen," pleaded Talbridge. "You can't breathe a word of this around here! I'd lose my job if they knew I had done any of this. Yes, I'll confess to what you might think is a porn addiction, if that makes you happy. And yes, I did express to Susanna that I wanted her. Went a bit too far there. But I have not been by Dayspring since I stopped going there for counseling! Why would I even want to kill her? So she said no to me. Plenty of women have. There are plenty who have said yes. I've just moved on from the nays and toward the ayes. Killing someone wouldn't settle the scales at all."

"So then you have an alibi?" asked Tori.

"I was here all day yesterday, then went home."

"We're more interested in the hours of eight o'clock in the evening to midnight on Monday," Ballack said, enunciating the time words slowly.

"I got a pizza from Little Caesars at Olive and Fee Fee Road and went to my house right by Parkway North. I was there the rest of the night."

"But no one can prove that?" said Tori. "I mean, no one was with you."

"No," Talbridge said, "but this girl I've been seeing—Tonya—called me on my land line around nine-thirty. She could verify it, and I'm sure you could always check phone records or something like that if you were in a bind. Here's her number and mine in case you want to check yourselves and match it up." He wrote the phone numbers on a package receipt sitting nearby.

"Perhaps," Ballack answered, taking the paper. "But I think that will be plenty for now. We've kept you from your job long enough."

Talbridge rose to leave, but as he touched the doorknob, he looked back with a begging glance. "I didn't kill her. I wouldn't even have wanted to. You have to believe that. And please, you can't let the office know anything. Please."

Tori waved him out and waited until the door closed before turning to Ballack. "I don't get it. Wants us to believe he's innocent but he's now heading down the hall to cop a feel on the next X-ray."

"I'm not saying it's right, Tor," said Ballack. "And we need to make sure his alibi checks out. But unless he was playing clueless, he had no idea when Delcliffe died."

"He is the strongest candidate so far, Cam, but only because nothing else makes sense. It's not impossible, but it would be tough to successfully plan out a murder of that type. An outsider who gets in, unseen by Darci Cooper and Trent Fogarty, and hides in Susanna Delcliffe's office. He'd have to expect she was there or going to be there."

"Again, possible," Ballack said, looking at the ceiling. "With his training, he might know something of what happens when you sever the renal artery. But he strikes me as such an impulsive individual, and this killing has all the hallmarks of careful planning. Someone knew her schedule, her habits. It points to a male staff

186

member of either the counseling center or the church with some axe to grind."

"So what now?" she asked him.

Ballack tore his eyes away from the ceiling and began to move his wheelchair toward the door. "I'd call Zane and Missy to have them follow up on Talbridge's phone call claim. Meanwhile, let's go see Dad."

33

Unable to get through to Zane Hull, Tori called Missy Crabolli and updated their progress, requesting they tackle the issue of Talbridge's claim. Crabolli in turn apologized for Hull, who had dropped his cell phone on the ground and caused it to act strangely ever since. Crabolli also mentioned their meeting with Victor James had come to naught. The conversation had broken down when James wept uncontrollably over memories of childhood physical abuse, which he said Susanna Delcliffe had worked hard to guide him through. Her own voice seemed taut and rigid, and she signed off promising that they'd connect when they found something out about Talbridge's alibi.

It was a quick elevator ride that brought them to the third floor, and soon they were heading west into the main hospital area. Ballack was surprised to see none other than his own father heading into the chapel when he saw the two detectives approaching.

"Now that's coincidental," Martin Ballack smiled, squeezing his son's shoulder lightly and giving a side hug to Tori. "I was just heading in here with the liturgy sheets for this afternoon."

"What's this afternoon?" asked Tori.

"Communion at one o'clock. That's why taking an early lunch with you two fits my schedule. Come on in the chapel, I'll lay these out, and we'll be ready to go in a sec."

"They've got you running all around, huh?" asked Ballack as they entered the small chapel. No one was present, even for quiet reflection or prayer, as Martin placed the bulletins at the rear of the chapel, checked the water font, and made sure there were enough prayer request cards near the back box. Ballack moved forward and gazed at the stained glass windows. Some hospitals, he believed, could really mangle these colored portals, but he thought the unlikely predominant combination of browns, reds, and yellows in these windows calmed the soul as well as any. His eyes moved from left to right. The panel displaying the creation of sun, moon, and stars—the miracle of the birth of the universe—was followed by the one in tribute to St. Luke, doctor and theologian, graced with the medical profession's caduceus. Finally, the Tree of Life—intersected as it were with the Greek letters of Chi and Ro for the name of Christ—surrounded by flames and crosses to symbolize love and faith.

"It's not Cologne Cathedral, buddy," Martin's voice rang out, and they retired to his office. Martin pulled out his lunch from a small refrigerator in a common room and they sat down around his desk.

"Tuna?" asked Ballack.

"That's right, and you can tell by the proper landslide of mayonnaise that Mom had no role in making this batch," Martin smiled. "What about you two? Lunch?"

"Ate earlier at Kaldi's," explained Tori.

"Well, I don't want to feel guilty chomping away by myself, so here," said the elder Ballack, upon which he promptly reached into a desk drawer, fetched two Mr. Goodbars, and slid them across the desktop to each of them. Ballack snatched his and began methodically unwrapping it. Before Tori got a chance at hers, she felt the familiar buzz of her cell phone against her hip. Exhausted by the caller's persistence rather than weariness, she sank back in her chair with a sarcastic grin.

"Sorry, Martin. I need to take this," she said. "I'll be right back." And rising from her chair, she ducked out into the hallway.

When the door shut, Ballack's demeanor changed, and with a serious expression he turned toward his father.

"Dad, we don't have a lot of time, and I don't want to keep you from your work, but there's something I need to know."

"Official police business?" asked Martin Ballack.

"Yeah. I know I haven't told you, but a counselor at Dayspring Clinic was killed two nights ago."

Martin looked at the door as if wary someone was listening from the other side. He fixed his eyes on his son and muttered, "Ah, Dayspring. Well, isn't that interesting?" His chocolate brown eyes betrayed an angry glint of fire.

"You've dealt with plenty of ministers and you hear plenty of things, Dad. I have to go through the painstaking process of interviewing suspects and following the clues, but it doesn't mean ignoring scuttlebutt and innuendo."

"Good thinking. You can believe the stuff that floats through the ministerial fraternity more than, say, what you read in the papers. I'll tell you this. Paul Merriwether has always been a chess player with people. Some of the people I've gotten to know over the past few years are ex-Dayspring members. They've mucked through a variety of reasons for leaving, but the unifying thread has been that once he feels your usefulness is gone, so are you."

"And who exactly has been telling you that?"

"Some are just folks you discover passing through the rye, but there was one guy, a former student at Covenant, whom he really rubbed raw," Martin said, moving his fists in a twisting motion to emphasize the image. "He ended up here doing a few CPE units, wanting to work toward chaplaincy in hospice, and so I worked with him a bit. Theo Ellis was his name. If you're interested, I can dig up his contact information, but he may not tell you any more than what I have to share. Began there at Dayspring Church as a college and career ministry intern. And he was doing great, been there for eleven months, enjoying himself, staying under the radar, when it happened."

"What happened?"

"Merriwether was out one weekend, and Trent Fogarty was going to preach in his place. But Fogarty came down with the flu. The youth pastor was out on a retreat, and basically everything was falling through on finding someone to preach three services that weekend. Theo stepped in and, on all accounts, did a phenomenal job. But that was the beginning of the end. Merriwether couldn't stand for the rest of the congregation talking about Theo's preaching skills. He thought —or so he might have felt—that anyone who could compete with him on stage was a threat. Three weeks later, Theo was summoned to a meeting of the elders where they stated it looked as if his abilities were not a good match for his present job and that he should consider another field of ministry."

"An elders' meeting, huh?" Ballack muttered, recalling the similarity between this story and Susanna Delcliffe's last night.

"Anyhow, Theo ended up taking seminary classes at Covenant and I met him through the CPE program. He still hasn't recovered fully from the way he believed Merriwether pulled the strings over there, but he's managing."

"Still? How do you know that?"

"I'm a genius, cubbie. He and I grabbed a cheeseburger one day. He talked. I listened. If my memory serves me correctly, Theo's exact words were 'I'm glad to be free of Pastor Ass.' I believe that qualifies as a slight lack of recovery."

"One would think."

"Don't get me wrong," stated Martin, "In the public eye, Merriwether is a friendly individual, happy and jovial. If I had to guess, he wouldn't have murderous inclinations, although I know you'd hold off on those assertions until all the facts are in. And it's not a total ecclesiastical bedlam of steamy hypocrisy like your last case. There was more of a reason to watch your back in the territory of the Cathedral. But I wouldn't be surprised if his leadership has led to the tragedy that occurred the other night."

"What do you mean?"

Martin leaned back in his chair, rubbing his hand across his face and searching for the right words. "I mean how he leads dictates the environment there. He's looking to build his own kingdom of permanence at that church. An ego like that can turn people off, and they either put up with it or leave the church. But it can also rub off on others, and they are the ones you have to worry about. They are the ones with the most to gain by solidifying their own power base. And they might collaborate rather than work alone."

"That's a pretty cynical view of the church," remarked the younger Ballack.

"I live and breathe, son. I live and breathe," Martin replied as he popped the remainder of his tuna fish sandwich in his mouth. "There are three things in life that are certain. Number one is how much I love Mom, you, Jill, and Christopher." He paused, his eyes growing misty at the memory of his late son. He tugged at his shirt. "Number two is that if you want to look presentable, use spray starch. And number three is that the manors in the kingdom of God are often built by the blood of the innocent. So watch your back. I mean it."

Ballack opened his mouth to respond, but at that moment Tori burst through the door. Her posture had slumped, her gait haggard, and her eyes were puffy and darting. It was obvious the phone call had been disastrous.

"Something wrong?" Ballack asked, although one look at Tori's ashen face answered that question definitively.

She crashed in the chair, throwing her head back and then straightening again when Martin offered her a tissue.

"That was Paula's school," she began. "They were the ones trying to connect with me all morning. Paula hadn't been at school at all today after she had checked out yesterday."

"How could she check out if you hadn't given them the go-ahead?" asked a shocked Ballack.

"I don't know, but I'm going to find out, but I can do that only when I find her," Tori replied, tears beginning to pour down her cheeks. "Because no one knows where she is."

34

"And where is that to leave me, Tori?" Ballack barked from the passenger seat. They had returned to the Sprinter in the parking garage off the second floor. Tori was quickly coming unglued, scratching her head, wringing her hands, and stumbling over the next thing on the agenda. She nearly hopped into the van before she realized she hadn't even let down the ramp for Ballack. During the ramp's descent, she was muttering that she needed to find her daughter. She had pulled out her cell phone to call her ex-husband for any news when Ballack had asked what she was doing. Upon hearing her plans to find Paula's location, he had put his foot down vehemently.

"Seriously, Tor," he continued. "We're in the middle of a murder investigation. We're still within the seventy-two hour window of the killing, and you want to go off the reservation. That's wonky enough, but what am I supposed to do about that? Are you taking off in this thing and leaving me to scoot down Woods Mill Road on my own?"

"Cameron, my daughter didn't go to school today, and I don't have a single clue where she is! I at least need to call Eddie and figure out the next step."

"Then you let Eddie deal with it! He's not tracking a murderer. You and I are. If the Kennedy assassination opens up again within the next hour and he's assigned to it, that trumps what we're doing. But it won't."

"He's a landscaper, you idiot." Tori snarled back.

"That's my point. If a rosebush dies, that's an act of God. What we're doing is a matter of justice! Get that through your head! Look, if I was you, I'd be worried to. But you can't drop everything to deal with it right now."

"I've still got to find out where she is, stupid!"

Ballack clamped his mouth shut to avoid making a comment that was sure to do more damage. He needed to calm himself down since Tori's constitution was out of his control. He slowed down his breathing, trying to plot the next move himself. He needed to keep his partner focused. He needed to stay focused. They could always readjust for later. He could justify that, but not a midday abandonment of their mission. He looked over at Tori. She had started the van but was staring straight ahead, locked in a pained trance. The angles came together in his head and intersected together into a clear strategy.

"Okay, Tor," he began, thinking off the top of his head. "Call Eddie and put together some sort of game plan on Paula. But do so driving to Dayspring. Go to the church. I'm calling Zane to let him know where we're headed."

"Why are we going there?"

"We're getting in some guys' faces."

"Which ones?"

"All of them."

35

Ballack directed Hull and Crabolli on to Six North Café for some hidden camera snooping. "I want you there for a brief stop. At least, I hope it's brief. Go speak to the manager and request to see the security tapes from one week ago."

"Where are you going with this?" asked a skeptical Hull.

"I want you to check the security tapes for the morning of April the fourth. They should have at least one angle that scans the majority of the restaurant. Look for Trent Fogarty and Paul Merriwether somewhere in attendance with Susanna Delcliffe. I want to nail them in case they're hedging on having met with her."

"And if the manager gives us any grief?"

"Tell him you can always get authorization," said Ballack. "I mean, come on. It's not like we're arresting someone there. I doubt you'll get any filthy libertarians like me squealing for civil rights when they've got their hands sunk into bagel dough and coffee beans up to their wrists."

"Will do, C.B.," replied Hull.

Ballack wasn't about to end the call. "Hey, by the way, anything on Talbridge's phone call? I know it would normally take a day or two to find something, but I do believe in miracles."

"Miracles? An atheist like you?" asked Hull.

"Agnostic, you jerk," smiled Ballack. "And you don't have to buy into a divine being to believe in miracles."

"I'll let you talk to Missy about the phone log. She's letting me behind the wheel, and I can't talk and drive at the same time."

"That's reassuring," said Ballack to no one in particular as he waited for Crabolli to grab the phone.

"Okay," she said, "I have a friend who is an inroad on this sort of thing. Don't ask how. She said she could check and have the results in an hour or two. She actually apologized it couldn't be faster."

"No sweat, Missy," Ballack replied. "It's just to eliminate Michael Talbridge. Let me know what goes on at Six North and then meet us at the church. We're going over to meet with Mulgakov and Warrick. See you then."

Tori got off the phone with Eddie seconds after. "He's quitting to check things out. He said he'd call the minute he heard anything, but the sooner I can get off work the better."

"Where's he starting?" inquired Ballack.

"I gave him a list of Paula's friends, but I told him to go after her boyfriend first. He's got to know, and if he doesn't then everything's hitting the fan."

36

The educational wing of Dayspring Community Church had been converted into an ad hoc counseling center virtually overnight. Ballack was impressed with the seamless transition but knew well enough that, if they eliminated Michael Talbridge, their search began and ended here.

Karissa Emerson had returned to work, seated behind a table and filing area that served as a makeshift reception area. As Ballack and Tori exited the elevator and started toward her, she rose from her chair and met them halfway.

"Hello, Detectives," she said in a voice still marked by shakiness. "Can I help you?"

"You can, Mrs. Emerson," said Ballack in a friendly tone. "We wanted to know if Ethan Warrick or Seg Mulgakov happened to be in today."

"They both are," declared Karissa with the full confidence of one who could keep straight an endless number of schedules. "You will need to wait on Ethan. He's in a session with someone and is only halfway through. However, Seg happens to be free for the time being. His next appointment doesn't happen for another twenty to twenty-five minutes. I can see if he's completely available."

Mulgakov was available and bade the detectives to a spare classroom down the hallway. The functional space was bordered by an array of folding chairs. Very likely it was used for children's ministry during the week. If Mulgakov was upset over the change in environment, he didn't show it. He pulled his chair into the center of the room and faced them both.

"I apologize for interrupting the flow of your day, Mr. Mulgakov," began Ballack, "but we do need to ask some follow-up questions as part of our investigation into Susanna Delcliffe's death. I know you spoke to Tori yesterday, and if you could spare some time presently it would be most helpful."

Mulgakov smiled, an easygoing grin with no pretension whatsoever. "You're not intruding in any way. Whatever I can do to help."

Ballack looked at his laptop screen and scanned his notes regarding Mulgakov's earlier testimony. "You were originally from Bulgaria?"

"I was," said Mulgakov. "Grew up in the classic mold. Soccer player, hard working student, put up with the Communist Party, and—once the Cold War thawed out—our family openly began going back to the Orthodox Church."

"Went back?" asked Ballack. Mulgakov was unfazed by his questioning.

"Openly," said Mulgakov. "We had been nominal churchgoers. I myself had been baptized at Alexander Nevsky Cathedral in Sofia. Because the church and the Communists had an uneasy partnership for some time, it was difficult to fully commit in return. I've been in America since 1994, first as an exchange student. I was able to play soccer at Bucknell, which you know from yesterday."

"Of course, you told Tori about your move toward seminary after your religious conversion. But what about your move toward counseling as a career," inquired Ballack. "What brought that on? What was your motivation?"

"To be honest, it wasn't any of the typical 'I-want-to-help-people' altruistic motives," the Bulgarian said, smoothing his black hair and suppressing a laugh. "Some people are shocked by that but it's true. Early on, even into my first position at the Pittsburgh clinic, it was more about solving a puzzle. Sort of like watching an hour of *House* but from a psychotherapist's viewpoint. I liked the challenge of figuring out what was wrong, where the pieces could line up, and directing how the puzzle should go together. I know that's not the usual compassionate way. And yet I think there was a little bit of idealism on my part in all of it. If you show someone the way they should go, if you enlighten them, they will naturally want to solve their problems."

"The educational fallacy," noted Ballack.

Mulgakov nodded. "Precisely. It was during my final year in Pittsburgh I made a deliberate shift and began meeting my clients halfway, taking a more encouraging stance. I realized I was objectifying them and needed to see them as real people. Basically, I moved in a direction that the clinic there wasn't comfortable with. Thankfully, a friend of a friend knew Trent, who passed on my resume to the church. And so I ended up here six years ago."

"Do you go to Dayspring for church? Or are you still Orthodox?" The question was Tori's, and her voice—after her extended silence—startled Ballack.

"Neither, actually. There was some gentle pressure in the past, coming from Trent mainly, about becoming a member here. Trent always said that in case Susanna ever followed any outside offers that came up, we would need a new assistant director. And the church bylaws, as you undoubtedly know, specifically state the director has to go to Dayspring for church. Trent feels it would be a good idea for the next assistant director to be a member here, but to tell you the truth I have no desire to fill that role."

"You don't?" asked Ballack, his suspicions barely cloaked.

"No," Mulgakov shook his head. "I am content with where I am, how I am, and who I am. I don't pursue that position because I don't need it. And to be honest, at this stage, it would be difficult."

"What do you mean by that?"

"Two things. For one," he leaned toward them, lowering his voice, "I'm not particularly a fan of the church here. There's a little bit too much control coming from that direction over us in the counseling center. I'm sure Pastor Merriwether thinks he's doing us a favor by overseeing things with a careful eye, but I'm not seeing much good fruit from that approach."

"Because?" The question came from Tori, who seemed to be asking along more for the sake of distracting herself from her daughter's plight than anything else.

"I think we would benefit from a more independent approach," said Mulgakov. "Trent is an assistant pastor at the church, and this only deepens the control issue. All I can say is that if you have a clinic in which the staff has the freedom to explore its own direction with strong, mentoring leadership, then you have a great place to work."

"Dayspring isn't a great place to work?" asked Ballack. "And you're not the biggest Merriwether fan?"

Mulgakov frowned, then smiled slightly. "I didn't say that."

"You didn't have to. I was just following your logic."

"Well, it's a place where I can do good, where I can make some quality impact on the lives of others. I don't have to have everything fall into place for all that. But no, to be perfectly clear, I think Dayspring's counseling ministry would be astoundingly fruitful if Pastor Merriwether would be more—as you say—hands-off. Yet it's not like I have to put up with the church side of things, like I said. I go to the Journey."

"All the way downtown in the city?" asked Ballack.

"No, I attend the west campus. We used to be in the chapel at Missouri Baptist and now moved into a facility down the road south of Manchester. I've been a member there for four years now. I like the church, the pastor, where the whole thing is headed. And it's not like this is a secret either about how I feel."

"You've told them?"

"Told him, to be exact. Please, Detective. I grew up in the shadow of a Communist powerhouse that crumbled within my youth.

203

I've seen bigger institutions than Paul Merriwether wilt away. What do I have to be afraid of?"

"That's reason number one, though," said Ballack, index finger emphasizing the singularity of Mulgakov's explanation. "But you said to become assistant director now would be difficult. For what reason?"

"Well, that would be because of a certain female," said a grinning Mulgakov, who straightened up in his chair and returned his voice to normal decibels. "I don't know if you met her since she was sick the other day, but Katie Fish and I have been dating for about five months now. It's a relationship that looks like it could have genuine possibilities, and if I would be assistant director, I would feel strange being her boss. That's more my side of things."

"There's no taboo against intra-office dating?" asked Ballack, wondering what wasn't off-limits in this environment.

"I know it can be something that, if it goes wrong, can upset the balance of the workplace. But Katie and I are quite comfortable with each other and are always talking about where we are with our feelings, with each other. We're well grounded, and if this didn't work out, we could still be colleagues and friends."

"Hardly according to the book," said Ballack, "but if Dayspring is fine with it, why should I plead caution." He looked at his screen, then back to Mulgakov, who all of a sudden had a sallow look on his face, as if he were going to be sick.

"Are you all right, Mr. Mulgakov? You look like you're going to throw up."

Seg Mulgakov gripped the seat of his chair tightly before relaxing his hands. He swallowed hard before returning Ballack's glance.

"I am now," he nodded. "I'm sorry. I don't know what came over me. Probably something wrong in my salad." He chuckled, then looked at the wall clock. He suddenly opened his briefcase on the desk behind him, grabbed a piece of paper from inside it, and began scribbling on the sheet. "I'm terribly sorry about that, and that I need to end this discussion so abruptly. But my next appointment is due soon. Is there a possibility that I could speak with you later this evening, if that's okay?"

Ballack looked at Tori, who shrugged unnoticeably, and then back to Mulgakov. "That would be fine, sir. I know you have Detective Vaughan's card, but here's mine as a backup."

Mulgakov took the card from him without looking, continuing to write before he placed the paper back in the briefcase and closing it. "Thank you both," he said. "I hope you find the killer, and sooner rather than later."

"That's the goal every time," said Ballack, looking past him toward the desk, "but accuracy is more important than speed. We just want to get the right person."

"I'm sure you will," said Mulgakov as the detectives opened the door to leave. He placed a friendly hand on Ballack's shoulder. "I know you will."

37

With a minimum of explanation and surprisingly no resistance, Zane Hull and Missy Crabolli were able to get access to the security tapes at Six North Café. Eager to join their colleagues at Dayspring, they nonetheless knew they couldn't rush observation. Crabolli slid into a straight-backed chair in the manager's office while Hull leaned up against the wall beside her. She had no trouble finding the correct date and began moving deftly through the frames.

"Give me a few minutes," she said. "And we should be on our way." Her straight blond hair was snatched back in a ponytail and provided a sharp contrast to her black pullover windbreaker that covered a bright red shirt. Hull's eyes moved professionally from his partner to the screen.

"Let's split the difference, Missy," he said. "You look at the left side of the screen and I'll take the right."

Crabolli said nothing except for a slight grunt of approval. She kept moving through the tape, rewinding at points when she thought she saw Merriwether in a booth or Fogarty at a table, but she was disappointed both times. Another four minutes went by before Hull said, "Stop."

Crabolli did so, but she was looking at something else on the screen. Frozen, she couldn't tear her eyes away. It couldn't be, she thought.

"Rewind it," Hull said. Crabolli was still staring at the still images.

"Missy," pleaded Hull. "Go back a few seconds. I see our little group in the back at a table that can barely hold them. But we've got someone in the way, so can you please go back?"

He looked at his partner. Her jaw was locked tightly shut, but her lips quivered. Her fingers, poised over the buttons of the remote control she held, shook violently and she dropped it loudly to the ground.

"What's the matter with you, Missy?" Hull's frustration simmered and he grabbed the remote off the floor. Straightening up, he returned the image to the spot he intended. Ignoring Crabolli, he moved closer until his eyes were inches from the screen. He smiled broadly.

"That's them," he triumphantly declared. "Merriwether, Fogarty, and Delcliffe. The two pastors are caught red-handed. Let's get over to the church and let Cameron know."

He didn't expect Crabolli to do a backflip of joy in such a small space. But neither did he think he'd get a profound silence from her. And when he turned to ask her to hurry, he saw the absolute last thing he expected. Her face was contorted with fear and tears poured down it like a waterfall. She was looking past him to another portion of the screen.

38

Ethan Warrick laid the file on his temporary desk and pulled himself out of his chair. His previous session had gone over the time limit. Cases like this one—one with vast evidence of emotional neglect—were matters that he could navigate ably. But specifics were more difficult to pinpoint than the heavy-hitting sins of verbal, physical, and sexual abuse. He didn't see many of those dysfunctions come his way anymore. The past seventy minutes had worn him out, and since he had done a greater share of the talking with his client, he was suddenly thirsty. A Pepsi might be in order, he told himself, opening his door to head to the soda machine in the kitchen of the church's fellowship hall. He crossed the expanse that could hold nearly two hundred hungry churchgoers for the midweek fellowship meals. Shoving his right hand into his pockets, he jangled around looking for enough change. His fingers grasped two quarters and were pinching a third when he heard a voice call from behind.

"Mr. Warrick, while we know you're busy at this point, is there a chance we could speak once you've grabbed your drink of choice?"

Warrick wheeled around so fast that a stream of coins flew out of his pocket. There, sitting in the corner of the shadowy room, were Detectives Ballack and Vaughan. He was taken aback by the shocking greeting, but even more so by their mismatched demeanor. Ballack wore the smirk of an investigator with unflappable confidence. The face of Vaughan—whom Warrick remembered from his interrogation yesterday—was an impenetrable mask, icy and cold. Warrick sized them both up, looking from one to the other and back again. Whether due to his having survived Vaughan's questions yesterday or some other reason, he found Ballack's façade especially chilling. An assurance bordering on cockiness belied the fact that this man was the brother of his soon-to-be fiancée. Warrick shook loose his cobwebs and looked directly at Ballack.

"Yes, absolutely," he said, "but this venue is hardly the place. My temp office is in the Fireside Room, if you'd like to join me in there after I grab a drink. Can I get you one as well?"

"No, thank you," said Ballack, "Although Tori might differ with me."

"That's true," said Tori. "If there's a 7 Up in there, I could use one."

Warrick held up a hand as if to say he'd be a minute. When he disappeared into the kitchen, Tori turned to Ballack and whispered, "What do you make of our queasy Bulgarian?"

"Nice to have you back," said Ballack. "As to Mulgakov, hard to tell. Maybe he had a shot of recognition or what he thought was a moment of remembrance. In a situation like this, where he was away on the day of the murder—and everyone verified it—it's hard to know what he could have recalled about a situation for which he wasn't present. If he does know something, we're not cracking it now. Nor does he want us to, given that he put that paper in his briefcase."

"A briefcase," sniffed Tori. "Communist turned preppie. Who brings a briefcase to a therapy session?"

Ballack raised his eyes as Warrick returned with a Pepsi and 7 Up and led them to the far end of the hallway. The room was aptly named, with a large fireplace that seemed to get little use. Warrick gestured Tori to take one of the plush chairs near the window and for Ballack to join her. He took a padded fabric chair and cracked his soda can open, taking a sip while Ballack looked over his laptop screen again.

"Cameron, it sure must be frustrating having to bounce around the way you've had to here," he said. "Of course, I don't know what more light I can shed for you."

Ballack chewed for a moment on the delicious irony that he knew of Jill's impending news flash on their dating relationship. He kept his poker face on as he mentally prepared for the questions ahead, but he did feel the need to draw a line in the sand.

"Three things to begin with," he replied to Warrick. "We always have confidence that any bit of light we get is a positive thing. Secondly, bouncing around to various sites is part of the job. And once again, while you are in that chair and I am here, you'll address me as Detective, not as Cameron."

The tone of Ballack's words sent a chilling vibe amongst the three of them. He had spoken them with no variance of inflection, but their stony delivery had positioned he and Warrick on opposite sides of the track, and with Ballack as the true authority. Tori celebrated inwardly. It was truly incredible to her how her partner could assert this kind of clout toward someone he obviously did not like, yet do so in a completely professional manner.

Warrick sheepishly rolled his eyes and said, "Okay. I get your point."

Ballack got right to the point. "No problem. Now that Susanna Delcliffe is dead, who will become the assistant director of Dayspring Counseling?"

Knocked off stride by the opening question, Warrick grappled for the correct words. "Well, quite frankly, Detective," he said, emphasizing the final word, "I find that to be a strange opening question. Shouldn't we be grieving her loss rather than casting a strategy for filling her position?"

"When someone is killed in her office the day after Easter, and when this person is the assistant director of the organization where said office is located, I think that legitimizes the question."

If Warrick had been considering a sarcastic response, he managed to squelch it. "I imagine that is an issue for Trent and Paul to consider, in conjunction with the board of elders."

"As they do make that consideration," Ballack replied, looking out the window, "what are the qualifications and essentials they'll look for in a new assistant director?"

"Well," said Warrick, "They do look for someone who shows staying power with the counseling center. It's not as if you need to be on staff for ten years before you jump into the inner circle, so to speak."

"It's not like becoming a cardinal in the Catholic Church," put in Tori.

"That world is a different planet for me, but I'll take your word for it. Basically what they are looking for is potential for leadership. Someone respected by the rest of the staff. An individual who can be trusted for the long term. Someone committed to the vision of the counseling ministry at Dayspring and to the church's vision for ministry."

"Was there ever any question about Susanna Delcliffe not meeting those qualifications in any way?" asked Ballack.

"I can't say for certain. If there was any trouble, I neither instigated any nor was aware of any. There were some conflicts regarding Susanna, but at the end of the day I hardly see how those differed from any other minor skirmishes people may have when they are working side by side, day after day."

"What about her vision for the counseling center and the dovetailing of her views with the church?"

"You'd have to speak with those on the front lines about those matters," Warrick said. "Of course, she wasn't a member at Dayspring, so there may have been some question about her commitment to it."

"I thought that was only a requirement for the director, to be a member of Dayspring Church," said Tori. "If it's not for the assistant director, then what's the uproar?"

"There's been a move pushed lately that both the director and assistant director be members of the church. The board of elders is studying the issue for pros and cons—although I don't see why they need much time to 'study' a detail like that—and they are probably going to vote on it soon, possibly at next month's meeting, Trent tells me."

"So the chances were that Susanna Delcliffe might have been removed from her position on a technicality?" asked Ballack. When Warrick hesitated, he continued. "That does seem to be the reasonable implication, doesn't it?"

"Again, you'd have to ask Trent Fogarty." Warrick crossed his blue jean-bedecked legs and brushed a hair from his white long-sleeved polo shirt.

"Who would be a prime candidate to move into her position?" Ballack leaned forward as he asked the question.

"Several could be considered." Warrick's timbre was slightly defensive.

"Namely whom?"

"Darci Cooper could be an obvious candidate, but a year here at Dayspring doesn't give the church much to go on to gauge the staying power question. But she enjoys it here and she attends the church, too. Peggy Kimball has the edge on the rest of us in terms of seniority, but three years ago she and her husband stopped coming here for church and started going to Chesterfield Presbyterian down the road. Seg would be a fine choice. Five years in Pittsburgh before here, and six years at Dayspring. But he either doesn't want it or need it. And he doesn't go here for church."

"What about you?"

"Me?"

"You've been here almost four years. That's not too far from Fogarty's time here. You're not as experienced as the others, but it hardly seems as if that's taken much into consideration. The emphasis, it seems, is staying power. Who is in it for the long haul? That's you as much as anyone else. Stability. Isn't that what the church—the counseling center itself—would be seeking?"

Warrick permitted himself a smug grin before addressing Ballack's assumptions. "I would think there's less stability than meets the eye, Ca—I mean, Detective. Not that I would want that to rule out any chance I have with Jill." He paused, and Ballack knew he was trying to check for a reaction on his part.

Failing to crack Ballack's stoic exterior, Warrick went on. "My parents were killed during my college years at Wisconsin. They were in a convenience store. Dad was buying some sodas, Mom was getting a paper. Thugs came in and robbed the place. Wrong place, wrong time. The clerk was riddled with bullets first as Dad pulled Mom down near the window. They might have survived, but one of the punks stopped for good measure on the way out and capped them both in the head. It was a tragedy I still haven't completely recovered from, and it certainly makes me an anomaly to the rest of the world around me. I mean, come on. Twenty-eight years old. No other family to speak of. Not the easiest foundation on which to build. Carving a sense of self-identity out of that was extremely difficult. I wouldn't say that's a model of stability."

"No," replied Ballack, "but some might look at that background and say that's enough tragedy on which to build a sense of compassion and empathy. That alone could position you as a top contender."

Warrick was clearly tiring of the present angle and leaned toward the detectives. "I think you can lay those matters to rest. And by the way ... Detective. Why would you assume those qualities about me? You've barely made an effort to get to know me even though Jill and I have been dating for two years now."

"It's a murder case. It's the hand we've been dealt. We're putting together a puzzle," Tori bluntly said.

"Then shouldn't you do it with the right pieces and go after the right people," Warrick asked her. Looking at Ballack, he took one more sip of his Pepsi and stood up. "Sorry, but my three-thirty is here, so our time is up." He grabbed his papers, stood erect, and motioned toward the door, indicating their interrogation was at an abrupt end. "I hate to be so hurried, but I don't like to keep my clients waiting."

Ballack held up a hand as a gesture of gratitude. "Completely understandable. Thank you, sir. We'll be in touch if we need to."

Ethan Warrick nodded kindly as Tori stepped outside the room. "Thank you ... Detective."

Ballack wheeled past him and—considering Jill's future missive—whispered, "You know, when leaving, 'Cameron' is fine."

39

Ballack zoomed through the automatic doors of the church's gray brick and green steel structure to find Missy Crabolli's black Chevrolet Cruze in the middle of the lot. He saw Zane Hull leaning up against the driver's side door, toothpick in his mouth and sunglasses covering his eyes. Ballack scooted ahead of Tori and approached Hull, attempting to gaze around him into the car, hoping that Crabolli would materialize from the interior.

"Don't bother, C.B.," Hull said quietly. "Something came up."

"Something came up?" Ballack repeated.

"Quiet," hissed Hull as Tori came alongside the car. "I don't know what happened, but Missy's done a complete one-eighty degree turn from before."

"What do you mean?" asked Tori, looking at her cell phone screen for any sign that Eddie might have called.

"Come over here," Hull motioned, and they followed him to a point a few parking spaces from the car. "Okay, here's the deal. The good news is that we caught Merriwether and Fogarty on video. They were there Wednesday of last week eating with Susanna Delcliffe. I even got to see her leave in a huff. But on the same tape, Missy noticed something that spooked her good. She's barely been able to talk or function since then."

"What? Like catatonic?" asked Ballack.

"More like whatever was on that screen scared the absolute crap out of her," said Hull evenly. "It took me literally twenty minutes just to get her out of the manager's office," he went on. "At that point she broke free and ran to the bathroom. Then it was another ten minutes. That's why we didn't get over here until now."

"You could have called," said Ballack, arms spread and palms up. "Something civilized, you know."

"Why don't you kiss my rear end, Cameron?" snapped Hull, in a rare usage of Ballack's Christian name. "When she came out of there, she was shaking like a leaf in Hurricane Katrina. Her breath stunk, too. It was obvious she had been throwing up the whole time. I tried getting to what it was all about, but she wouldn't breathe a word. Whatever it is, she's in grade-A shock right now. I don't know what to do."

"We're neck deep in a murder investigation!" Ballack voice popped with frustration. "It's not like we can pull an ostrich and bury our heads!"

"Is that what you're going to tell me while Paula's missing?" yelled Tori.

"Paula's missing?" Hull was stunned.

Ballack put up his hands, trying to ward off a two-front war. "I'm not saying you're doing that, Tori. And I'm not saying that's Missy's attitude, either. But we at least need to talk about where we are on all this."

"I don't think you can expect much out of Missy."

"It is really that bad, Zane?"

Hull lifted his sunglasses so Ballack could see the whites of his eyes. "It's frightening, pal. Some sort of deep psychosis stuff right now. If we do get her out of the car and sit down to define where things are now, you'd better be thankful if all she does is lay down in the fetal position and quiver for an hour."

Ballack ground his teeth. He wanted to fire back at Hull, but deep down he knew that he was dealing with two teammates incapable of overcoming their emotional avalanches. Privately, he had more compassion for Tori. After all, he knew what she was facing while none of them could divine what had put Crabolli in the throes of shock. He also knew to push things now could break the inner resolve of both women. He needed them for the entire course of their investigation, not merely for the following hour.

"Okay, listen," he said, looking Hull straight in the eye. "What's your estimation of what she can do? If she can't hang with a quick sit-down on where we are at this stage, does she at least need to come inside and be with us?"

"She won't be anywhere near effective," replied Hull.

"I'm not anywhere close to one hundred percent," said Tori, "but I'm sure going to be on the same page as everyone else. I'm staying. But I'm looking at her right now in the car and I can tell you're going to have to drive her home, Zane. And she can't be left alone right now."

"I don't think she wants to be left alone," said Ballack in a kinder tone. "Talk to her, Zane. Let her know we need to meet but she doesn't need to participate. But it's probably important she be with us. If you've been with her the entire time since the fright sighting, you can't let her out of your line of vision."

"Then where are we meeting?" asked Hull.

"Tori, do you still have the key to the center that you got from Karissa Emerson?"

"Right here," she replied, pulling a nickel-plated key on a small circular chain.

"Let's go in and sit in the lobby," said Ballack. "Missy can lie down if she needs to. We'll have privacy since the center isn't opening up until Friday morning. Sound good?"

"I'll try to talk her out of the passenger seat," said Hull, turning toward the car with a quick stride.

"What will you do if Krieger asks why we packed it in before five?" asked Tori when they had settled in their chairs. Crabolli lay on the sofa facing them, but her eyes were vacuous orbs.

"He's never asked before," smirked Ballack. "What are the odds he'll nail us tonight? I think given the circumstances, he'd understand. Heck, even I do."

"Softie," replied Tori.

"Let's do this," declared Ballack, "and figure out where we are going tomorrow. We've already covered our client suspects. While neither Victor James nor Dave Slayden are in the suspect lineup, what Slayden told you makes us think Merriwether or Fogarty could be dirty on this one."

"Something wrong, that's for sure," said Hull. "But unless Delcliffe had some sort of axe to grind, I don't see anything stirring that pot."

"Can you check with Phil Delcliffe as to otherwise?"

"Maybe, if …" Hull gestured toward Crabolli.

"Forget it. I'll call him from home," said Ballack. "David Stump checked out fine. Michael Talbridge claimed to be at home with a phone call verifying that."

"By the way," interrupted Hull, "We got the call back from Missy's friend. I took her cell phone away and fielded the call while we were leaving Six North. The call was legit. If Talbridge was the one home receiving the call, then he's clean."

"One more soul eliminated from the pool of suspects," grumbled Ballack. "Right now we're back to the male counselors here at Dayspring, plus Paul Merriwether."

"What are the odds that Mulgakov and Warrick trump Fogarty and Merriwether?" asked Hull.

"Tori?" Ballack motioned for her to explain.

"Both denied being interested in any promotion," she began, "although from our perspective Mulgakov made a better case for his apathy. Warrick named several people that he thought were in line to replace Delcliffe, and he never identified himself. He mentioned Mulgakov, Kimball, and even Darci Cooper, which seems odd given she's the newest one on staff."

"Personality wise, who was less credible?" asked Hull.

"Not that it makes any difference, but Warrick was much less gracious."

"Alibis check out?"

"Among the males, only McDougal—the one on vacation in Florida—and Paul Merriwether check out fine with no doubt. But Merriwether could be lying. We have assertions from Fogarty, Warrick, and Mulgakov, but nothing verified by outside sources."

"What if this has nothing to do with climbing the ladder?" Ballack cut in. He had been listening, but the sudden thought jolted him and it was out of his mouth before he could restrain himself. "Or what if it does partially, but this is more of an issue of revenge or dislike, and a murder committed out of revenge could generate the possibility of moving on up the ranks here?"

"That's your motive?" Tori was stunned.

"I don't know if the connection is there," replied Ballack, "and it's hard to justify ladder-climbing as a motive in such a small entity like this place. However, there may be a link twinning them together."

"If there was," said Hull, "Susanna Delcliffe was unaware of it. Nothing in her private electronic journals bear out anything of that nature about her colleagues. She was gracious toward all the other counselors, the males included. The only frustration or hatred leveled at anyone at any point was toward Fogarty or Merriwether. And since they outranked her, it's hard to think they'd be concerned about promotion."

"Her husband seemed to think there were issues strewn all over the road," said Tori, "from what Cameron says. Of course, we're re-checking with him."

"Cameron, I can do that," said Hull. "After I get Missy home. You worry about your report for Krieger. What else?"

"We need to get with Katie Fish as soon as possible," said Ballack. "Apparently she and Mulgakov happen to be an item. She might know a few things. However, given our circumstances we might need to wait until tomorrow morning for her. We've checked the schedule on Karissa Emerson's desk and she will be in the office first thing Thursday. The lineup is she and Mulgakov just before nine. Fogarty in at nine-thirty. Kimball at ten along with Cooper. Sneller and Warrick at eleven and that's all."

"Your brother-in-law doesn't come in till lunch?" asked Hull.

"He's not my brother-in-law," said Ballack in a tense voice. "Nor will he be, according to Jill."

"Really?"

"Really, but he doesn't know that yet. In a way, I feel sorry that I know that and he doesn't. Let's finish this for now. The fingerprint scans brought back nothing. That means we have to dig in on our interviews until someone cracks or elicits a contradictory statement that can wedge this thing open."

"So what's the plan?"

"That depends," said Ballack, "on what happens tonight. Tori, if things are okay with you and Missy tomorrow, we can meet for breakfast around eight-thirty."

"First Watch on Ballas okay?" asked Tori.

"Remember last time we set that?" recalled Hull. "Everything came together the night before and we got the huge break and never got to First Watch."

Ballack smiled at the memory of the final pursuit of their case involving the Archdiocese the previous September. "Maybe that's our good luck charm. How about this, guys. I'll call out tomorrow morning once we're all awake and confirm First Watch, but do wait for my call. Perhaps we'll get a big lead tomorrow."

It was at that point that Tori's cell phone beeped. Looking at the message, her tense body uncoiled with relief.

"That was Eddie. He located Paula. She was with a friend but seems insanely upset. He's taking both of them to my apartment, so we need to leave in a bit.

Hull nodded his relief and walked toward the sofa, taking Crabolli by the arm and pulling her gently upward. She offered no resistance, and Ballack wondered what had broken within her that caused her to be so withdrawn yet accepting of a man's help. He heard Tori jangle her keys and then felt he should say one more thing.

"Everybody, I know this is going to sound atypical coming from me," he said. "Take care of these personal matters but don't hesitate to ask for help. What you have going on within you is more important than what you have going on here and now. And if you don't take care of yourself, you'll be less effective for the team. Please, I really mean that."

As he said this, he started his wheelchair toward the front door of the center, and as he passed Missy Crabolli, he saw a faint hint of light come from her eyes and a smile of thanks form on her lips.

40

Following Eddie's instructions, Tori headed straight home after dropping Ballack off in the late afternoon. Thanks to traffic, it was some time before she was able to get back to her apartment at Westbury Place. The sun had gone from a pleasant orb to a blinding spray of light in its descent toward the horizon, and Tori felt the beginnings of a brutal headache coming on. She rolled to a stop, turned off the ignition, and yanked out the key. Feeling dehydrated, she forced herself from the van and began the slow trudge toward her door, a million questions rushing through her heart as to why Paula had skipped school.

The scene that greeted her was hardly the norm for what went on in her living room. Eddie sat in a blue fabric recliner, rising as she entered. He wore a sturdy white tee shirt with his jeans, obviously having kept his work clothes on. Tori was amazed how good-looking Eddie remained. His sandy hair clung to his skull and even his bushy mustache exhibited rivulets of sweat. His hands were leathered but clean, evidence of a day's honest toil. Tori paused for a moment, reflecting that although their marriage had wrecked, a crisis like this could unify them for a fleeting time.

"She in the back?" asked Tori as she moved toward her ex-husband, not knowing exactly what drew her toward him.

"She is. Tracie is with her. Paula needed to use the john for a second."

Tori stopped in front of Eddie and hesitated, knowing the gulf she was about to cross. But this wasn't about them. It was about the dread of that moment, of being scared beyond comprehension by the disappearance of their daughter, and she leaned forward and threw her arms around Eddie, who took her in a brief but sincere embrace.

"Um, guys?"

It was Tracie, entering the living area from the hallway that led to the bathroom. Beside her came Paula, walking unsteadily but with a slight, hopeful smile. She walked slowly toward the sofa and sat down, hands clutched tightly together. Tracie sat on her left. After a few seconds, Tori left Eddie and lowered herself on the sofa to Paula's right side. Eddie, choosing to be comfortable for whatever transpired next, plopped back down in the recliner but rotated his body to face Paula.

It was Tracie who took the initiative. "Paula needed to share something with you about not being at school today, but she wanted me here and she wanted both of you to know it. I agreed that would be for the best. My mom dropped us off here and should be back soon, so we need to talk now."

"That's fine," said Tori, "and we're glad Paula's okay. But Paula, honey, could you let us know why I got a call that you hadn't been at school all day and I've been frantic until now?"

Paula spoke for the first time. "That's not a good sign, if you were upset then."

"Of course, I was upset! I had no idea where you were or if something happened to you!"

"Tori," pleaded Eddie.

"Listen, Eddie ..." Tori began.

"No, Mom. Both of you listen." Paula's voice was clear yet trembling. "I never went to school because I needed something today. I texted Tracie, and she was able to pretend to be sick and get out after her third-period class. She offered to come along with me to see her mom."

Tori was now genuinely confused. "The school didn't know where you were, and you were with Tracie and her mom the whole time? Why? For what?"

"My mom's a nurse at Barnes St. Peters, Mrs. Vaughan," reminded Tracie.

"I knew that, Tracie," began Tori, "but what does that have ..."

She stopped. She halted when she saw the fresh tears flowing down Paula's face. And her heart nearly stopped when she looked downward as her daughter opened her clenched hands, revealing a single plastic stick with double pink lines.

41

A chorus of laughter spilled from the deck as Ballack glided up the stairs from the basement on his chair lift. Rhoda had come early for her shift, having some hours to make up for the nursing agency. Ballack simply wanted to grab a couple of things from the refrigerator to make a sandwich, and once he located the roast beef, some cheese, and bread he whirled around and went to the sliding glass door in the rear of the house. His father was standing by the gas grill checking the status of a few bratwurst and sliders while three other men milled around the deck. Ballack immediately recognized Bruce Whittaker, the father of his good friend Graham, but he was less familiar with the other two. His father noticed him through the screen and drew near to pull the door open.

"You're home early," he noted. "Everything okay?"

"The rest of the team has some other matters to attend to, so I let them have an early night."

"Tori, too?"

Ballack decided against letting his father know about her plight. "Her also."

Martin Ballack nodded as Bruce approached and offered his hand. "Good to see you again, Cameron. Graham wanted to know if you wanted to go to a Cards game next week. He can get right field terrace tickets, so seating won't be an issue."

"It never is for me there," smiled Ballack. "I'll call him in a day or two. I'm smack in the middle of a major case at present." He turned to the other two men and put forth his hand. "Cameron Ballack."

"I'm Kip Stearns," said the first, standing at six feet, five inches and weighing a good two hundred sixty pounds. "I'm a pastor at Kirk of the Hills. Good friend of that reprobate tending our meat over there."

"Kip thinks that anyone who can stand him for more than fifteen seconds is a friend," remarked Martin. "And so he holds onto them like grim death, which may not be far off for him given how I cooked his burger."

"Nice to meet you," said Ballack perfunctorily.

The younger man grasped Ballack's hand in a firm grip. "Skip Ross. I'm a new associate chaplain at St. Luke's and Martin invited me over tonight for dinner and to make it a fourth."

"Explains the poker chips and cards on the kitchen counter," mused Ballack. "Dad? Just a heads-up. Dana might be coming by in a bit, and so if she heads down below while you all are throwing down some Leinenkugels in the middle of some Texas Hold 'Em, it's completely normal."

Martin arched his eyebrows. "Completely normal, huh?"

Ballack rolled his eyes in return. "Okay, you got me. Relatively normal." He turned to head back inside. "Whatever that means anymore."

After putting his sandwich together, grabbing some chips from the counter and a soda from the fridge, and putting everything back where it belonged, Ballack headed back downstairs on the lift. From there it was all eating and Rhoda checking his vitals until dessert, which Rhoda had provided once again in the form of her famous chocolate chip cookies.

"I'll never guess your secret ingredient, girl," he said admiringly as he bit into his second cookie.

"It changes every time. Extra vanilla extract last time, gin this time around," she replied.

"I guess that explains the heightened sense of self-esteem," Ballack joked as the roaring laughter and masculine insults floated down from upstairs. "I guess Mom's out with some of her friends for her to allow the Fantastic Four to cut loose on our property."

"She told me it was a girl's night out."

"Good for her," said Ballack, who stopped when he saw a figure of a person darken the sliding glass door at the back of his suite.

"Expecting someone?" purred Rhoda.

"Yeah, it's Dana. Tell you what. Let her in and then you can head upstairs for a bit. I'll text you when you can come back down, but this has to be a private conversation for now."

"Will do," she said cheerily, crossing the floor and letting Dana in. "I'll be upstairs rolling my quota of joints in case you need me."

Dana looked confusedly at Ballack as Rhoda disappeared. "Well, to each their own," she smiled.

"Better than manufacturing counterfeit money," Ballack replied, returning her smile. "Rhoda has a different line for every occasion. Never boring."

Dana slipped her purse off her shoulder and sat down opposite Ballack in an easy chair. Ballack, attempting chivalry, asked, "Cookie? Or do you want a drink?"

Smiling, albeit painfully now, Dana shook her head. "No, thank you. I grabbed a bite on the way over."

Ballack looked her over. In a way, she seemed more beautiful than ever. She must have come directly from work, possibly from an afternoon of grading sophomore English essays at the Whitfield School. Dana was gracefully adorned in a light blue v-neck sweater over a white top, with khaki slacks and brown shoes. She pulled her Scrunchi out, eliminating her ponytail and allowing her light brown hair to spill around her shoulders. It would seem to Ballack to be an exquisitely lovely picture if not for the fact that Dana was tapping her index fingers and thumbs together, more rapidly than he had ever seen before. Whatever the news roiling within her, it had turned her into a volcano of nerves.

Finally, she leaned forward, taking a deep breath before trying to look at Ballack, but barely pulling her eyes from the floor.

"Cameron," she said, her voice barely above a throaty sigh, "I haven't been completely honest with you about my story."

Her eyes remained riveted to the floor. From above, Ballack could hear Bruce Whittaker let out a celebratory whoop over a hard-fought hand won.

"Dana," he said, losing patience with the lack of eye contact. "Whatever you're going to say, the floor isn't going to understand."

She lifted her head and revealed her eyes, the lustrous gray eyes that had been what arrested Ballack's attention fourteen months ago at St. Basil's. Unlike then, however, now they were flooded with tears.

Ballack prepared to cross the Rubicon in front of them, not sure if she would follow. "Dana, I don't know how this will fall out, but nothing will work unless you tell me."

"It's been so painful," she wept. "And I'm so worried about what it could do."

Weighing compassion alongside his impatience, Ballack rolled forward until he was a foot from her. "Dana, if you remember, I've been through pain of my own. But putting this off won't make it easier."

She was still weeping, her hands over her face. He took her left hand in his right.

"Dana, just tell me."

Her right hand remained over her mouth, but it slowly dropped into her lap as her breathing slowly returned to normal and she realized the truth could wait no longer. She gripped his hand tightly and shut her eyes as she began her tale.

42

Zane Hull went to the rear window of Missy Crabolli's small two-bedroom home in Overland. The glass pane gave him a view over a postage stamp-sized yard, one which he estimated would need only six lengths with a mower to cut the entire lawn. The entire neighborhood was one of tiny residences and starter homes that looked as if they'd sell for around sixty thousand dollars each. He had helped Crabolli into the house and onto the sofa, where she could attempt to get her bearings. As he dialed Phil Delcliffe cell number, he recalled the brief back-and-forth Crabolli managed on the way there.

It was when he had passed a white Pontiac Vibe as they went past the Delmar exit on Interstate 170 that she finally spoke. "I'm sorry I ruined the evening for everyone."

Startled by the sound of her voice, Hull managed a weak reply. "That's okay. What's happened, happened."

She looked out the passenger window as they approached the exit for Page Avenue and he readied himself for a westward turn. He didn't want that sound bite to be the end of it. "Do you want to talk about it?"

No response, so he had let the matter drop. Now he heard Phil Delcliffe pick up the other end of the line. "Delcliffe."

"Mr. Delcliffe, this is Zane Hull from the Special Investigative Division. Do you have a minute?"

"I have several if you're in need, Detective. What's the occasion?" Despite the witty rejoinder, Delcliffe's voice was somber, exhausted.

"We've gone through your wife's journals line by line, and it is true that there was no love lost between she and Fogarty, nor she and Merriwether. However, she doesn't mention anything that gives us any impression they posed a physical threat to her if she gave them any resistance. I know this is a long shot, but can you think of anything Susanna might have said regarding any potential physical threats? From anyone at Dayspring?"

Delcliffe was silent for a few seconds. "To be honest, she mentioned nothing about a vibe of danger she sensed from anyone. However, there were several things she mentioned over the past couple years that were rather intriguing."

Hull moved into the hallway toward the bathroom as the line flared with static. Behind him, he heard shuffling feet enter the kitchen and then the refrigerator open. Trying to focus on Delcliffe's words, he nonetheless could pick up a couple of glass knocks, followed by the sound of two bottle caps clattering to the counter's surface.

"Susanna told me something that always stuck in the back of my mind," Delcliffe continued, "but now that you brought this up it jumped forward. She would wonder if there was a competition among the men at Dayspring for the most buff staff member."

"What did she mean by that?" asked Hull. He heard Crabolli's footsteps getting closer.

"Basically that a number of them worked out like fiends and they were not only in top aerobic shape, but quite physically strong as well. They all had memberships at the West County YMCA in Chesterfield. Fogarty wasn't among the regulars, but apparently Merriwether could bench press more than his weight. Or so he claimed. Ethan Warrick doesn't do a lot of weightlifting per se, but he does that P90X crap and runs a lot. He is pretty wiry, but Susanna mentioned the tendons in his joints are tighter than the average bear, and he has to pace himself through his workouts. And Seg Mulgakov was an incredible soccer player, but he told her about a few instances from when he lived in Bulgaria. It seems he got in a number of fights on the street with older and bigger guys and could pick them out of his teeth. Wouldn't know it to look at him now. He's a fairly quiet, if intense, person. I've met him a few times."

It was more information than Hull thought he would get. "Well, thank you, Mr. Delcliffe. That fills in the gaps a bit."

"No problem," the widower muttered, clearly fighting back his own emotions. "I just wish it wasn't necessary to have this conversation."

"Neither do I, sir. But hang in there. We're doing everything we can."

Hull hung up the phone and backed up a step. He had been so intrigued by what Phil Delcliffe had told him that he had forgotten about Crabolli. He bumped into her and, startled, whirled around. She was standing before him with a Busch Light in each hand, one of which tilted in his direction.

"Thirsty?" she asked. He took the bottle as she drifted past him into the living room. He followed her from a few paces behind. She had clearly started on her beer well before he did, for she drained the last bit, placed the empty on an end table, and went back to the refrigerator for another.

Hull began to feel uncomfortable. It was one thing to play the role of the strong tower when Crabolli's inner resolve had melted. Now that she was on two feet and walking with a less feeble spirit, Hull sensed the balance of power had shifted. It was then that he realized that—having come here in her car—he had no way of getting home. He brushed his fingers through his hair, looking up to see her re-enter the room halfway through another beer, with yet another in her hand.

"Can you sit for a minute?" she asked softly.

Indeed, where was he going? He sat down after a slight delay. The sofa was firm and uncomfortable, like he was in a doctor's office. She sat down next to him and, without hesitation, powered down her second beer in the last four minutes.

"Thank you for putting up with me," she said.

"Taking one for the team," he joked, then in a more serious vein he said, "You had me worried. Everything okay?"

She shook her head no. "It was that video. If we hadn't been looking for Fogarty and Merriwether on it, I'd have never seen it and we wouldn't be calling it a day."

Hull felt that curiosity was a danger he couldn't afford, but his brain was slower than his mouth.

"What about the video?"

Crabolli sucked in a massive breath of air, rubbed her eyes, and then looked into Hull's eyes. Deep within.

"Do you want another beer?"

Again, there it was—the inner reminder that he was too precocious for his own good. And once again, his inner resolve was as sluggish as a drugged mastodon running a marathon.

"That would be nice."

She returned, not with two beers, but with four.

"What did you do, rob Friar Tuck's?" Hull said in a pathetic attempt at being comical.

"I thought I saw my father's murderer in the video."

The words pierced him as sharply as an Aztec javelin. Hull couldn't process this without any transition. "What?" he asked, vigorously shaking his head.

Crabolli bit her lip. "I know we've never talked about my family. I told you my dad had passed away when I was in high school. He was a cop in Kansas City. He got caught in the crossfire of an inner-city drug bust. It was a group called the Fremont Street Hustlers. One of the junkies—they were called ghetto babies—capped him with a clean shot through the neck. My dad never had a chance. The kid was a high school senior, eighteen years old, and he ended up doing time, but I knew he had a chance of parole."

She paused before going on. "He walked past me at the trial and said I'd better get myself out of the city, because if he ever got out of prison, he was coming after me to finish the job."

Hull sat wide-eyed through it all, then looked down and saw that half of his second beer was gone. "That's why you became a cop, because of your dad."

"Thanks to Zeus Taker. That was his street name, my dad's killer. As in Zeus the Undertaker. I wanted to be part of bringing scum like him to justice, but I wanted to do so as far away from him as possible. And I thought I was, until this afternoon. That's when I thought I saw him."

"At Six North?" blurted Hull unbelievingly. "Why would you see a thug like that at a Ballwin cafe?"

"He may be a punk, but he can blend into any crowd. All the gang communications between KC and here run deeper than we realize. Still, it would be ridiculous for someone like him to be there. I looked more closely. It wasn't him."

Crossing yet another of his internal barriers, Hull leaned toward her. "Still, given what you went through with your dad's murder, it makes sense how spooked you'd be," he said in the most comforting voice he could find. "Sorry. I just couldn't figure out what happened."

Crabolli drank the rest of her beer as the outside shadows darkened the room. "Thanks, but as you can guess, I'm still pretty freaked out by the memory." She turned toward her partner and said in a barely audible voice, "And it means I really don't want to be here alone tonight."

43

"I do have confessions to make," said Dana, "not all my own doing, but everything over the last nine years has been marked by fear."

Ballack remained quiet while she continued. "Fear of what someone could do to me, fear of what could happen if I didn't go along with things, fear of God's hatred, fear of things becoming known." She paused before burying her face in her hands again. "And fear of what you will say," she sobbed.

Firmly but gently, Ballack leaned closer. "Neither of us will know, Dana, unless you tell me."

Without looking at him, she began.

It was supposed to be an ordinary night like any other during the spring of her senior year. Parkway West had won their fourth consecutive girls' soccer game, this time storming from two goals down against Marquette for a scintillating last-second victory. Dana's beautiful crossing pass had found Rena Makosky's left foot for a one-timer that nudged around the goalie with twenty seconds to play. Dana was in a buoyant mood as she said good night to her parents, headed to the Wild Horse Grill with Rena's family before spending the night at their house.

Rena's brother, Erik, had said little over dinner, but what little he had said was directed toward Dana, who was so exhausted from the game that she didn't have the energy to give him the time of day. Had she been more alert, she would have sensed his inner anger building over what he viewed as her rejection. But she didn't realize her mistake. Not until later, anyway.

It was one o'clock in the morning that she stepped out of Rena's gigantic bedroom to make her way to the hall bath. There were no lights coming from the rooms nor a night light to mark the path down the hall. She had just managed to find the door frame to the bathroom with the tips of her fingers, and she was about to search for the light switch when the unthinkable happened. Strong arms grabbed her from behind and a hand clamped over her mouth as she was dragged backwards into a bedroom as the door shut. A box fan was blowing at full speed to attenuate any sounds. Erik quickly and roughly forced her to the floor without a sound. She struggled, wanting to cry, but stopped when he heard his menacing voice.

"Don't even think of calling for help, you little pop tart. Maybe this'll teach you to not ignore me."

In complete shock, she couldn't stop him, couldn't utter a whisper of desperation. And for the next ten minutes, it was his breath, his rage, and her silent tears. She never remembered how she got back to Rena's room. In the morning, she told Rena she had torn her robe on the door and the bruise on her cheek came when she bumped against the frame in the darkness.

"I couldn't bring myself," she said, "to speak to a guy, to look him in the face for some time after that. Part of me, sad to say, believed him that if had said something to Erik at dinner, he wouldn't have assaulted me."

"Does he still live around here?" asked Ballack.

"No, he's long gone."

Ballack sat, glaring silently into space, wanting to take her hand, but wondering why she was about to go on. But he knew there was more. There had to be more.

"I didn't date much at college when I got to Missouri State," she went on. "Not initially, anyway. The assault was still a recurring nightmare. I was literally looking over my shoulder whenever a group of guys was nearby. My heart rate would go up when a guy tried to talk to me. It changed with Dieter, in part because he knew how to be charming. He always knew how to do that. I see it now. I even saw it then but wouldn't call it for what it was. He was always interested in self-promotion and knew how to say the right words to get me to come along for the ride."

Ballack remained quiet. Although he had dispassionately pursued the case toward the successful arrest over a year ago, personally he had no use for Dana's former husband. Ballack, though an agnostic, maintained the Orthodox Church suffered a black eye with someone like Dieter Witten making it through St. Basil's Seminary and landing in a church as a priest. His diffident attitude toward Dana while alive, as well as his philandering activity, put him in the husbands' hall of shame, in Ballack's opinion.

"What I'm telling you now, I've never told anyone, not even my parents. They know about what Erik Makosky did, although I told them well after the fact, and I never specified his identity. Dieter and I got engaged after he received word he'd been accepted into St. Basil's. We went out that night and celebrated, but it soon got well beyond that."

Ballack gritted his teeth. He was in no mood for those details.

"Dieter had a bit too much to drink and became aggressive," Dana went on. "His roommate was gone for the weekend and he had the whole apartment to himself. Things got out of hand that night. He knew he could move in fast enough where I reached a point of no resistance. It was bad enough to bring back all the memories of Erik again. And then three weeks later, I discovered I was pregnant."

Before he could prevent it, Ballack let out a powerful breath. Dana briefly glanced at him before clasping her hands to her face again, looking downward.

"Dieter screamed at me when I told him. He said we couldn't allow this to derail his plans. *His* plans, he said. His plans for entering the ministry couldn't be knocked off course. I said why couldn't we have the baby, give it up for adoption, and then put off seminary for a year. That's when he just lost it. Said he wouldn't go through with the marriage. Basically, he badgered me and verbally beat me down until I caved and … and …" And then she could say no more.

The silence hung in the air like a summer morning mist, and Ballack realized that whatever Dana's story was, the next line was too awful for her to say.

"You had an abortion," Ballack finished her thought, "so that everything had a chance of being normal."

241

She wept loudly, a wail that dissipated into silent chokes, her soul still raw from the memory.

"And you had no idea," he continued, "what my reaction would be."

"I … I haven't … I haven't known what to think … for a while," she said, finally looking up. "The bereavement group I've been going to isn't exactly that, so I haven't been up front with you on that, either. It's not for losing a spouse. It's several women who try to find post-abortion healing, especially for those who have had them years ago and are just now dealing with the memories. I haven't told you that because I didn't know what you'd think. I didn't know what I'd think if you reacted against me. But I knew all that was out of my control. I found myself praying this wasn't a wreck. I was praying that you'd be pro-choice even though I'm not and be able to put it behind you even though I can't. And I prayed so much and so hard I forgot what I was praying for."

She stopped, then looked in his face, into his stony brown eyes that betrayed no emotion or hint of what he could possibly say.

"What is it, Cameron? I've told you. Can't you just tell me what you're thinking?"

Please, Ballack prayed to no one in particular. *Please.* He swallowed hard.

"It's kind of hard," he said slowly, "to muster something on the spot. I mean, we've known each other for over a year. You've just dropped this on me. I hope you weren't expecting an instant statement."

Dana said nothing.

"But I will say what I am thinking right now," he continued. "As long as you understand it's a quick response. The first thing is I could never blame you for all that happened which was beyond your control. I want you to hear that. I want you to believe that. I can't blame you for something that isn't your fault."

Dana remained silent as Ballack went on. "And on the whole Dieter thing, all you've established is who he was. Nothing more needs said about him. As far as the abortion goes, there's no reversing past decisions. And it seems that you've been dealing with the fallout of that for some time."

He looked for any sign of emotion on her face, which was difficult when speaking about Dieter. She was merely looking at him with eyes that could not decide between pleading and resignation.

"But what I do have a problem with," he said, barely obscuring his rising irritation, "is that while I've laid bare every tragedy and struggle in my life, and although I've spilled everything about me to you ... above and beyond anything I've ever told to anyone else, you haven't trusted me enough to reciprocate. Even when I've told you that I know there is more there, that something is amiss, that something is wrong and not normal, you've hedged on every opportunity to share yourself with me."

Ballack had practically spat out the last phrase.

"I ... I can't justify why," Dana began. "I think I just felt you'd reject me."

"You thought that someone who knows what it means to be disqualified out of hand for almost every opportunity," Ballack replied in a punchy voice, "who has enough baggage of his own, who was up front with you, and who practically invited you to do likewise … you assumed I would do that?"

"I'm not saying they were the right reasons, Cameron."

"In my world, that means you're not following the evidence."

Dana snapped. "Why don't you stop talking like a detective? You're not on a case right now. I was assaulted! I had an abortion! Don't you get it? Those aren't the easiest things to just bring with anyone, let alone with you!"

She had said more than she intended. Ballack smelled blood. "What?" he growled.

Dana dipped her head, knowing she had hung herself.

Ballack refused to let it go, but he kept the anger out of his voice. "What did you just mean by that?"

She took a deep breath before responding. "Sometimes you being a detective scares me. Like you can investigate any nook and cranny of my past. And if you can do that, you can judge me for it."

"You know I don't. I don't know how you could assume anyone could judge you when you've never told anyone."

"Because I always believed it would be there. Growing up in church, hearing it four years at St. Basil's, you hear about how sinful it is, any extramarital sex, abortion under any circumstance. You live under the weight of that reality, and you keep silent lest anyone would know. You tolerate your husband because you're afraid of what it means if you're on your own. You live a moderate deception because it's more manageable than the painful truth."

She looked at him and went on, "Can you see why I was scared? Why I felt you couldn't understand?"

Ballack readied himself before responding. "Dana. Listen, honey. I'm not saying you should have told everyone, but the fact you couldn't trust me is what speaks volumes. And you've had a unique, evil hand of cards dealt you. That's not my problem with this. It's that you felt it was a good thing to hide behind it and never trust me."

Dana looked into his eyes, the hope in those gray pools fading fast. "Does this change how you feel about me?"

"It doesn't mean I love you any less, Dana," he said, measuring his next words. "But if you can't fully trust me, it means you don't fully love me. And I won't go on like that if you can't trust me completely. You're the one refusing to believe that you're loved, refusing to believe that you're fully accepted. Not me. If you believe we can work through this and you'll hack through the pain and that I'll be by your side, then choose that. If you can't commit to that, then you need to choose that. But I deserve to know. I've dealt with people rejecting me because I'm weak, because I can't walk, because I'm not normal, because I'm a little esoteric. But if you can't trust me, don't be with me."

Dana's body slumped under the quiet force of his words and for a couple of minutes she sat in a quiet trance, staring at her hands, then in Ballack's face, then down at her shoes. Ballack felt within himself that he had never seen a more beautiful woman, no matter how tortured or scarred or despondent. If he could have dived within her, he told himself, he would do everything in his power to turn her heart toward this gift of hope.

He took her hands in his own and she looked at him once more.

"Dana, your past might be broken, but your future is untouched."

Her head dropped again, and his soul and his pulse froze, awaiting her word. She leaned toward him so that her cheek touched his. He could feel her hot tears smearing his face. Her breathing was shallow and unsteady.

"I want to believe. I know you love me, Cameron. And I love you. It's just …"

Her voice trailed off. She kissed him lightly as a new eruption of sorrow burst from within her. She quickly snatched her purse and stumbled toward the back sliding door, exiting through it with a wail as she vanished into the night.

44

The cool breeze rippled over the back patio of Seg Mulgakov's two-bedroom, one-bathroom home near the corner of Highway 141 and Manchester Road. Almost perfectly equidistant between church and work, he had purchased this starter home for less than one hundred fifty thousand dollars and had spent most of his weekends making it more presentable for any interested buyers in the future. He wasn't absolutely certain if anything would work out long-term with Katie Fish, but if marriage was down the road, he knew she would likely want something larger than his present cubicle. Baseboards, paint, and the occasional caulking dominated his Saturday mornings, and the small domicile was already showing the fruit of his labors.

This night was not to be spent inside, however. He had finished a draining racquetball game and was enjoying a beer on his back patio with an acquaintance. Mulgakov, a devotee of the O'Fallon Brewery, had worked the cap off a frosty bottle of Hemp Hop Rye while his companion opted for the Smoked Porter beer. The sun was about to disappear behind the tree line to the west, and as if its disappearance were a marker, Mulgakov turned his words to his friend. There had been a reason he wanted to spend the latter moments of this evening with this acquaintance on his back patio, he said. The events of the last few days of his life had vexed him terribly, and he needed to vent to someone, even if it was a casual friend he didn't completely trust.

"You're still able to do your job, aren't you?" asked his friend.

"I am," Mulgakov responded, "more so because we're working at the church and not at the center for the time being. To do otherwise would spook me."

"Come on! You're a resolute guy. I wouldn't think something like this would spook you so easily!"

Mulgakov frowned. "You know, that's what I'm talking about. It seems like everyone except for me has been going about the last couple days as if everything is totally normal rather than descending into flippancy."

"Flippancy?"

"Maybe that's too strong of a word, but really—I don't see how anything can be normal when the cops are in the middle of it all."

"You told them the truth, didn't you?"

Mulgakov's frown increased. "And why would I do otherwise?"

"Well," said his friend, finishing off the bottle of Smoked Porter. "You haven't exactly been forthcoming about your thoughts."

Mulgakov leaned back in his chair. It was time, he thought. No turning back. Even if it brought the church and the counseling center down.

"I keep thinking about Monday night," he finally said. "When I called you. It's just a weird thing happened before you signed off."

"Oh," said his companion gently, grasping for something in a jacket pocket. "What was that?"

"I thought I heard a ring. You know, like an annoying metallic voice. Seemed far enough away, but still somewhat distinct. Freaked me out at first. I was wondering what you were doing there, if that was the case."

"What do you mean?"

"Hey, I heard the noise, didn't I. That's all I'm saying. I didn't dream an alarm."

"Oh, come on, Seg," his friend said soothingly, assuringly. "Just because you heard that doesn't mean it was there. I told you I was at home. You've been to my house. I have an alarm there in the entryway. Same thing. Same message."

Mulgakov leaned back, recalling that night.

"Same message?" he said, unbelieving.

"Same."

"Thirty seconds?"

His friend's gaze hardened. "Yes, thirty seconds. For as long as I can remember."

Mulgakov kept his curdled emotions at bay. He waited until he was certain his voice was as calm as could be. "Well then … I must have read too much into it. I'm sorry. I didn't mean to imply anything."

His counterpart's face broke into a smile after several uneasy seconds. "No problem. It could've happened to anyone."

The two of them sat for another minute of quiet before the friend broke the repose. "You know what, it's been awhile since we did a power-down. Before I go, we need to renew that tradition of old."

"Oh, forget it," Mulgakov protested. "We both have work tomorrow. No way I'm going in to the office totally bombed."

"Who's saying you're getting drunk? Let's slam one more down," his friend said, getting up. "I'll even save you the trouble and get you one of your beers that tastes like a Nebraska granary."

"More like a Bulgarian one," grinned Mulgakov. "That's why I like it." He thought for a second. "Fine, for old times sake, we'll power down."

His friend disappeared and was back with the beers after a longer-than-expected hiatus.

"Had to use the bathroom," the friend explained. They clinked their bottles together. "Let's do this right before I go."

They both threw their heads back and the respective beers slammed into the backs of their throats. Mulgakov usually won these matchups of adolescent hijinks, but he had difficulty this night. The foaminess of the beer prevented him from making any headway, and this didn't seem to be O'Fallon's usual quality batch of Hemp Hop Rye. He pulled the bottle away with an ounce or two remaining, gasping for breath. He looked at his friend, who was grinning, bathed in the rising light of a waning moon. An empty bottle of Smoked Porter lay on the table, evidence of Mulgakov's defeat.

"That selection sucked," Mulgakov sputtered. "My throat feels like I swallowed bleach."

"I doubt the brewery uses Clorox," replied the friend. "You going to be alright?"

"Except for this bitter taste in my mouth," said Mulgakov, reaching for a bottle of water he had on the table. "It's like a pile of nuts gone rotten."

"Or it could be that you've finally woken up to how bad that stuff really is," laughed the shadowy figure that was his friend. "Well, I've kept you long enough. You have work first thing tomorrow. I'll take my bottles to your recycling bin on the way out."

"Thanks for dropping by," said Mulgakov, who felt slightly woozy.

He sat there for about ten minutes, leaning back in his chair wondering why he wasn't feeling well. He gradually became extremely warm, and then was engulfed by a violent sensation of pressure on his throat and chest. It was as if he needed to loosen a tie and collar from around his neck, except he was wearing a loose-fitting tee shirt. He rubbed his throat and tried to stand when the awful truth hit him. He had heard no sound of the bottles dropping into the recycling bin. No evidence would be left behind. He tried to rise and his knees turned to gelatin, buckling underneath him and sending him crashing to the ground on his side. He clawed across the patio in pathetic lurches, trying to reach his cell phone back on the table. But he knew this was the end. He had opened his vault too wide and the result was now that Susanna Delcliffe was the first, but not the only, victim. He felt his tongue expand, choking him yet dry as sand. He felt the twitches come over him, one, two, three times. And then, silence.

Thirty minutes later, a shadow glided across the side of Seg Mulgakov's house. Taking two damp towels in hand, the figure wiped the bottles of Hemp Hop Rye clean on the outside, following that with a brisk wipe-down of the patio table and both chairs. Quickly bounding into the kitchen, the shape approached the refrigerator and counter, wiping slowly, meticulously, taking no chances. The shadow swept outside, closing the patio door with a towel-lined hand before sauntering over to the lifeless body of Seg Mulgakov. The individual leaned down and scowled into the leaden eyes.

"Couldn't take chances with what you knew, my friend. I'm truly sorry it had to be you, but this has been my life. This is where my days have been hurtling toward for nine years. Call it fate. Call it destiny. But you can't call it anything now, Seg. No one, and I mean no one, takes what is mine from me."

PART FOUR

A Salvaged Journey

(April 12)

45

Katie Fish hit the "end" button on her cell phone for the fourth time in the last fifteen minutes. Her boyfriend, renowned in the office for his punctuality, was now a full twenty minutes late. Seg Mulgakov was impeccable in being on time. Both she and he had a full slate of clients today, but beyond the professional courtesy she also looked forward to Thursday mornings since they opened the center together with Karissa Emerson. Normally, Karissa was extremely busy with setting out the coffee and snacks in the lobby, and so Katie and her man could count on a few moments of time for a solitary make-out session. It would be harder to come by here at Dayspring Church until they could definitely move back to the counseling offices, but there was always hope. But with the early morning hours slipping away, her anticipation faded to anxiety.

Karissa Emerson peeked her head into Katie's room. "Still not here?"

"No," said Katie, "and it's not like him, of course. I don't know what's keeping him. He's not the type to oversleep."

"You don't think he slept through his alarm?" quipped Karissa. "I heard on the radio that the power grid west of 141 on Manchester took a hit. Doesn't Seg live down there? You don't suppose that turned off his electricity and messed up his alarm?"

"Possibly," mused Katie, "but Karissa, it's still not like him. He's likely to get up with the first rays of the sun. I know we can't drop everything and go down and check on him, but can anyone else do so?"

Karissa thought. "I'm sure Trent hasn't left his house yet, and he lives a little over a mile from Seg. Let me call him and explain the situation to him and ask him to head over there and check."

Katie nodded, worry still flickering in her pupils. "Thanks."

Karissa patted her on the back, a chaste, motherly gesture. "I'm sure it's nothing. It's got to be something completely reasonable we're not thinking about." She picked up her desk phone and hit a speed dial button. Ten seconds later, she heard a click on the other end.

"Trent? It's Karissa. Are you on your way in yet? ... No? Good. Listen, Seg hasn't showed up yet and it's just Katie and I here. I know you have clients coming in starting at nine-thirty, but since you live the closest to Seg, do you mind swinging down there and making sure he's up and going? ... Yes, Katie has tried four times to reach him on his cell and got no answer ... Sure. Sure I can do that. I'll tell them it might be a ten or fifteen minute delay ... No, I'm sure you're right. You can make up the difference throughout the day ... That's very kind of you. Thanks ... Yes, I'll stay by the phone."

With a compassionate smile warming her face, Karissa turned to Katie and said, "He'll check it out. Just get to work and don't worry. It looks like your first client has arrived."

Fifteen minutes later, Paul Merriwether placed his coffee on his desk at Dayspring Community Church. A long night of very little sleep was behind him and he hoped today could be spent shielded from the world. A two-hour lunch with an interested publisher was the only parry into a day of expected tranquility. He booted up his computer and got into a file to begin finalizing his sermon notes for the weekend. It was then his cell phone jangled, nearly falling off the edge of the desk. Grumbling at his rotten luck, Merriwether looked at the incoming call number and figured he'd better take this one. Now what crisis of stupidity could this be?

"Hello, Trent. This had better be worth the interruption."

Halting breaths and choking gulps flooded the line. "Paul ... Paul. I'm down here at Seg's house. Sir, I've got really bad news! Really bad news."

46

The opening strains of Boston's "More Than A Feeling" rippled through the dark room, jarring Zane Hull out of a deep slumber. His back ached as he swept his right hand downward, following the soulful lament of Marianne walking away, until his fingers closed around the device he sought. Flicking his index finger across the screen, he woke the phone to life and croaked a weak "Hello" to his caller.

"Good morning, Zane," came the snappy voice of Cameron Ballack, with both anger and resolve in its tone, "If you aren't up and moving by now, get that way immediately and head out to Manchester Road."

"C.B., good morning first of all," offered Hull, trying to shake off the cobwebs, "but where on Manchester did you …" He stopped.

He was looking at a radio clock on an end table, which was confusing to him because his bed in his apartment on McKnight Road had neither of those items next to it. Nor did his bedroom have a ceiling fan, which he saw out of the corner of his eye. Red curtains, too, for that matter. And why was he sprawled out in a queen-sized bed? Why was he on top of the covers instead of under?

He closed his eyes and his heart nearly stopped. Why was he in another house? And why did he feel so hung over? He brushed his hands over his body. *Fully clothed,* he thought. *That's good. Still doesn't explain where I am, but it's still good.*

That's when he heard the painful groan gush out from under the covers next to him.

Oh, sweet Maria, Hull thought. *No, no, no. Tell me that's not her, and tell me this is a bad dream!*

"Zane!" Ballack bellowed into the phone. "Are you there?"

"Yeah," answered Hull, "I'm just tired and have the headache from hell. Did you say Manchester?"

"Meet us at Creve Coeur Avenue. First right after Highway 141 on Manchester westward bound. Got word from Dayspring that Seg Mulgakov's body was discovered there this morning by Trent Fogarty."

Hull was wide awake at the mention of death. "What?"

"That's all I can say for now. How soon can you get out here? And are you anywhere near Missy?"

Craning his neck to his left, Hull saw a head of smooth blond hair slide out from underneath a red comforter, followed by the creamy smoothness of Missy Crabolli's right shoulder. On it was a tattoo, a simple heart with a cross through it, and the word "DADDY" underneath. Looking more closely, Hull let out a sigh of relief and he saw she wore a navy tank top.

"Yeah, we'll be out there as soon as we can," he said, the events of the previous evening coming together in his addled mind.

"Are you near Missy's place?" barked Ballack.

Hull grimaced painfully, both from his headache and from the irony of Ballack's question.

"Yeah, I'm fairly close," he finally said, but as he did, Crabolli let out a loud moan. Ballack wasn't going to need good ears to hear that.

"Um, Zane," Ballack asked, "What the heck was that?"

"That? That noise?" Hull replied, thinking fast. "It was the television. I fell asleep on the couch last night and it was on now."

"I thought you said you're on your way to Missy's."

"What?"

"You said you were fairly close to her place. Wouldn't that mean you were on your way?"

Hull cursed himself for having to chase a bad cover with a worse lie. "Not on my way. I … I just meant I'm close to her place anyway. Shouldn't take much time to snake up McKnight, hop on the highway, and get to her place on Page."

He hoped for a reasonable assent from Ballack, but all Hull got from the lead detective was a few seconds of silence before hearing, "Why do I get the feeling you're not being totally straight with me?"

"C.B.!" Hull exclaimed, trying to drown out Crabolli's additional groans with a desperate interjection.

"Forget it," replied Ballack. "Tori and I just passed Chesterfield Parkway and so we'll arrive well before you do. Marcus is on his way and Sheilah's team will get there eventually. Just get in gear and move. We don't have any time to waste." And he was gone.

Hull dropped his phone to the floor, overcome by the reality of what was going on around him. He turned to his left in the bed only to be met by an equally hung over Missy Crabolli, who met his dumbfounded stare with one of her own.

"Oh, Lord help us," she exhaled, "What happened?"

"Nothing happened. And forget all that for now," Hull said, "We've got another body."

47

Ballack settled back in his wheelchair as Tori drove on and angled off the highway at Exit 22, making a southward turn down Highway 141 on which had become a familiar path over the past two days. She had been noticeably quiet this morning, begging off any driving chatter due to a lack of sleep. Ballack, who wasn't in any mood at the moment to speak about Dana's issues, allowed his partner this privacy, but as they approached the Clayton Road exit, he felt his stomach rumble.

"Mind getting a bit of breakfast?" he asked. Tori, who evidently had the same hunger pangs, nodded and turned off the road to the McDonald's at Lamp and Lantern Village. With the late morning start, they wasted little time in the drive-thru lane and procured a sausage McMuffin, apple pie, and an iced tea for each of them. Ballack was all for eating on the way and supposed they would do so. He was not prepared for Tori to swerve the Dodge Sprinter into a parking spot, shaking her hands and rubbing her eyes vigorously.

Quietly, he decided to let her get ahold of herself, so he munched on his breakfast sandwich and took a few sips of tea. Getting nothing from her, he asked, "Something with Paula?"

Tori shot a breath of air from her mouth at tremendous force. "She's pregnant."

Ballack's bite of sausage and cheese tumbled from between his teeth onto the floor of the van.

Tori wiped her eyes. "She's pregnant. That much is for sure." She stopped, shook her head, and continued. "Good night, that sounds bizarre just saying it to someone else."

"Was it that Will fellow, her boyfriend?"

Tori's jaw clenched tightly. "Ex-boyfriend. His choice. As soon as he found out the news, he dropped her like a hot brick."

Ballack was aghast, although simultaneously comforted that his news wasn't the only bad tale of the day. "He's not out of this, though, is he? Not by a long shot?"

Tori smirked painfully. "Jetting on my girl was the stupidest thing he could have done. It practically shows he's the father, not that there was any doubt. He's going to get a paternity test slapped on him so hard he'll think he was in the ring with Muhammad Ali." She went on to relay all the details of the family meeting last night.

"Ouch," said Ballack, "Although in Paula's defense, if I was a fifteen-year old girl and had just discovered I was pregnant and my life could change, I'd probably skip school, too. I wouldn't know where to turn."

"What do you mean, your life *could* change?"

"It could change. Just what I said."

"It will change."

"She's having the baby?"

Tori turned to him with a quizzical look. "Just because she's fifteen doesn't mean she can make a decision of this size. She's made a decision to sleep with a guy, she needs to face up to what she's done."

"And what if she can't? She is fifteen, as you said."

"Cameron, I know this is not an area we've really ever talked about, but even when you take me out of the Catholic Church, you can't take the Church out of me. And that includes on this issue. I'm not saying she has to keep the baby afterward. She can give it up to someone else through an adoption agency. But you can't just punish the baby for that."

"So you will force her to have the baby, but after birth, it is Paula's decision where to go from there."

"You have a problem with that, or is there a flaw in my thinking, O great Socrates?"

"Just dwelling on the irony of saying she's not capable of deciding whether or not to have a baby, but somehow she becomes completely trustworthy on what to do with the baby after delivery. Seems like the moment of childbirth seems an awfully arbitrary benchmark for when Paula would get a sudden ray of wisdom."

"Making your point with the subtlety of an elephant stampede, I see," said Tori.

Ballack shrugged his shoulders, the pain of Dana's words and walkout last night still fresh.

"Don't you think that even with all your challenges and medical issues, your parents made the right call, the one that is *good*, to have you?" asked Tori, trying to move the conversation away from Paula.

"That's run through my mind repeatedly since last night," Ballack said, aware he had given Tori a peek at his soul.

"What do you mean?" asked Tori, and Ballack proceeded to tell her about Dana's declaration from the night before. He spoke generically about the sexual assault but figured Tori could connect the dots. He was up front about the abortion tale and Dana's abrupt exit of the premises.

"So what was your reaction?" asked Tori.

"What reaction? I barely had a chance to process eight years of history in eight minutes. I tried to get her to realize it wasn't a deal breaker, but there's still a lot of fear and lack of trust. I can't live with that."

"You left her hanging on the whole abortion thing?"

"She left too quickly, but I did tell her it was something in the past, not the present. Is that what you're getting at?"

"Just confirming my suspicions that you're pro-choice," said Tori.

Ballack shook his head. "And that's where you're wrong."

"What? Then why did you give her a pass?"

"It's something out of my control. I can't overturn it. Neither can Dana. She feels devastated about it and has to live with that decision every day of her life. Just because I can't quite believe God exists, I don't want her thinking that He might have taken forgiveness off the table."

"If you're such a skeptic, how can you hold to that? No one in your camp, to my knowledge, is against abortion."

"Actually," Ballack replied firmly, "I'm not anti-abortion. I said I'm pro-life. I wouldn't be able to stop it myself if I tried. Maybe it could be a legitimate option in cases of rape or the rare times the mother's life is threatened in childbirth, but I try to avoid those arguments. But I think true pro-lifers deal with more than the abortion issue. It means fighting for opportunities for physically and mentally disabled people. It means quality medical care for people who are both healthy and sick. It involves honoring and taking care of the elderly like my grandparents. It would mean not getting involved in unnecessary wars as a nation. It should get the government red tape out of the way of drug development and research for disorders like mine and other diseases like Parkinson's. So abortion is not the only game on the field."

"But you believe a fetus is a human being?" Tori ventured, her voice betraying her curiosity. In truth, she was happy for this bull session, as it deflected a bit of the worry she felt for her daughter.

"Start the van and let's get going," Ballack said, looking through the windshield. When Tori pulled out of their parking spot, he continued. "But yes, I believe a fetus is an unborn human."

"Without any religious reasons whatsoever?"

"That's right. It's based completely on logic and critical thinking. You think the religious right and the Catholic Church have cornered the market on this one? Plenty of atheists and secularists line up with me."

"How so?"

"Okay. Can we agree that when a baby is born, it's a human?"

"With the exception of Hitler?"

"Seriously, Tori," he said as they got onto southbound 141.

"Yes, it's a human."

"And for it to be a human, it would have to have potential to become more and more the finished product it is at birth, right?"

"I suppose."

"If someone has potential to be something, that 'somethingness' has to be at the core of their being in some measure all along the way, right?"

"I suppose."

"Meaning a baby that is human at birth was human in some measure all along in the womb."

"Okay, professor, is that your only card?" Tori asked as they passed John F. Kennedy High School.

"Nope. What about this? Can a man and woman create anything other than a human being?"

"Other than what resulted from Geena Davis and Jeff Goldblum in *The Fly*?"

"Obviously you believe the answer is no. No human being has ever given birth to a manatee or a rabbit or a Venus flytrap. It would have to be human, and that takes us back to my first point."

"Well, class needs to be over soon, Cameron, since we're coming up on our target." She slid into the exit ramp for westbound Manchester Road.

"Which means we can close with a rhetorical question," he said.

"And the closing question is what?"

"If scientists found a living cell on a distant world in our galaxy, what would the headline be?"

"I'm guessing something like 'Scientists Discover Life In Other Worlds', or something like that," replied Tori.

"So if we would call that life, then why isn't a group of living cells in a human womb granted the same accord?"

Tori put her palms up in a quick you-got-me gesture before grasping the steering wheel again. Ballack looked out the window, still wincing from the salt in his wound from the night before. "But all that being said," he quietly uttered, "I still admit I wouldn't know the first thing about how to steer through a voyage like unintended pregnancy. I'm not a woman, and it seems rather unfair to excoriate someone for making a painful decision when they're in a bind like that."

"So you say it's a human being, but you can't be dogmatic about a decision made by someone else?"

Ballack sighed. "I land between those poles, for better or worse."

Tori made the right turn at Creve Coeur Drive and saw Trent Fogarty's car and the now-familiar outline of Marcus Broadnax's blue Honda Insight. "Well, to be fair, partner, you never cease to surprise me."

Ballack shook his head as he looked at the gathering on the back patio of Seg Mulgakov's house. "To be honest, I'm sick of surprises. Especially ones like we're getting into now."

48

Thanks to their breakfasting delay, Ballack and Tori hadn't been out of the Sprinter for very long when Hull rocketed into the driveway past them in Crabolli's car. Both detectives emerged, looking haggard and sleepless. Ballack expected this from Crabolli after her emotional turn from yesterday, but normally Hull looked slightly more put together than this. His hair, far from being carefully styled as usual, was unkempt and flying in every direction. Dark stubble marked his face and he stifled a yawn as he approached Ballack.

"Good morning, sweetheart," Ballack chirped. Crabolli walked right past them with her sunglasses shielding her eyes, straight toward the crime scene. Hull intended to follow her, but Ballack prevented him from doing so by circling in front of him.

"Might I ask how everything is?" Ballack inquired.

"Pounding headache," Hull replied.

"Not to mention your wardrobe needs some inspiration. That's what you were wearing yesterday." Ballack pointed at Hull's shirt.

Hull took a sip of a cup of strong coffee in a QT travel mug. "And your point is what exactly?"

Ballack smiled and shook his head. "I'm saying you look like the sad result of a mating whirlwind between Lyndon Johnson and a Chia Pet."

Another sip of the coffee. "Cameron, why don't you just go ahead and tell me I look like yesterday's garbage?"

"I thought I just did," answered Ballack. He feigned turning around but just as quickly whirled and faced Hull. "Zane, if something's going on that could affect the case, I think you owe me that knowledge. You know, out of professional courtesy."

Hull looked troubled. "I will," he said, "but can I ditch this hangover first?"

"I have some Bayer if you need it," said the nonplussed Ballack. "Let's move." They began traversing the driveway and then crossed the side lawn when Ballack decided he needed to be even more pointed.

"Zane? Wait right here."

Hull stopped and turned. His posture was barely, but noticeably, slumped and his sunglasses fogged up from steam whenever he took a sip of his coffee. Ballack calculated one sip every five seconds. This sort of caffeine overdrive was unknown, he surmised.

"Take off your sunglasses," Ballack said quietly, not wanting to be overheard.

Hull looked away. "Why, C.B.?"

Ballack rolled to a stop three inches from Hull's shins. "Because I want you to."

Exhaling his annoyance, Hull pulled his shades from his head. Looking straight at Ballack, he asked, "Satisfied?"

"Yeah, right. Satisfied that you show up here with bloodshot eyes, wild hair, on no sleep, and same clothes as last night? Satisfied that you're looking as if getting sent to hell would be an upgrade? Don't insult me."

"Can we get to the stiff?" pleaded Hull.

"Before we do, Zane, let me just say this: You can do whatever you want on your own time, and whatever went down between you and Missy last night ..."

"Listen ..."

"No, you listen," Ballack said in a pooling anger, "Don't try to deny it. I don't care what you did or do, or if nothing occurred. But don't shred the cohesiveness of our team or screw up the pace we need on this investigation. We've got another death, by all looks of it a murder. This case is going to kick into high gear in a few minutes and I need you to run with me on the same path at the same speed. Got it?"

Defeated and knowing it, Hull withdrew from any argument. For whatever frustration Ballack felt toward him in that moment, he was supremely confident Hull could absorb his outrage and channel it toward a determined charge down the home stretch. Hull gulped down the remainder of his coffee and nodded his head. "Got it."

"Are we okay?" asked Ballack.

"We're okay," Hull replied, and without a word they moved toward the back yard scene.

Marcus Broadnax was straightening up as all four detectives gathered around. Ballack saw Crabolli, adorned with her own pair of sunglasses, struggle to get to her feet from a crouching position. Tori pulled out her notebook with her ballpoint pen poised for action. There was a larger, thicker binder under her arm that looked like a personal organizer.

"Okay," began Broadnax, "First of all, is this a connected death to the previous one?"

Ballack nodded. "Second one from Dayspring. Licensed professional counselor. Name is Seg Mulgakov. We had interviewed him about the first murder."

"Well," responded Broadnax, "here is the short version." He rubbed his latex-gloved hands, but Ballack noticed he kept them well away from his face or any of them. "Death likely at about nine o'clock last night, given the rectal reading and judging from the rigor mortis. Sheilah will be able to tell us more if there are any fingerprints at all, but there don't seem to be any outstanding details that lead me to believe this is a violent act like assault. No marks, bruises, or punctures at all."

"Natural death or no?" asked Ballack.

Broadnax gestured at Tori, who pointed toward the back door of the house. "The door was unlocked. Went quickly through and saw the front door was, too. No signs of breaking and entering. No signs of struggle. He either died alone or someone he knew and trusted might have been here when it happened."

"Or caused it to happen," said Ballack.

"That's where I lean," replied Broadnax with a raised finger. "Don't get to close, but when I examined the victim's mouth there was a reddish stain and a smell like almonds."

"Poisoning?" The question was Hull's.

"I would say that's your most likely scenario, guys. Around his body, there is still a ruddy complexion. That means the skin tissues and the bodily organs aren't able to use oxygen in the blood. That's not a hereditary trait. It has to be forced on someone."

"What sort of poison are we talking about?" asked Ballack. The mention of almonds brought back the memory of Dieter Witten's death that preyed on his tree nut allergy. Of course, that brought Dana's face into his mind's eye. He shook himself loose from the pain. He had three comrades facing their own problems. As the lead detective, he couldn't add to the emotional inefficiency.

Pulling his gloves off, Broadnax discarded them in a biohazard bag before cleansing his hands with sanitizer. He stood up and faced them again. "With this particular smell, I'd say the best odds are on potassium cyanide."

"Potassium cyanide?" exclaimed a wincing Crabolli. "How can it create that much red color and that pungent of a smell?'

"Because it's probably a massive amount," said Broadnax. "Once Sheilah checks out the prints on the beer bottle, I'll take it for the lab work. But if you mix KCN—that's the formula for potassium cyanide—in with anything, you can't see it. Highly soluble. If it's in that beer, we'll know in no time once we can investigate it. It acts on the acid in the digestive system and keeps the body from using oxygen. From the looks of things we definitely have some sort of cardiac arrest here as a result. But it's one the murderer wanted us to know happened this way. That's why the bottle is left behind."

"Odd for this guy," said Hull.

"Yeah. It looks like he had worked out earlier," said Ballack. "Strange for someone in such good physical shape."

"Given everything you see, that is odd," said Broadnax. "And the almond smell is usually slight when coming from cyanide, especially hydrogen cyanide. That's what the KCN turns into when reacting with acid. A lethal dose of KCN can run around two milligrams dosage to every pound of human weight. But for the smell to be that acute on his mouth, you're talking a devastatingly high dosage. Something that was designed to finish him off quickly, where there would be no doubt."

"Where the victim couldn't fight back," said Tori.

"Someone would have to know the correct dosage and how to ramp it up," put in Ballack.

"Or," corrected Broadnax, "have no clue but would rather overcompensate. But that's unlikely. If this is KCN, the perp in all likelihood knew how to utilize it."

"If that's what it is," said Hull, looking into the blue sky and not at Mulgakov's body.

Broadnax looked hard at him, wagging his fingers with a snapping motion of his right wrist. "I'm giving you my best guess. Given the presentation of the body, I'd say it's a good one."

"You were right on the Delcliffe death," said Ballack flatly. "I'd say that's earned you the right to an educated guess here. Anything else, Marcus? Would beer—given that was the target—be an efficient conductor for the potassium cyanide?"

"One of the better fluids to do so, especially if there are hints of citrus in with the hops and grains," said Broadnax. "The altered taste might be noticeable to anyone with a strong sense of smell. In this case, we'll never know."

No one responded to this, so Broadnax looked around the group. "I'll be able to give you the clinching report after I get him on the table. We're backed up today, though."

"Might take a while?" asked Tori.

"Might take a miracle," replied Broadnax. "Do your thing with the body and I'll get it later. Stay away from the mouth, though. Residue, and all."

After Broadnax went aside to speak with Sheilah Grimshaw and her forensics crew, Ballack turned to his colleagues.

"Okay, here we go. Sheilah and her group will be tearing this place apart for a strand of hair or a print smudge. If this death is like the first one, I don't think they'll locate a thing, although it won't be for lack of trying."

"You think Freud did both?" asked Crabolli. It seemed to take all her strength to form that sentence.

"He did both," said Ballack, looking at Mulgakov's glassy eyes. "Two counselors from Dayspring wiped out. The question is why, because at first glance Delcliffe and Mulgakov are unrelated in their positions, backgrounds, and mentalities."

"So what's our first step here, C.B.?" asked Hull. "Snoop the house or ask around the neighborhood for unusual activity?"

"You and Missy hit all the houses on this street and find out the normal stuff. Any sightings of people, cars, license plates, anything out of the ordinary. Rapid fire items shouldn't take you to long, and the walking around will do you both some good in the fresh air. Tori, if you could please get the portable ramp from the Sprinter and we'll check the kitchen and other places inside the house provided we're not bumping into Sheilah and company. As small as this place is, it shouldn't take long." Ballack turned toward the house.

"Think you'll find something packed away that will give away the killer?" inquired Crabolli.

Ballack stopped, his brain rapidly connecting to the afternoon before in the spartan classroom. He smiled, thankful his attention to detail could come in handy here.

"What is it, Cam?" asked Tori.

Ballack shook his head, laughing. "Just get the ramp. Let's get inside. And the first thing we need to do is find Seg Mulgakov's briefcase."

49

"And why, may I ask, are we doing this?" Tori wondered as—with gloved-lined hands—she placed the briefcase on Mulgakov's small dining table. Ballack pulled up next to her.

"To find out why we're here," he replied. "I sure hope we can get through this carefully yet quickly. I sense another long trip back to Dayspring."

"One problem, partner," Tori said glumly, clicking the open tabs of the briefcase to no effect. "And that is, this thing is locked. You want me to go about prying it with a crowbar?"

"A crowbar isn't necessary, Tor. Take both locks and set each combination to six hundred ninety-four. That's six-niner-four."

"Excuse me?"

"Just do it. We're fighting time. Hopefully, Zane and Missy have worked the lead out and are lolling around the neighborhood finding out anything that can help us track down Freud."

"Why that number?"

Ballack smirked. "I should be remembering it correctly, but I think that's it."

"You're not just screwing with me, are you?" demanded Tori. "Because if you are … oh … oh. There is a God."

Ballack didn't necessarily agree with her last statement, but he couldn't stop grinning at the result. Seg Mulgakov's briefcase opened as if moved by a divine hand.

Tori laid her trembling hands on the table. Her daughter's pregnancy, and now Ballack's eccentric willpower to remember the most incidental details. She wanted to return to Paula's world, and yet Ballack's single-mindedness—recaptured since his confession this morning—forced her further on the terrain in this universe.

"You noticed this when?" she finally croaked.

"Yesterday when we interviewed Mulgakov, he went pale as he wrote something and he placed it in his briefcase. I happened to watch him rotate the combination. He obscured the left side, but I had a clear view of the right. It was a gamble, but I figured the number was the same on both sides."

"The briefcase was almost ten feet from us!" exclaimed Tori. "Even I remember that. How in the world did you see the combination?"

Ballack pulled a dollar bill from his wheelchair's side pouch, pointing to the top of the pyramid on the back. "The all-seeing eye. It views everything," he smiled.

"Next question is how you remembered a strange number like that," said Tori, looking in the briefcase. "Hard to imagine that's a birthdate."

"It was somewhat easy," declared Ballack as he sidled up to the table and viewed the case's contents along with her. "If you keep Mulgakov's nationality in mind."

"What does being Bulgarian have to do with six-nine-four?"

"It's actually six in ninety-four. Remember the World Cup we talked about at breakfast yesterday morning? Bulgaria's star player was Hristo Stoichov. He was the leading scorer. The leading scorer with six goals total. In the 1994 World Cup. Six in ninety-four. Not just a mere combination code, but a living tribute."

"I still don't see how you could see it, or come up with that," Tori gushed, thumbing through two files and a book from the case. "I swear I'd love to spend a day in your brain and know how it works."

"Maybe like a road map of West Virginia," replied Ballack. "What's in the flaps?" He pointed toward a cream-colored sheet of paper, the edge of which was barely visible. "I think that was the paper he wrote on when we questioned him yesterday."

Tori lifted the page from the rear flap of the skinny accordion file. She unfolded it and read. "It says, 'Confront tonight and ask why with Delcliffe." She stopped, unconvinced she had just read those words.

"Six. Ninety-four," said Ballack softly. There was a long pause.

"You check his cell phone there on the sofa, Tor," Ballack finally said, moving toward the kitchen. "I'm seeing what he had in the fridge."

50

The sun was high in a cloudless sky when Ballack and Tori left the house, circling around to the front and running smack into Crabolli and Hull who were coming up the driveway.

"You both are looking better," said Ballack. "What's the news from the other houses?"

"Thanks, sweetheart," responded Hull, who gestured to Crabolli to begin.

"House next door is vacant," began Crabolli. "Not a lick of furniture inside. So it leaves the two across the street. The four-bedroom directly across from here was a no-go. According to the couple in the house cater-corner to here, it's occupied by a few teachers who have gone in on renting it together. But that couple was our only link with any hard knowledge. They said a car took off from in front of here a few minutes before nine."

"They just happened to be looking out the picture window at that time?" asked Tori.

"Retired couple. Richard and Mary Foley were in their living room. Richard said he had just made some hot chocolate for the two of them. He sat down with a book by the window while Mary played piano. Their porch light was off, so what Richard saw was likely sketchy. Said the car looked like a compact, but he wasn't sure."

"If it's someone from Dayspring, that doesn't help us," quipped Hull. "I don't think I've seen a midsize or above in that lot."

"Well, Mulgakov's car is here and intact," redirected Ballack. "Although, we didn't find his car keys anywhere. The fridge is decently stocked and there was a notable supply of beer. To be precise, a twelve-pack carton of O'Fallon Hemp Hop Rye and a sixer of O'Fallon Smoked Porter. The rye beer was minus two and the Smoked Porter was down two. Searched his wallet and found a receipt from the Schnucks at Baxter and Manchester and the beer was one of the purchases. The receipt was dated yesterday at three-thirty-eight in the afternoon, soon after we talked to him."

"Meaning that if Freud—assuming this was Freud—drank with him before killing him, they polished off a combination of four last night," said Tori.

"Good math skills," joked Hull.

"Shut up, jackweed," snarled Tori, but a stern look from Ballack kept her at bay.

"And given that we found the bottle of the rye in front of Mulgakov on the patio," said Ballack, "and we discovered an identical one on the kitchen counter, I'm figuring Freud either drank the porter with Mulgakov or made off with a couple of them."

"Are we to go to Dayspring and ask everyone their favorite beverage?" asked a dazed Crabolli.

"We won't ask them that. I just kept that in play as a mental hook, but Tori found something even more noteworthy." Ballack pointed to Mulgakov's cell phone in her hand.

"Three separate communications of interest last night," she began. "We know the recipients because they are banked in

Mulgakov's contacts. There was a text to one Dan Cooper to remind him they were still playing racquetball at six-fifteen last night, but it would have to be a quick game, as he was meeting with someone soon after. That text was sent at ten minutes until four in the afternoon, followed by two more matters. There was a conversation with Ethan Warrick at five after four. That call lasted two minutes and fourteen seconds, and hot on the heels of that was a text to Trent Fogarty. That text said, 'Something critical came up today, and I think you and I need to have a face-to-face talk. Very important.' And that was it. Sent at four-oh-nine. He called Katie Fish last night, apparently in transit from the YMCA or wherever to his place. That was it, although Fish called him last night around ten and then four times this morning when he didn't show. I listened to her voice mail. Frantic girl."

"Two texts and two calls to four different people last night," Ballack sighed. "And within four hours of the first communiqué, Sergei Mulgakov was dead."

"Looks like we're headed to Dayspring," said Hull.

"And we have three persons of interest," Tori added. "Two at Dayspring and one in Dan Cooper. We need to talk to each of them as soon as possible. I think we can discount Katie Fish unless it's to offer condolences."

"Gotta figure who this Cooper guy is first," reminded Crabolli.

Ballack shook his head. "Zane, you interviewed Darci Cooper our first day there. Did she mention her husband's name?"

Hull looked as if the hangover lifted like a thunderhead over the ocean. "Geez, that's right. She said Dan. I wrote it down and never made the connection."

"So we have three darts in the air. Let's run up to Dayspring and gather the entire staff. Given the text to Dan Cooper is the clearest lead from the phone, we need to check with him ..." Ballack trailed off, aware of an incoming call on his own phone.

"Ballack," he said, answering the call. "Yes, sir. We're headed to the church. Yeah, no need to come here ... Excuse me? ... Excellent. That might not be everything we want but it's more than I expected. Thank you, sir. Good bye."

He hung up and pointed to the cars. "Let's go. Tori, peek in and tell Sheilah to come up to the church or call and brief us when she's done. That was Krieger. He has warrants for personnel files. It's not much, but it could be enough. Let's roll."

51

They were headed north on Highway 141 when Ballack's
phone went off again. Looking at his caller ID, he thought it strange
that his sister was calling him just before lunchtime. He needed to
focus, and against his better judgment, he answered after three rings.

"Can you grab dinner with me tonight?" His sister's voice was
remarkably blunt.

"Tonight?" Ballack's head was scrambling to jump to this
tangent. "You are aware I'm smack in the center of a murder
investigation? Depending on how things go today, I can't say. I won't
give you a written guarantee."

"You obviously forgot my birthday is tomorrow," Jill replied.

Ballack rested his forehead in his left palm. "And you and
Ethan aren't going out for one more free meal while you work up the
courage to dump him?"

"He wanted to take me out tomorrow," she sighed listlessly,
"but I'm going over there today after he's done at six."

"And?" asked Ballack, already guessing the answer.

"I'm telling him it's over. I'm sure he'll be upset, since he was
probably going to pop the question over dinner tomorrow. But I can't
do it. Call it a pre-emptive strike."

"So you're an Israeli missile to his Iraqi nuclear reactor,"
Ballack chuckled, shaking his head. "Well, I'll tell you what. Let's
compromise. Call me around when you get out of his place and we'll
see what's up then. But are you sure you need to talk to him today?"

"I want this done with, Cam. It's not that he isn't a decent guy and all. I just don't want to marry him. And if I don't want that, why stick around?"

"It's just that …" Ballack paused, not wanting to divulge anything about rooting around Dayspring, especially since he couldn't be certain Warrick had told Jill anything or not.

"What?" Jill implored. "It's just that what?"

"Never mind," said Ballack, confident that his nagging sensation meant nothing. "Call me when you get out of his apartment, and I'll let you know if the dinner is a go."

"Will do," said his sister. "And let Tori know she doesn't have to drop you anywhere. I borrowed the van from Mom since my car is in the shop today. New muffler and all. Wherever you are, I can pick you up and take you home if you want."

"Fine," replied Ballack, feeling a cough coming from his suddenly irritated lungs, "but just remember, we might not have had our closing meeting and I don't know where we'll be on this case. So no promises."

"I never know where you are on anything, brother," she responded. "Keep your phone on. Just try to make it happen. I need someone to help me decompress from this." And she was gone.

52

It was Ballack's first visit to the conference room in the
Dayspring church office. With all counselors here for one more day, it
would be the most convenient place to amass what remained of the
entire staff. The beige walls were decked with a series of photographs
depicting the progressive erection of the church building. The red
fabric office chairs, all on cast rollers, surrounded the long table, and
once again Paul Merriwether took his place at one end. Assured that
everyone was present except for Katie Fish, Ballack entered the room
as the double doors in the lobby opened from afar. A tall, bearded
fellow held up his hand to Ballack and waved several sheets of paper.
It was Stu Krieger with the warrants, just in time.

"Good day, boss," Ballack said to Krieger when the SID
Commander entered the room. "I see you got the goods."

Krieger, known for a significantly gruff appearance and
attitude on the job, actually mustered a slight grin as he shut the door
behind him. "More on these later. Don't let me keep you."

Ballack looked around the room. As before, the other
detectives stood, each keeping vigil over a different side of the table.
Peggy Kimball, Audrey Sneller, and Trent Fogarty sat on the side
nearest the door. Ethan Warrick, Darci Cooper, and Karissa Emerson
sat to Ballack's right. Emerson had demanded to stay and comfort
Katie in the basement when Merriwether had relayed the news to her
that Mulgakov was dead. But Ballack and the rest of the detectives had
unanimously rejected that point. They needed as many people with

them as possible to discern reactions and ask questions regarding this suspicious death. Being accommodating to others' emotions had to take a back seat to the truth.

"You all, with the exception of Miss Fish, remember me and the other members of my team from Tuesday morning," began Ballack, "when we came here on the death of Susanna Delcliffe. Although this latest tragedy has not occurred on Dayspring's campus, it is no less heartbreaking. Seg Mulgakov was found dead at his home this morning by Trent Fogarty. I am truly sorry to have to tell you this news, which some of you already know. But this redoubles our efforts to find the killer, so we will once again insist on your full courtesy and cooperation."

Both Peggy Kimball and Audrey Sneller began crying uncontrollably at the news, shaking violently in their seats. The tears flowed down Karissa Emerson's cheeks again. Trent Fogarty and Paul Merriwether both put their hands to their faces and covered their eyes. Ethan Warrick leaned forward and began breathing heavily with a troubled look on his face. Darci Cooper, after letting out a gasp and a few tears, turned to Ballack with fear erupting from her throat.

"For the love of God, is it so hard to find a killer? Susanna's dead! Seg is dead! We've lost two of our colleagues, two friends! And you are insisting on our courtesy?"

Ballack knew Darci Cooper was spooked out of her wits, or this was a good cover. He just didn't want her getting control of the conversation, so just as suddenly he interrupted. "Insist we will, Mrs. Cooper, even as you all grieve. We will need to ask some questions, hard questions, but the more truthful you are in very trying circumstances can make all the difference in our finding the killer."

Merriwether spoke next. "I'm sorry, but is there any reason to assume there is one killer? And if you are asking some 'hard questions,' as you put it, are you not insinuating that you consider these deaths to be the result of someone's actions within Dayspring itself?"

"Paul," said Ethan Warrick somewhat sharply, "I think the detectives can handle this, and we need to realize they need to look at every option!"

Ballack waited, giving space for one of his team members to enter the fray, but none did. He looked down the table at the pastor. "Both attacks made on people here make us believe it is the work of one person. True, there is the chance there are more, but if so, they are working in coordination. As for believing this is an inside job, we neither assume that nor reject that as a possibility."

He looked around at the other counselors. "We will have to take some time for questioning, and we'll need to raise those questions with specific people in here. Also, Commander Stu Krieger is here from the Special Investigation Division, and he'll need to speak with Mrs. Emerson and Pastor Merriwether when we break for questioning."

"I can speak with them in the pastor's office, if that's okay," demurred Krieger.

Ballack nodded. "If that's the case, I want to speak for all my colleagues and say how sorry we are that you have had to endure these losses. Please remember that, even as we continue to do our duty around here. And I realize you all would like to get back to your true offices as soon as possible. That should be tomorrow if all goes well."

The counseling staff took that as an unspoken blessing of dismissal. Before they could move, however, Ballack held up his hand.

"In the meantime, we will need to meet with two of you. Mr. Fogarty, if there's a chance you could meet in your church office with Detectives Hull and Crabolli. The rest of you are dismissed, with the exception of Mr. Warrick."

The surprised Warrick was in the middle of smoothing his dirty blond locks, and the mention of his name change his visage to a quizzical one. He looked from Ballack to Tori and back to Ballack before casually shrugging his shoulders.

"Want to meet downstairs in my functional office?" he asked finally. "I've got a client coming in thirty minutes."

"No," replied Ballack, waving the last of the staff out of the room and ramming an authoritative finger on the table. "Here will be just fine."

53

Ballack nodded to Tori, who pulled Seg Mulgakov's cell phone from its recharging cord plugged into the wall. He was relieved his partner had her head on straight today. It had been Tori who remembered to look around Mulgakov's house for the cord before they departed for Dayspring. "Never know how long of a day it'll be," she murmured.

Tori approached Warrick as Ballack adjusted his own voice amplifier for his trach. His throat and lungs were burning with the weariness of the last few days, but he was determined to make no misstep or flaw in pursuit of Freud from here on out. He looked at Warrick's face as Tori showed him the phone screen.

"Do you recognize this phone?" she asked curtly.

Warrick glanced at it briefly and looked at the doorway. "Must be Seg's. His picture is on the screen."

Tori flicked two or three buttons, having figured out this step while Ballack had been addressing the staff. "Do you remember this call?"

Again the brief look with the gaze toward the doorway, as if seeking an escape pod to materialize out of thin air. "Well, that's my number," offered Warrick.

"A call that occurred at five minutes after four o'clock yesterday afternoon to be precise, Mr. Warrick," Ballack intoned. "According to the direction of the arrow icon, it seems to be a call that originated from your phone."

"So it is," replied Warrick.

"In and of itself, it's just another phone call," said Tori, "but in the context of its timing, we find it interesting. Soon after this call, Seg Mulgakov texted someone else and told that person that something had just come up that he needed to discuss with them. Now you wouldn't happen to know what that issue would be?"

"And why would I?" Warrick's voice held a trace of antagonism.

"Because from another communication of his," Ballack said firmly, "in which Mulgakov said he needed to get together with someone and find out why that individual was here with Delcliffe. Would you happen to know what he meant by that?"

"Here with Delcliffe?" asked Warrick. "I'm sorry I can't be more helpful, but I have no clue what Seg would have intended."

"When we spoke with him yesterday," said Tori, "He wrote those words down as a reminder to himself. We came upon that note today when we explored his house."

"And you're sure it was the exact one, I'm guessing," said Warrick. "Well, if he did write it down, it wouldn't be referring to me. I didn't even see him last night. I was at home, at my place in Des Peres."

"All night?"

"Yes, if you're wondering that."

"As a matter of fact, we were," said Ballack. "But can anyone verify that you were there?"

Warrick let his silence speak for him.

"You okay, partner?" asked Tori.

"I am," said Ballack, "but every now and then I wish we could have a beer on the job. You drink, Ethan?"

More silence.

"Ethan?"

"What does that have to do with anything?" Warrick asked.

"It doesn't. Just wondering. Do you have a preference?"

"Are these really the questions you intend for me to answer?" snapped Warrick. "My friend and colleague is dead, and you feel the need to question me about my choice of beer?"

"If you don't like those questions, how about this one? Do you understand our interest in any text or phone call with Seg Mulgakov? Given that it's likely he had some desire to speak with whoever was with Susanna Delcliffe in which appeared to be her final moments? Whoever fit that category, if he knew it was liable to identify him as Delcliffe's murderer, might have motive to rub out Seg Mulgakov as well."

"And to that, I'll repeat what I said earlier," growled Warrick. "I was home the whole time. I never saw Seg at all last night. So there is no story you can stitch together that implicates me! Because I can't be accused of a crime I never committed!"

Ethan Warrick's face was turning red. A vein rippled down the left side of his head into his temple area, as crooked as a mangled pipe cleaner. Ballack took a hard look at him, a chill rippling through his body.

"If that's the way you see it," said Ballack.

Tori cast a sidelong glance at him.

"It is," said Warrick, his voice going lower. "Look, I know you have a job to do. I know you have to be impartial and check out everyone here. But I would hope that you'd at least consider things on a personal level, too. I'm a counselor and a team player. I'm someone committed to emotional healing, not physical destruction. I've seen enough pain to last awhile. I certainly wouldn't want to inflict it on someone else."

Ballack considered this in silence, again feeling sorry for Warrick given what Jill would be telling him later. Tori watched him, waiting through an agonizing stretch of quietude, although she knew such feigned serenity masked the vigorous thought going on within him.

In that moment, Ballack shrugged his shoulders and moved toward Warrick with an extended hand. "Given that," he said, "perhaps you have a point. And I'm sorry if you felt I was rough on you. That wasn't the intention."

Warrick quickly accepted the handshake. "No problem. To both of you. And now, if you'll excuse me, I need to head downstairs for my first appointment."

He left through the door, and as he did, Darci Cooper went walking by.

"Mrs. Cooper," called Ballack as loudly as his struggling voice would allow. He signaled Tori to follow and to bring Mulgakov's cell phone. "Sorry to interrupt you so soon after our group session, but we need to ask you a question."

Darci Cooper stood uneasily before them as they approached her in the church lobby. "Yes, Detectives?"

"Could you happen to tell us where your husband works?"

"My husband?"

"Is Dan Cooper your husband?"

"He is. I just got off the phone telling him about Seg's death. May I ask why you're asking?"

Tori flipped out the phone, already logged to the text between Dan Cooper and Seg Mulgakov from the afternoon before. Ballack began talking.

Forty seconds later, heads turned in the church office as Darci Cooper exclaimed, "You can't be serious!"

54

"You know, you could have pulled out a grenade on her if you wanted her scared out of her wits," laughed Tori as Ballack gestured for Crabolli and Hull to join them outside in the parking lot.

"I know," replied Ballack, "but I wanted to see her face. And admit it, you wanted to, as well."

Hull and Crabolli drew near. "Any word from Fogarty?" asked Ballack.

"There's nothing we didn't expect," said Crabolli. "Fogarty actually said he never read the text until this morning when he checked his phone after Karissa Emerson called him. Quite indignant, pretty nervous. That head bob thing to his right shoulder! Annoying. But he claimed to have been out to dinner with his wife last night and paid via credit card. His wife is bringing over the receipt to prove his alibi."

"His wife is driving in?"

"Says she handles the finances."

"Did you ask where he had been last night? Or did he offer that first?" asked Ballack.

"I asked," offered Hull, who was on his third cup of coffee for the day, and it was paying dividends. "Why do you ask?"

Ballack looked at his laptop screen pensively. "Just a thought I had."

"Great," said Tori. "When you get those thoughts, the biggest loser is Blue Cross and Blue Shield."

"Krieger will get you set up on the personnel files, although we might need to comb through all those together," reminded Ballack. "We expected a fight on the client records and didn't go after them, mainly because we'd lose but also because I don't think they'll be helpful at this stage of the investigation. Still, I think there's some gold we can mine from personnel files on anyone in that office. We have some other things to cover in the meantime—Tori and I have to go bug Darci Cooper's husband—and the files will likely take several hours to comprehensively cover, but we can't afford not to take the time."

"Okay," said Crabolli, "Get with Krieger and hit Merriwether's email. But upon what assumptions are we proceeding? We're still banking on Freud working alone? And that he's a male?"

"Mulgakov's death could go either way," said Tori, "but it's likely we're talking one male targeting both. The question is whom."

Ballack nodded. "We keep an open mind, and it would be helpful to speak more definitively with Katie Fish if she's up to it. For now, this is all to go on. Let's get moving because this will be a long night."

The four of them separated into their usual pairs, and as he and Tori approached the Sprinter for departure, Ballack felt a sudden pang of necessity. He pulled out his cell phone and dialed, waiting through three, four, and five rings. Finally, the voice mail engaged.

"Hi, you've reached Jill. I obviously can't answer the phone now, so please leave a message."

The beep was so soft that Ballack nearly missed it before saying, "Jill, it's Cam. Give me a call back as soon as you get this. Important."

"Important?" asked Tori, bringing the ramp down to earth.

"Another thought I had."

"And you know what happens when those erupt."

55

The offices of J.W. Terrill oversee the stretch of Highway 40 that intersects with Maryville Center Drive. Sharing building space with two other companies, the structure faces the newly built campus of Westminster Christian Academy to the west and looks northwest toward Maryville University. Tori pulled into a handicapped spot south of the building and went through all the usual motions to set Ballack free from the van. Two minutes later, they were on the second floor convincing a skeptical receptionist they were there to speak to Dan Cooper on a matter of great urgency. The girl, with short auburn hair and a gray pantsuit, called Cooper on the intercom and then directed them back.

For someone who had lost a good friend and just been told so by his wife, thought Ballack, Dan Cooper was doing remarkably well. He seemed slightly rushed during introductions, and his hair was somewhat out of place, but he managed a solid handshake and asked both detectives to seat themselves near his desk.

"Did the receptionist offer you anything? Coffee? Soda?" he asked.

"No, she didn't, but we'll be okay," said Tori. Ballack thought it unwise that she declined for both of them as his throat was bothering him more and more. He asked for a bottled water.

"She just got hired a week ago," explained Cooper. "Still trying to remember the little things to make people welcome." He pushed the intercom button. "Mandy, could you bring a water back here for the detective?"

Ballack got right to the point. "I know that your wife has likely told you of Seg Mulgakov's untimely death, as well as of Susanna Delcliffe's death a few days back. While I understand that he was a friend and this could be a difficult time for you, would it be possible to answer some questions?"

"I suppose so," Cooper said haltingly, as if he had been crying before their arrival. "I certainly want to help."

"How long have you been working here, Mr. Cooper?"

"Eight years. I interned at Terrill while getting my MBA and they offered a position in insurance soon after. Being working in retirements and investments the last two years. It's been a good experience. Great people to work with."

"I see you share space with Morgan Keegan."

Cooper nodded. "We do. Of course that façade will change in the near future. Raymond James just bought them out last week, so that'll mean a new sign."

"How long did you know Seg Mulgakov?" asked Tori.

"Three years. Darci and I go to The Journey for church, so our friendship precedes when Darci got on at Dayspring. Met him there, and then I saw him at West County Health and Fitness another time. We both play racquetball—I should say played—together and usually did that twice a month on average. That's actually where we were yesterday evening. We had a six-fifteen game reservation at one of the courts there. Seg was willing to play, but he had texted me late afternoon and said it needed to be a really fast game. When we met at the club, I asked him why and he seemed incredibly uncomfortable discussing it. He said he had to get away no later than seven and meet someone."

"Did he say where he was going?" asked Ballack. So far Cooper's testimony checked out with the text they had seen.

Cooper shook his head and swallowed hard. "No mention. That's not like him either."

"Not like him?"

Cooper shrugged. "I was worried he was seeing someone else. You know, other than Katie, his girlfriend. Poor girl. This is going to devastate her."

Ballack wanted to stay on task. "He didn't mention a certain location? A restaurant? Going home first? Anything?"

"Nothing."

"What car do you drive, Mr. Cooper?" asked Tori.

"The silver Volvo with the Romney bumper sticker on it out in the lot. Why?"

"Just asking."

"Because you wonder if I had something to do with his death because he and I saw each other yesterday evening?"

"You never saw him at all after the racquet club last night?" Ballack queried.

"Never again, sadly."

"Where were you the remainder of the night?"

Cooper sighed. "I actually went back up Kehrs Mill Road from the club, hit Clayton, and came back over here to the office. It was about eight-thirty by the time I arrived here. I had stayed longer to lift weights and run after Seg left. I was here doing some work for a new client until about nine-thirty, upon which I went home."

"Home is where?"

"Up near Olive and Woods Mill. That bank that has the nice stone fountain on Olive just west of Woods Mill? We live in a development behind there."

"So you got home at nine-forty-five or thereabouts?" asked Tori.

"Give or take a minute."

"Your wife can verify if we ask her?"

"I'm sure Darci will have no trouble doing so."

Recalling Broadnax's judgment on time of death, Ballack knew this didn't let Cooper off the hook. "Can anyone verify that you were here during the time you claimed last night?"

"I don't know about security cameras," said the slightly miffed Cooper, "but I used my electronic key fob to get in. The security staff for the building would have the record of that entry even if they don't have my face on film."

"But technically anyone could use your entry fob," said Ballack. "That's why a visual would be helpful."

"Are you doubting me?"

"I didn't say that. I'm merely distinguishing what we know and what we can't say for sure. Did anyone see you enter the building last night?"

He could sense Cooper's frustration rising, but the investment executive calmly said, "No. Not to my knowledge."

"Did Seg Mulgakov come to your home very often over the last few years, or you to his?"

"Several times for both," Cooper ventured warily.

"How often? Say how often per month?"

"Maybe once a month. When he came to my—our place—it was usually to have dinner with Darci and myself. Lately, Katie has been in that equation, so it's been the four of us. Whenever I went to his place, it was normally after playing racquetball and it revolved around having a beer from his fridge."

Of course, thought Ballack.

"Any particular beer?" he asked.

Cooper's brow furrowed. "What does that have to do with the price of tea in China?"

"Just asking. For the sake of argument, assume it has to do with something."

Before Cooper could answer, Tori broke in. "It wouldn't have anything to do with that picture over there, would it?"

Ballack followed her extended finger to a small photograph, adhering to the side of a tall file cabinet, held on either with tape or Sticky-Tac. It showed a broadly smiling Dan Cooper with his arm around Seg Mulgakov, with Darci Cooper and Katie Fish on either side of the men. From the date stamp, Ballack reckoned it was from the most recent Oktoberfest, and from the background, they seemed to be in the middle of Soulard. But the noticeable things were the beer bottles in their hands. Mulgakov was clutching his Hemp Hop Rye, while Cooper's fingers gripped a frosty cold O'Fallon Smoked Porter.

56

"I feel like we're dancing around things," Tori declared as they curled off the north outer road onto Highway 141 heading south, back to Dayspring. "Racquetball, text messages, and beer, but no clear motive. Why would Dan Cooper murder a friend? For that matter, why would he kill Susanna Delcliffe?"

Ballack was listening, but he was dialing Jill's cell phone at the same time. "I have no clue, and that's the sticking point. He's the last one we clearly know had seen Mulgakov, and no one saw him last night at Terrill. That doesn't put him in the clear, but it doesn't implicate him either."

Jill's voice mail clicked on again, and Ballack groaned through the greeting. "I don't believe this."

"Why are you trying to reach her?" asked Tori.

"My reasons," he shot back, "are my own." The voice mail elicited its muted beep. "Jill, it's Cameron again. Listen, call me. It's im-por-tant! It's about two in the afternoon. Call me before you go over to Ethan's this evening for your little chat."

"She doesn't know he's an amazingly unlikely prospect in a murder investigation, does she?"

"Unless Ethan Warrick has told my sister, then no."

"You paranoid that he's not so unlikely?"

"I never said that. I just think she needs to hold off on having her 'dear John' talk until after this runs its course."

"Oh, please! Do you realize how long this could take? He could propose to her by then! There are worse tragedies."

"Speaking of tragedies, it seems like Miss Fish came up here to mourn with us for a few moments," said Ballack as they pulled up in the counseling center's parking lot. A lonely blue Hyundai Accent sat backed in to a spot near the front door, and Ballack—remembering Fish's face from one of Dayspring's pictorial counseling brochures—recognized her sitting in the drivers' seat.

Tori pulled the van up next to Katie Fish and eased the window down. "Miss Fish, I assume there's a reason why you're here."

"Everything is so empty now, so gray, so meaningless," said Katie Fish in the waiting area of Dayspring Counseling Center. She gently wiped her nose with one tissue and dabbed her eyes with a second one. Her black hair fell to the middle of her shoulder blades, covering the top of her royal blue button-down blouse. Her white slacks were carefully creased. An ankle bracelet hovered above her left foot, while the second toe on her right foot bore a ring. Even in her grief, thought Ballack, she showed enough fastidious care for her presentation.

"It won't be meaningless," encouraged Ballack, "if we can catch his killer. Anything you tell us, or can remember, can be helpful."

"And you're sure he was killed?" Fish asked.

Ballack hesitated, so Tori responded in his stead. "Upon close investigation, it was apparent he had been poisoned. It wasn't a common toxin, so from all appearances this was a deliberate action."

Fish stared wide-eyed at Tori, then at Ballack.

"Miss Fish," he said, "He was murdered."

Shaking her head, Fish's lips quivered as she sought words she forced out through tears. "Then it makes complete sense why he said what he did last night."

"Last night?"

"I asked him if he wanted to go out for frozen custard after he got done with playing racquetball."

"When did you ask him?"

"Around three o'clock. I called him and asked him. He seemed incredibly troubled when he told me no, so I asked why. He said something had come up in his mind about Susanna's murder and he needed to speak with someone about it."

"He didn't mention who that someone was?"

Fish shook her head. "He didn't. He told me he'd figure out when to let me know, but that he wanted to handle the first leg of the conversation himself."

"And he didn't tell you why?"

"No, except that he just wanted me to be careful."

Ballack leaned back in his wheelchair. "For the likely reason, as it seems, that he was about to confront Susanna Delcliffe's murderer because he had discerned who it was."

Fish whirled toward Ballack. "What?"

"We figured as much," said Tori, "from a note he wrote himself. We found it in his briefcase this morning at his house."

"I don't suppose," said Ballack, looking full in Katie Fish's eyes, "he told you about that little detail."

"No," she meekly said. "All he said was that the sharks are the ones we least expect to have teeth."

The chimes announced that the front door had opened, and within seconds Missy Crabolli and Zane Hull followed the voices and arrived in the waiting area. Ballack gave a look meant to say, "Got anything?"

"I see you beat us here," said Hull. "What now?"

Ballack looked at Katie Fish before going back to Hull.

"It's time to hunt sharks."

57

The shark-hunting quickly went from bad to worse. For the next two hours, the team sat in Trent Fogarty's counseling suite sifting through all the personnel documents imaginable. Reading, re-reading, and passing each file on to the person to their right—hoping they would catch something the previous one missed—was appealing to Ballack's meticulous nature but gradually wearing out the others. They took two short breaks, during which Ballack lodged unsuccessful calls to Jill's cell phone. She had never gone this long without responding before and Ballack began to grow concerned.

At four-twenty, the four of them were rubbing their bleary eyes over two orders of Little Caesars pizza and breadsticks. Hull had strongly volunteered to go down to Manchester Road to pick up the food since he was about to "go postal" with the sheer volume of reading. Nothing of interest came from the information in the female counselors' files, so much of their attention turned to the men's dossiers.

"So what's the over-under on us barking up the wrong tree?" asked Tori. "We have the other two pastors at Dayspring along with Merriwether. What about them?"

"Those are a no-go," said Crabolli. "When we were going through Merriwether's email, he said that Hobbs was with him at the board of elders meeting with him, and that he called Hobbs at his home around nine-fifty that night."

"Where does Hobbs live?" asked Ballack.

"According to Merriwether, off Carman Road somewhere."

Ballack calculated the driving distance mentally. "No way he could have done Delcliffe and been home to take the call. What about the youth pastor?"

"Chris Malone was at a baseball game up at Parkway Central, and then he hung out with some kids having frozen custard at the Silky's near Olive and Mason. Home around nine-twenty. His place is in Robinwood West off Ross Road."

"Less confirmation there," said Tori, "but if it holds, he could be off the hook."

"Can't see a motive there, either," reminded Hull.

Ballack pushed some buttons on his phone.

"Again?" asked Tori. "Just let her call you back."

"I'm not calling Jill," Ballack replied. "I'm getting a mental enema, and I'm putting it on speaker."

"Hello?" The voice on Ballack's phone was clear and unmistakable.

"Scotty Bosco, do you want to have some fun?"

"I thought you might be in a quagmire," said the lieutenant. "Only reason you ever speak to me anymore."

"We're sitting around going through personnel files because everyone's been interviewed and one of our top suspects has to be lying but we haven't put it together."

"Take over the investigation, Scotty," pleaded Hull mockingly.

"So you want my advice?" said Bosco. "Here it is. You either have to re-interview your big guns …"

"Yes," groaned Ballack, his voice now officially raspy.

"Or you look past the usual stuff in the personnel files and go for the quirky things you believe wouldn't give you the answer under any condition. Because this might be that time."

Ballack heard a woman giggle in the background.

"Scotty?" he said, quickly taking his cell off speaker.

"Yeah."

"Please tell me that was Debra."

"Gotta go."

"You've been a big help, as usual."

"Cam, just use that big juicy brain of yours, Mister Prodigy. It's your training. You didn't get an education in this art for nothing."

It hit Ballack right between the eyes. How could he not have considered that?

"Thanks, Scotty." He hung up.

The other three were staring at him, awaiting the next step.

"Freud is here," said Ballack, rubbing his hands. "And I know what we might use to hang him. But we need to move fast."

58

The motor in Ballack's brain seemed to have gone to supersonic speed. "Go to the college and graduate school transcripts for each of the counselors I mention. Mulgakov, Delcliffe, Fogarty, Warrick, Cooper, and from the church files we have I want all three pastors looked at."

"What's the rush?" barked Hull.

"Give me a file, and I'll update you as I go," Ballack snapped, grabbing Paul Merriwether's file and rifling through until he found two transcripts, one from the University of Tennessee and the other from a seminary in Charlotte, North Carolina. "Scan the courses they took, the years they were there. Ask yourself what doesn't belong. Any unusual training, anything that makes you think they'd have the skills to pull off two very different murders. Any crossover with what we know about Susanna Delcliffe and Seg Mulgakov."

"That could be anything!" exclaimed Crabolli.

"I know it's a fragile connection," maintained Ballack, "but we haven't probed it yet. I realize that to be fair, we need to get ahold of Dan Cooper's somehow as well, but let's pore over these first."

"Fogarty has a couple transcripts from college days," said Tori. "Apparently he began at the University of Illinois and was in Army ROTC. But he transferred after one year and entered North Park at Chicago."

"You're wondering if the military training could bring on murderous aggression?" asked Crabolli.

"Not saying, just mentioning what's there," Tori said, never taking her eyes off the page.

Ballack looked around the room. "This suite doesn't give off the impression of a GI Joe or someone who can kill someone with his own thumbs."

"You're telling me," said Hull. "Unless he's hiding his own strength, he's got one of the weakest handshakes I've ever received from a man."

"Aha!" yelled Ballack.

"What?" replied Tori. "You speaking in tongues?"

"Zane," Ballack said to Hull, "You might have cleared it up for me."

"Clear it up for me then," complained Hull. "I can't make heads or tails of Warrick's transcript."

Ballack's eyes narrowed, and Tori saw that rare glint when her partner believed they were closing in. For the life of her, she didn't know why now.

"What about the transcript?" Ballack said.

Hull looked over a white sheet of office paper trimmed in red. "Warrick's undergrad one from the University of Wisconsin. Psych major, which of course we'd expect, but he also has a biology minor. The kicker is this notation in green stamped ink on the paper after his junior year. Four letters. N-M-C-H."

"N-M-C-H?" asked Ballack.

"Probably nothing," said Tori.

"If it's nothing, why is it splashed across the transcript?" asked Hull. "I've never seen it on anything else."

"How many transcripts have you seen in your life?" said Crabolli, whose two years at Meramec were more higher education than Hull could claim.

Ballack sat erect in his wheelchair. "Missy, go to the phone on Fogarty's desk there." He began typing as rapidly as his hunt-and-peck method would allow, looking up at the clock on the wall. "Four-twenty-eight. We have no time to waste! Listen, this is important. Identify yourself as someone else, Karissa Emerson, whoever. And call this number …" He rotated toward them to show them his laptop screen.

"The registrar's office at the University of Wisconsin at Madison?" said a genuinely befuddled Missy Crabolli. "And why?"

"Pose as Karissa Emerson," he said breathlessly, "and tell whomever you speak to that Dayspring is in the process of interviewing in-house for a new assistant director. You have a question about what N-M-C-H means and you are wondering if it refers to academic distinction, some training capacity, or something. Just that you need it clarified."

"Whoa, whoa, this is going a little too fast for me, Cam—" Crabolli pleaded.

"Just do it!" yelled Ballack, pointing at the screen. "We have maybe thirty seconds for you to place the call, because office hours there close at four-thirty! Just do it and make it up as you go. Put it on speaker."

Shocked, Crabolli nonetheless stumbled over to the desk phone and dialed the number Ballack had showed her. One ring passed into two, and with three rings Ballack despaired that the delay had cost them. But just as the fourth ring began, the line scrambled, followed by a feminine voice saying, "Registrar's office. Brooke Helton speaking."

"Uh, good afternoon, Mrs. Helton," Crabolli began. "This is Karissa Emerson at Dayspring Counseling Center in Saint Louis, Missouri. Our assistant director is moving out of state, and so we are beginning the search for her replacement. Part of that process is looking in house, and one of our candidates is Ethan Warrick, who graduated from your university in 2005. We have his transcript—no need to send us another—but we did note a point on the document that had a code with the following letters: N-M-C-H. We aren't sure what that means or if this refers to some sort of special course or training Ethan might have had, but as he is one of our top candidates, it would help to know."

Ballack raised his eyebrows, impressed with Crabolli's ability to expand on his format.

Miles away, Brooke Helton responded. "Well, Mrs. Emerson, I don't know. I'm relatively new in the department and that's an unfamiliar code to me. To be honest, the office is closing for the day now and some of us are leaving for dinner in a bit. And, pardon my ignorance, isn't that something that this person would know and you could ask him yourself?"

Ballack's heart sank. Hull smacked his forehead. But Crabolli, strangely calm and resolute, nodded and said, "True, Mrs. Helton, but that's our exact problem. Ethan is on vacation and doesn't want to be interrupted. One of those trips where you turn off your cell phone and computer and crash at a cabin in the woods for days. We really want to get cracking on this, so if you could inform us, we'd be in good shape to advance this process."

"Wow," silently mouthed an impressed Tori. Ballack saluted Crabolli, who smiled.

The hesitation on the other end kept them uncertain, however, until Helton said, "I guess that's fine, but we truly are closing for the day and our reservations are for five."

"Dammit," hissed Hull, to which Ballack quickly put his finger to his lips, glaring at him fiercely.

"However," said Helton, "if you are waiting on the information and are needing it now …"

"We are," said Crabolli impatiently. "Our board is meeting tonight at eight for preliminary discussions, and it would be helpful to have that detail going into it."

"Then here's what I can do. The university is on my way back home from the restaurant. If you don't mind waiting until around seven, I can stop by here and see if I can find the information you're looking for. Just to repeat, you said the letters N-M-C-H, right?"

"That's correct," said a relieved Crabolli, "and just to be safe, since I won't be at my desk, let me give you my cell phone number." Crabolli then dictated her number and Helton dutifully confirmed it.

"No problem," said Helton. "I'll stop back here. Expect a call around seven, or as early as six-forty five."

"Must be going out with friends or alone," muttered Hull when Crabolli signed off. "Who'd spend that little time out if it was a hot date?"

"That's not my concern," replied Ballack. "Missy, great job! Above and beyond the call of duty."

"To the end, C.B.," she said, perking up considerably.

"So what now?" asked Tori. "We've got a couple hours before she calls us."

Ballack pivoted his chair toward Fogarty's doorway. "Down the hall. Let's bring the pizza and the files."

"What for?"

"Change of venue, Tor. We'll think better with a change of venue."

59

"If you don't mind waiting, honey, I can take a shower," he said with a smile.

Jill Ballack creased her brow. "Take a shower when I'm here?" Her comment was not laced with disgust as much as confusion. Her firmly drawn lines on physical activity in dating splashed into other areas, and when Warrick had casually mentioned his potential ablution, she exhibited clear discomfort at the idea of being in the apartment with him naked, even if in separate rooms.

Warrick rolled his eyes. "It's okay, babe. I'll take my clothes in the bathroom and change in there. Just make yourself at home and I'll be out in ten minutes."

He kissed her on the cheek and turned on his heel down the hall of his Des Peres apartment just off Ballas Road. Jill watched him go with a guilty pang in her tender heart. Two years of dating coming to this, to an admission that—although she adored and cared for him deeply—she couldn't picture a future with Ethan Warrick. Maybe it was the fact he was a counselor and she couldn't fathom being emotionally dissected by his psychological assertions. Perhaps it was the ease in which he discussed the travails of the office, a world she found alien and troubling. His facility in describing how professing Christians acted behind one another's backs was a significant turn-off. To be honest, she thought, it was not one dominant reason she could give, but rather the mélange of several layers of personal weariness. All of this forced her to recall her mother's firm yet tender guiding advice from years back: "Remember, Jilly. If you're not comfortable with someone, then you're not called to marry him. Don't ask questions, just get out, and the truth will match up later with what your heart feels."

Jill looked at her cell phone and saw a plethora of calls from her brother. Not now, Cameron, she thought. He could find out the juicy details and blow-by-blow account after the fact. For now, she had to think by herself, for herself. The thought of how Warrick would take a break-up—during or after dinner at Brio—sent a sudden chill through Jill's body, and she scolded herself for not bringing a light jacket along. Perhaps Warrick had something that would suffice for tonight, although she felt guilty doing so when she was only going to shatter his heart in a couple of hours. She walked down the hallway toward his bedroom, hoping to see if there was something in his closet that she could wear nonetheless. She looked down at her fingers as she turned on the light to the massive walk-in closet area, and she saw the white gold promise ring Ethan had bought her only eight months before.

It took her very little time to locate an orange Denver Broncos pullover windbreaker, likely a relic from his seminary days in the Mile High City. But when Jill pulled it off the hanger, the slick polyester fabric fell out of her hands and to the floor below. She stooped down to procure it, pulling it off a pile of scrapbooks in a box when she froze. It wasn't the presence of scrapbooks in a man's closet, but rather the contents sticking out of them.

A green album with gold trim was bulging with pictures and newspaper clippings from several years back. One sheaf in particular was sticking out, two stuck together with Scotch tape. Quickly and quietly, Jill lifted the book from the box as her curiosity got the best of her. Flipping to the exact page, she saw the two items side by side that revealed the truth. One was an article about the devastating professional judgment of plagiarism, a conviction leveled in the court of public opinion, and the ruin of a talented yet troubled therapist in Racine, Wisconsin. The other was a clip from *Psychology Today*. While Jill had no interest in the technical and wooden language of it, she did notice the name of the columnist. It was a name that was familiar to her from conversations with Ethan. But nothing was as disturbing as the photograph that joined the two sheaves together, one of an athletic youngster with dirty blond hair standing admiringly next to a sweet yet noticeably older woman on a cloudless summer day.

So engrossed and rattled was Jill in absorbing the painful truth before her that she had not noticed the shower had stopped running several minutes before, that the bathroom door had opened soundlessly, and that the footsteps coming down the hallway and into the bedroom advanced noiselessly on the thick gray carpet. She did feel rather than hear the approach of the demon from behind her, but before she could turn around her neck was seized in an overpowering grip. And before she could summon a defensive scream, the same hands that clenched her threw her sideways at tremendous force against an unforgiving wall. The last thing she remembered before the

319

darkness enshrouded her was the sound of a scrapbook being neatly tucked away in the box from whence it came.

60

"So we're here because the change in venue might trigger something to implicate Freud?" asked Tori, as they had moved everything out of Fogarty's suite to Ethan Warrick's office. They had continued searching every nook and cranny of Warrick's file, but no further revelations were springing to life. The time was rapidly approaching quarter till seven and Crabolli had her cell phone turned up to maximum volume. There would be no missing this news.

"Let's think about what we know about him. Psych major, bio minor," said Ballack. "What other details are important?"

"The fact that he's got that stupid code on his transcript," said Hull.

"His parents died, didn't they? He's played that trump card with you guys, right?" asked Crabolli.

"Let's find out about that," said Tori. "Can you Google it for us, maestro?"

"Already there," said Ballack, whose fingers were doing their pained dance on his keyboard. After several seconds, he found what he was looking for.

"Here it is," he called out, "From the *Wisconsin State Journal* on September 19, 2002. Frank and Karen Warrick were murdered at a 7-11 store around ten o'clock at night during a robbery that left four people dead and two others wounded. So far his story checks out. That'd be during his sophomore year of college, so the ... um ... ah, that's interesting." And he stared at the screen. "Good heavens, we should have checked out his story from the start."

"Care to enlighten us, oh noble Buddha?" mocked Tori.

"What's on there?" asked Hull.

"It's what's not on there," said Ballack. "No mention of Ethan being their son."

"Wouldn't that be more appropriate for the official obituary?" inquired Crabolli. "That's usually when those snippets make it in."

"Then I have to wonder why it mentions that Frank and Karen Warrick, ages thirty-six and thirty-five respectively, are mentioned as having left behind a ten year-old daughter Christina. No mention of an Ethan, let alone one working toward a college degree and getting drunk at Camp Randall Stadium cheering on the Badgers."

"Thirty-six and thirty-five," whistled Hull. "Which means for them to be Ethan's folks, she'd have to get knocked up in high school."

Ballack felt Tori stiffen standing next to him, sadness and rage concurrently flowing through her.

"Easy, girl," he whispered softly. A tear fell from her left eye.

"There's that, yes," Ballack continued, wanting to deflect from the painful issue of teenage pregnancy, "but the absence of Ethan's name to the inclusion of another makes me wonder."

"Wonder what?" asked Hull.

"That this whole I-lost-my-parents thing isn't the truth, but a full-blown swerve that he's attached himself to for some other reason."

"You mean," shouted Crabolli, "that he just made it up?"

322

"Not that, but that he took a real life incident, worked it so that it was part of his own story as a cover for some other reason."

"But we see it's not his family," said Tori.

"We do," replied Ballack, "but that's because we looked it up and discovered it. No way he could be their child, but maybe he took a calculated risk that no one would ever find out or be in a position to snoop around."

"That's so whacked out," gushed Hull, collapsing into a chair.

"It's not the only thing whacked out or off center," said Ballack, pointing at the wall. "This office is the picture of order. Clean desk, immaculate carpet and furniture, and nothing out of place. Except for one thing that's been bugging me since the minute we came in here."

The rest of them followed his finger toward the wall. A framed picture of a beach scene at twilight hung there. The four bodies in the scene, positioned on a length of sand, were silhouetted against a vast stretch of water facing the sunset-cloaked invasion of darkness. Two taller individuals were in the center with shorter companions on either side. That, however, was not what grabbed Ballack's attention.

"Nothing else in this room is out of place except for that picture," he said, "and if you'll notice, it's tilted leftward and it seems to be pushed out a little from the wall, as if something's behind it. So if you could, Zane, lift it off the nail."

Hull eased out of the chair and approached the wall. Lifting the frame, which was heavier than it appeared, he looked behind the picture and did a double-take.

"The cardboard backing is coming away from the frame, and one of the notches holding it in place is broken off," Hull said. "And … well, well, well."

"What?" Ballack asked, sensing everything was coming together.

"It looks like there's a note stuffed down in here," Hull answered, putting his hand in between the backing and the picture and retrieving a single page that appeared to be printed off a computer.

"Piece of the puzzle?" asked Crabolli.

"Looks like Freud left something behind," said Ballack, as Hull opened the page.

"Warrick is Freud?" exploded Tori. "Are you that certain, Sherlock?"

"Putting everything together," said the unflappable Ballack. "First things first, Zane. What does the letter say?"

Scanning the note quickly, Hull let out a massive breath. "It's a letter, and it has some of the quirks of a suicide note without saying goodbye. Strange though, that the name at the bottom is just a letter. The letter A."

"Other oddities?"

"Yeah," said the sudden-white Hull, "It's a full-blown diatribe against Susanna Delcliffe. Whoever 'A' happens to be, or was, apparently Delcliffe was a whistleblower who accused this person of plagiarism. Must've really screwed this person up something fierce."

"Let me see that," requested Ballack, and no sooner were the words out of his mouth than Crabolli's cell phone erupted with noise.

"Area code 608," she said. "Madison, Wisconsin."

Ballack nodded for her to answer, his eyes never leaving the paper.

"Hello, Mis— … excuse me, Karissa Emerson speaking," she said, wincing over her near-stumble.

With the speakerphone not on, the others could only guess at what Brooke Helton was saying on the other line. Crabolli held up a finger and nodded vigorously, signaling they had definitive news.

"So you found it out after all?" she said, and in the following seconds her eyes widened. The silence in the room was replete with tension, no one daring to take a breath. So pregnant was the pause that no one was ready for the shock of Ballack's strained voice shouting out loud in the laconic air.

"It's 'name change!' That's what the letters mean! Freud changed his name!"

61

"Get off the phone, Missy," Ballack hissed. And Crabolli did.

"Are you trying to make everyone crap themselves?" yelled Hull. "What was that all about?"

"Shut up. He's right," Crabolli said. "He's absolutely right. How did you know?"

"Did she tell you his former name?" Ballack asked her.

Crabolli nodded.

Ballack showed them all the paper that Hull had pulled out of the frame and pointed to the salutation.

"Lord have mercy," exhaled Hull. "It's him. But how were you guessing beforehand?"

"Several factors, and I need to go through them quickly because we don't have much time," Ballack said in a rushed cadence. "This morning we asked Warrick about the phone call yesterday afternoon between he and Mulgakov. He admitted to that but also maintained he never saw Mulgakov last night."

"Meaning?"

"We never asked him about last night. The call came during the afternoon. So when he tipped his hand without us forcing it, I sure paid attention."

"Better than I did, that's for sure," confessed Tori. She didn't know whether to be angry about missing that detail or that she allowed her concern for her daughter overwhelm her performance on the case.

"Not your fault, Tor," comforted Ballack, as if he was reading her thoughts. "The second thing is that when I shook Warrick's hand afterward, it felt like my hand had been crushed underneath a school bus. He's got an incredibly powerful grip."

"So you're thinking that …" Crabolli said.

"That could connect with Susanna Delcliffe's death. The ribs snapped like dry wood? The bruised back and the bleeding into the abdominal cavity. Broadnax all but told us you'd need to be knowledgeable about that physiology and strong enough to knock down a rhino to pull that off."

"And as far as the knowledge goes," marveled Hull, "that would connect with the biology minor. That's some serious insider information. He's got a few classes in anatomy and physiology on here."

"Could be," thought Ballack, "and the picture's note gives us a valid motive. Whatever accusation of plagiarism went down between Delcliffe and this 'A' person—who from the tone of the note seems to be a female—it was bad enough to cause a serious demise."

"Maybe disgrace?" said Crabolli. "Maybe suicide?"

"Whatever it is, Warrick has been keeping it secret for years. So secret and so atomic that he was willing to get a counseling degree and pour his energies into getting hired here, of all places! And the only reason?"

"Susanna Delcliffe was here," Tori gasped. "In his crosshairs. All along."

"Only now," Ballack rasped, "that doesn't bode well for my sister."

"You don't think he'll do anything to her, do you?"

"She was going to break up with him tonight," Ballack said in a sickly tone. "Even if she doesn't know all this and he doesn't know we know all this, it can't be a good cocktail. I need to …"

"Hang on, C.B. Hang on," interjected Hull. "Can we just do the rational thing and just go to his place and do this the easy, normal way? I know this is your sister and all, but you have a professional obli—"

And at that precise second, Ballack's cell phone woke to life, and the strains of Nickelback's "Burn It To The Ground" never sounded so ominous.

"Please," he said, as his friends crept close. "Please."

"Hello. Jill?"

"It's me," Jill said. She sounded out of breath, as if she had just run three miles in the summer heat. "Are you free now?"

"Free?" It was the last thing Ballack had expected to hear. "I … um. I can be. Are you done with your night with Ethan?"

"Yeah. Yeah, I am. I was hoping I could talk to you about it. You know, relationship recovery and all that."

"Are you sure you're okay, Thrasher?" Ballack asked, hoping the use of her nickname would snap her from her apparent stupor. "You sound like you've run a half-marathon on downers."

"I'm fine. Really I am. Just need something to eat."

"Where do you want to go?"

He could have sworn he heard her sniff audibly, as if she was crying. "Can we figure that out when I see you? Where are you now?"

Ballack didn't want her knowing the exact location. "Near Chesterfield. And what do you mean when you see me? We can meet wherever you want to get me a bite."

"No, I mean … Listen, I'm feeling kind of morose. I feel bad because I never got by the cemetery last week for Christopher's birthday. I know it's dark, but I wanted to go by there, even for a minute. Can Tori just drop you off at Bellerive and I can take you from there? I can even take you home and Tori can leave early."

"Drop me off?"

"Yeah. I've got the van, remember? Just meet me at the headstone and we can go soon after."

Ballack felt it, that abject sensation of foreboding and evil. Something wasn't right about this. Think, he told himself. What's going on? He closed his eyes and cleared his head. "Use your options," he whispered to himself. "Get her to tell you in some way."

"Are you sure about meeting you at the cemetery?" he asked desperately.

"Yes, at the cemetery," she said in a voice that was frightfully firm to him. "You can meet me there. About an hour? I'm going to be with Christopher."

He nearly dropped the phone. "You … what? Be with?"

"I'm going to be with Christopher. I'll see you there. Goodbye, brother."

Bug-eyed, Ballack clicked off. He looked at his squad mates vacantly. His chest felt like it was about to spasm, and he wanted desperately to vomit.

"Cam? Where do we need to go? What's the problem?"

Breathe, he told himself. *You're no good to your team otherwise.* He looked up into their concerned faces. His hands were shaking as he turned his wheelchair power on and began to move toward the hallway.

"We need to move fast, and listen to me as we go. Call Krieger now. We're going to Bellerive and we need to draw up the plays in the dirt on the way."

"Draw up what?" pleaded Tori as she jogged to keep up.

"The plan. My sister's going to die in an hour if we don't have one."

62

Fifty minutes later, under a first quarter moon that gave minimal luminescence, Tori descended from the Dodge Sprinter and stood in the small parking lot in front of the offices at Bellerive Cemetery on Mason Road. She began the usual process of lowering the ramp, unlatching Ballack's wheelchair from its clamps, and letting him out of the van. She raised the ramp upright and closed the side door, resting her head against the van and biting her lower lip.

"You sure you know what you're doing, buddy?" she asked.

"It's the only way," he whispered, looking up at the two-story brick building. He saw, even in the darkness, that Jill had already arrived, given the presence of their mother's Honda Odyssey. "Listen, Tori," he continued, his voice barely above a whisper. "We couldn't just pursue Freud when a hostage is in play. This is the best we could do on short notice, but as long as we stick to the plan, we might come out of it alive."

"Oh, please God."

"You keep the faith, girl. Get going and I'll see what I can do with Freud on the battlefield. I'll start heading up there."

Tori nodded slowly.

"Get out, Tori. Freud will think something's up."

Tori obeyed, and fifteen seconds later she was gunning out of the lot. Waiting until several cars zoomed past, she made a right turn and began heading north on Mason into the night.

Ballack popped a cough drop in his mouth and began the motorized climb up the graded landscape as Jill's form came into view. The flood of memories came back at hurricane force. Christopher's burial, which began his journey down the agnostic road, returned in all of its raw fury. The Easter return last year, fresh off his heroic stand at St. Basil's Seminary, saturated his recollections. But this menacing moment was here, and he was entering it completely vulnerable. And coming out in one piece was not guaranteed.

He was twelve feet away from Jill. She had struck a pose of plaintive meditation, not tearing her eyes away from Christopher's headstone even once. Had he not known she would be here, he'd have sworn it was a statue and not his sister.

Hearing him approach, his wheelchair coming over the grass, she raised her head. She was decked out in a Denver Broncos windbreaker, a long-sleeved tee shirt, jeans, and Birkenstocks. Her face was mournful, and as she spoke, she raised her hands toward her face.

"I'm sorry about this, Cameron."

Barely, but discernibly, her eyes looked beyond him and to his right.

"Jilly," he spoke evenly, "We can make it out okay."

Her eyes grew wide, disbelieving.

"We are," he added, "going to make it."

The click, a soft echo, resounded behind him in the gloom of the night.

"You both," came the satanic growl of Ethan Warrick, "are going to be an absolute pleasure to kill right here."

Ballack looked at Jill for the briefest of moments and winked at her.

"Why, that sounds like the lilting metallic throb of a Glock 21 with its silencer," replied Ballack in an incongruously cheery tone. The footsteps continued to his right, and Warrick came into view with the pistol discreetly and squarely aimed between Ballack's stony light brown eyes.

"And here I am again," chirped Ballack, "face to face with the vengeful mourner, the counselor, the murderer—Peter Van Sluys."

63

Killing her lights on the upward climb lest Freud should have superb vision, Tori snaked up the drive path in front of St. Timothy's Episcopal Church, just a third of a mile north of the cemetery. She coasted around the back end of the church, looking up at its squat copper-plated steeple for a second before sliding next to Crabolli's car beneath a lamppost that bore a purple banner celebrating the Easter season. She alighted from the van with three black ski masks and a pair of night-vision goggles for herself. She tossed two each of the masks and goggles to Crabolli and Hull.

"All set?" Hull asked.

"Thank God we had the van stocked with these. He's in position with a tracer on the rear of his chair in case something goes wrong with our goggles," replied Tori. "We'll be running uphill and it'll be a good five minute haul, but we can make it. Remember to slow down and not gallop over the lot. He'll hear us."

Crabolli smacked Hull on the arm. "I'm taking the west wall."

"You sure?" Her partner asked in part protest.

"Absolutely. If he's watching out at all, I'm more likely to be unnoticed at my size. There's only a sliver of coverage from that wall above the sidewalk next to Mason and I can wriggle up it better than you can. At least I have the better odds of not being seen."

Hull shrugged before he dialed a number on his phone and waited on the speaker.

"Yeah?" came a voice amid a plethora of rattling.

334

"Commander?" Hull said, seemingly anxious to keep even the rabbits on the church grounds from hearing him. "We're en route and will be arriving at the battlefield in five. Tori and I are going through the parking lot around either side of the building and Missy will stay low on the sidewalk under the low wall bordering Mason."

"Roger that, Zane," Krieger replied. "We're flying in high and will be swooping down over Laduemont for the final push. He may hear us, but it's a risk worth taking. We won't flip the lights on fully until we're on top of him, but trust me, we'll scare the bejesus out of him."

"See you there," said Hull, gesturing for the women to take off. He silenced his phone and jammed it in his pocket, taking off on a full sprint before loping along next to Tori. As he did so, he prayed fervently against all odds, begging the Almighty that the triad of souls would still be walking among the graves when the chopper came roaring in from the skies.

64

"Let's take a walk," Warrick grinned as he waved them toward a copse of trees some twenty-five yards away from where they stood. "Over there should be fine."

"You devil," Jill spat, fury and tears indistinguishable.

"Shut up, you little tart," Warrick sneered. "You might want to save your breath while it's still in your lungs. You and your brother are about to suffer the ultimate irony."

"What's that?" she murmured.

"I think what he means," Ballack purred in a strangely dreamy voice, "is that he's about to kill us on this same ground where our brother was laid to rest." He looked at Warrick, raising his right eyebrow childishly. "Isn't that the game, Peter?"

"Why," shrieked Jill, who was going insane in the face of Warrick's threats and her own brother's insouciance, "are you calling him Peter?"

"Right there," Warrick ordered, swinging the Glock toward Jill and motioning her toward a tree. "Cameron, you stay right here. And while we're on the subject, do you want to enlighten your dear sister about my original name before she follows you in death?"

"Now the whole death thing is up for debate," Ballack derided him, "but I can at least pull the road map of truth out one last time before your rear end gets kicked, Peter."

Warrick, taking his stand behind Jill and facing northward at Ballack, threw his head back and laughed. "Hilarious. Just the facts, *Detective*."

"We figured out the meaning of a certain code on your college transcripts from your days in Madison. Thanks to a quick phone call, not to mention a resourceful and gullible administrative assistant, we discovered that Ethan Warrick was originally Peter Van Sluys."

"Not bad," Warrick replied. "I'm impressed. And I don't impress that easily."

"Speaking of impressions, if you want to make a credible one on a cover for your parent's identity, make sure you pick a couple that could legitimately be old enough for the role."

"I beg your pardon?"

"You jacked the story of the couple who got capped in Madison and claimed them as your own tragic tale. You obviously grew up elsewhere."

"Wouldn't you love to know the details on that?"

"I really don't need to know where. I just figure that with your Dutch surname you were subjected to enough family discipline to inspire a Peter DeVries-like rebellion against a religious subculture that made you want to crack like a vase dropped from the Gateway Arch. Family dynamics colder than an ice storm in North Dakota. And I figured there was a loved one wronged by someone you determined to stalk until your brand of divine justice was complete."

"And how," Warrick snickered, "did you move those chess pieces around?"

"Because when someone forgets how to hang pictures right, I notice."

Warrick cocked his head slightly, confused.

"We found the little love note to you from the mystery lady whom Susanna Delcliffe nailed for lifting, pilfering, and God knows what else for the sake of professional advancement."

"Shut your mouth! Just shut that hole in your face, Cameron! You don't know what the hell you're talking about." Warrick furiously wagged the gun at Ballack, and as he did so, he swiftly moved behind Jill and wrapped his arm around her neck from behind, pinning her back first against his chest.

"Oh please, God!" Jill bleated through tears.

"The mystery lady was my aunt Angela. She was everything to me my parents weren't. She was more than that. She was my life. My life! Do you get that? No one was as talented, loving, or beautiful as she was." He snarled in Jill's ear. "Not even you, honey. But at the time Angela was headed out for a conference, Susanna's review of her first book—her big breakthrough!—hit every corner of the counseling world, and it was a career-ender. Accusations of dishonesty, lifting sentences and whole paragraphs from others without documentation, everything! Angela never recovered, and she died as a result."

"Killed herself?" asked Ballack.

"Might as well. Died of a broken heart, overwhelmed by sorrow, pills, and alcohol. Never had a chance to tell her goodbye, never had a chance to tell her how much she meant to me."

"You loved your aunt, saw yourself as her white night of vengeance, and you regarded Susanna Delcliffe as the twisted villain. Now that's irony."

"You don't know the first thing about what I've been through!"

"Why don't you get off your pedestal of pity?" Ballack's anger poured out of him. At that moment, as long as Jill survived, he had come to the point where he didn't care if he got wiped out, as long as he went down swinging his way. "All you've had to show for the last few years of your life is a trail of stalking one person who ruined another person's dreams. You went into counseling to prove that you were a better person than Delcliffe, and then you decided during your seminary days that it wouldn't be enough."

"You have to admit, though, that getting the proper references, having the best grades, dazzling others in the right internship and the most challenging practicum was an intricate enough web to make Dayspring recruit me."

"And when you arrived, you bided your time until you could strike."

"That's the hilarious thing," Warrick chuckled as he scratched his right temple with the barrel of the Glock. "Pure comedy. My time almost ran out. Fogarty and Merriwether made life miserable enough for her that she had all but thrown in the towel. Not exactly, but she was determined to make them fire her in broad daylight. The down side would be that she'd escape my justice. But on the bright side, I had a chance to take her out and pin the suspicion on Fogarty and the pastor since they were seen as her primary haters."

"And thus, you attacked her Monday night. In her office. You squeezed the life out of her, shattered her ribs, and smashed her kidneys so badly she bled out inside! That's justice?"

Warrick looked at him coldly, with soulless eyes. "Yes."

"Which could have left you in the clear," surmised Ballack, "except for the fact Seg Mulgakov figured you as the perpetrator."

"Ah, Sergei. He had to do the idealistic thing and give me a chance to turn myself in. He remembered calling me on my cell and hearing the Dayspring alarm in the background. He would put two and two together. It's a shame. He was a fine man and a decent friend. But you can't have friends who will sell you out."

"As opposed to an enemy like you who will do it anyway?" Ballack snapped.

Warrick clenched his arm around Jill's throat more tightly and pointed the gun at Ballack again. "Not the kind of thing you should tell someone who is a finger spasm away from sending you straight to hell."

The gun, sizing Ballack up from ten yards away, gleamed in the tricky moonlight that peeked through the tree branches.

"Straight to hell, huh?" said Ballack.

The gun held steady and Jill's jagged sobs downshifted into silence, and to Warrick's untrained ears, the status quo hadn't changed. But Ballack knew the playing field had tipped, for in the distance he could hear the low hum of a chariot of deliverance coming through the air.

65

Tori leaned up against the front door of the Bellerive offices, gasping for air and cursing that she hadn't quit smoking sooner. Hull was normally slower of foot but in better shape, so his recovery time had been less. They had each been careful, both to tread softly through the parking lot and to stay out of what they believed might be Warrick's line of sight. Now they were fitting their night-vision goggles over the ski masks for the final stretch of their rescue mission.

"I'll take the right side," whispered Hull, nearly inaudibly, as he pointed. "You go left. Remember, stay out of his vision. Hopefully, Stu will be here in a minute, but the minute we see Freud advance we have to move."

"Wait a sec," Tori mouthed, looking around. "I can't see Missy."

Hull had turned to look in that direction but whirled back when Tori's voice hit a decibel above secrecy. He covered Tori's mouth and backed her against the wall, using a fiery look to shut her up.

"If Freud saw her, there'd be shots by now!" he seethed. "Look, I can't see her either, but that's a good thing. It means if we can't see her, neither can Freud."

Tori shoved her hand away but silently mouthed her response. "Fine."

Hull inhaled and exhaled silently. "Believe her even if you can't see her right now. You ready?"

"Ready," said Tori, and she snaked around the left side of the building just as the oscillating thumps of a helicopter came into earshot.

66

"Here's the thing," said Ballack, working his way through a rotation of platitudes. "How are you going to beat all this, Peter? I mean, you've rubbed out a woman due to revenge and another colleague out of fear. But now things are going to sag worse for you than a Spanish moss in a cloudburst. Even if you rub us out, how will you beat the rap?"

"The rap?" Warrick jeered. "What rap? If your sister hadn't been sticking her nose in the center of memory lane, I wouldn't have had to do this. It has to be both of you. That's the functional part of this."

"And here?" The roar from afar was more noticeable. Ballack swore he could even see a shadowy gigantic hummingbird skimming over the tree line where Mason Road dog-legged to the south.

Warrick showed an evil grin. "The location is the art." He squelched Jill's whimpers by cinching his arm around her throat yet again. "All that remains is to shoot you between the eyes, shoot my pretty here in the mouth, and dash off. I've already written out your murder-suicide note in advance to be placed by your bodies. And there you have your morning news story all over town."

"More like the ten o'clock news tonight, depending how quickly we get done here," chuckled Ballack as he raised his voice. The blades thundered closer, and the trees on the verdant hill began to sway in the inky blackness of the night.

"Cam! Are you out of your mind?" Jill wept.

Ballack looked at his sister, the one who never had trouble expressing her loves, her doubts, her joys, her rages. The dear sibling who somehow held to her religious faith in perfect, if baffling, paradox with the evils of the cosmos. And here it was all vaporizing, but not for long. Hold on, Jilly, he thought, a few seconds more.

Warrick's menacing voice, which had all the melody of a chunk of granite being scraped on a cheese grater, rose in order to be heard about the rising din. "Ten o'clock is even better."

"I thought you'd be agreeable, Peter," Ballack yelled back, using the final reserves of his vocal cords.

"Don't call me that, Detective!" Warrick roared in the surrounding fury. So taken was he by the magnificent rage within him, thought Ballack, that he took no notice of the herculean albatross hovering behind them, or that his words were barely heard in the tumult. "That was the old self before I was reborn. And by God, you'll feel my rebirth now! So much for your claim that you'd kick my ass!"

"I never said I'd kick it!" Ballack bawled. "I said you were going to get it kicked, but I never said by whom!"

And the truth dawned.

Piercing downward from the sky, a bolt of white light blinded all of them like Saul on the Damascus Road. Ballack cursed as he saw Warrick did not lose his grip on Jill, but the voice from the heavens sounded comfort that there would be no rest for the wicked tonight.

"Ethan Warrick! This is the Special Investigative Division! You are surrounded and there is no escape! Put your gun down and surrender! I repeat, put down your gun and surrender!"

The white haze lit up Warrick's form as he turned back to face his wheelchair-riddled adversary. With the nightmare closing around him, he looked at Ballack and mouthed his utmost defiance. Ballack couldn't hear him, but the words were unmistakable.

"No surrender," scoffed Peter Van Sluys.

And the Glock popped in the resplendent brilliance.

67

Rather than following Tori and Hull directly, Crabolli had swung an indirect path along the road before hiding behind the Bellerive sign. She plunged herself down on the ground, careful to slide along the grass next to the sidewalk and making sure her head stayed below the wall's field level that was peppered by graves and the moldering bones of St. Louisans past.

It took an extra two minutes after she shifted her body fully onto the sidewalk, but she snaked her body slowly up the grassy incline, just slightly, where she saw three shadowy human outlines about thirty to forty yards away. In fact, it seemed to be two figures, one being enormously large. But as she adjusted her night vision specs, Crabolli saw the one on his right was actually Ethan Warrick with a firm rear chokehold on Jill Ballack. Ten yards to the left, seated in the wheelchair, was Ballack. And Crabolli could read body language even in the blackness of the night. Defiance emanated from their lead detective like steam in an Icelandic volcano.

Crabolli looked left, and she saw Hull, gun drawn, shuffling toward the southwest corner of the building as a southern breeze built itself into a full-blown gale. With excitement and trepidation, she raised her gun and aimed carefully toward the trees, waiting for the right opportunity. And then the searing white shaft erupted from above. She saw rather than heard the fear pulsate from Ethan Warrick from across the field. She could see Ballack sit up and grip the arm rests of his wheelchair a half-second before he looked back at Warrick.

Her heart stopped as she saw Jill Ballack pitch downward to the ground. With a scream from her lips, her foot pushed off the unforgiving surface beneath her. She launched himself upward onto the plain of graves, praying she would not fail her colleague now.

68

Watching his sister carefully, Ballack took a calculated gamble when he realized Warrick would make the fatal choice to shoot. He could only hope Jill would made some sort of sudden maneuver, and given the way Warrick gripped her from behind, he gambled on any disruption sending a bullet toward his right.

The blood in his veins ran frosty as he saw Warrick's tricep straighten out over Jill's shoulder and proclaim his refusal to fold his tent. It was in that nanosecond that Jill grabbed Warrick's left arm at the elbow joint with both her hands and dropped straight downward, jerking him over her in a painful somersault. The Glock erupted in the night with a snappy *pfft!*, and Ballack leaned as far to his left as he could. The bullet shot through the air seeking a fleshly home for its heated core, but the only shelter it got was the back pad of a power wheelchair after ripping through the sleeve of Ballack's upper arm.

At the sound of the gun, both Tori and Hull sprinted out of their positions with their guns out. Tori's view of Warrick was obscured by Ballack, and while Hull had a clear shot, his navigation of the terrain was not ideal. Plus, Jill was directly behind the target, and a stray shot could be a deadly commitment that would spill innocent blood.

Warrick screamed in pain as his head and neck twisted into the ground at an awkward angle. The Glock popped from his grip and fluttered along the springy turf, but not far enough away. Ballack saw his nemesis gather his senses and scurry toward the gun. He heard Jill gasp and begin to scream and saw Warrick's fingers curl around the deathly piece as the murderer scrambled to his feet.

Pop! Pop! Pop!

As if being lassoed by some planetary force from the east, Warrick lurched sideways, emitting a piercing wail before slamming to the grass, the back of his head splitting open upon impact with a double headstone. The first had whizzed past his ear; the second had grazed his shoulder and missed Jill's nose by inches as she attempted to stand. But the third shot had been the equalizer, having torn clean through Warrick's shoulder with significant force. All three had come from the steady, reliable gun of Missy Crabolli from thirty yards out.

Relieved that neither he nor his sister were harmed, Ballack nonetheless had his wits about him and noticed Warrick stirring slowly. The chopper was descending to earth gradually, but the floodlight enabled Ballack to pick up the Glock's location. He and his sister locked eyes as he pointed to a headstone marked to the memory of one George Timms.

"Jill," he called, "kick it away. Kick it away."

In seconds, his entire team was around them. Tori broke toward Warrick and cuffed his hands behind his back. Krieger's pilot was having difficulty getting on the ground, but that was the least of Ballack's concerns. He saw Jill pick herself from the earth and pull herself up by the right wheel of his Quickie so she could embrace him tightly.

"Thank you, thank you, thank ..." she wept, and her tears overcame what was left of her speech.

"You're hit, C.B.," said Crabolli matter-of-factly. "He get you in the arm?"

"Something grazed me," Ballack replied, out of breath, "but I heard a ping, so check to see if the bullet got lodged in my backrest.

Hull was looking at him with large admiring eyes. "You, my friend, have to be the gutsiest person I've ever met."

"I can't believe you called me that," smiled Ballack.

"Gutsy? It's high time I did."

"No, you called me your friend."

"High time I did that, too," said Hull, panting hard.

The helicopter swerved toward the lawn behind the office building as its choice for a landing pad. Suddenly Ballack felt Jill's chin leave his shoulder and he followed her gaze. Warrick was struggling to his feet, being raised off the ground by Tori and shackled cumbersomely. His eyes were dazed, almost vacant, but his demonic smile remained.

A blast of hot air shot from Jill's nostrils and she slammed her fists down on Ballack's armrest. Ballack himself looked into her eyes, eyes that belonged to his sweet sister who patiently would wait out any travesty, who could forgive almost every wrong he could imagine. But this look was one he had never seen before. There was no patience, no absolution, and anything of that nature. He saw only a heat-seeking missile of blistering hatred ready for launch. She leapt to her feet and started toward her ex-boyfriend.

"You!" she screamed at him. And the entire team looked at her, a rabid wildcat tearing off a Denver Broncos jacket that could just as well find a calling as a noose if she so desired. Warrick, standing wobbly, turned away from her.

"Hey, *Peter*!" she shrieked loud enough to be heard all the way to the Atlantic coast. "Stand up and face me, you jackass!" She flew at him, shoved Tori out of the way and, gripping his collar, slammed her knuckles under his chin. It was then that Jill Ballack reared back and began letting even more punches fly. Her very first one bisected Warrick's cleft and sent him flying onto his back, crunching his handcuff-laden wrists beneath his weight. She leapt on top of him, still raining down blows.

"You murderer!" *Thwack!* "You kill others ..." *Thwack!* "... and now you try to kill me and my brother ..." *Smack!* "... right here!" And she smashed her forehead against his listing temple, opening up a cut over his left ear.

"You psycho, are you trying to get him off all charges?" screamed Tori. She grabbed Jill around the waist from behind in a desperate attempt to stop the barrage. But she was no match for Jill's fury, as the younger Ballack fell back on top of her, knocking the wind out of Tori. Crabolli and Hull edged closer, as if afraid Jill would unleash her anger on them.

Jill crawled back to the groaning form of Ethan Warrick, clenching his collar in her left hand, and spat in his face. "Look at me!" she growled like a raging pit bull. "I want you to remember this face when they shove the needle in your arm and sent your buttermilk-sucking carcass straight to hell!"

"Jill," cautioned Crabolli, "let him go!" But her steps toward her were slow ones, caught between both professional need and vengeful resolution.

Jill ignored her, keeping her eyes on Warrick. "Because if there's any justice in this world, you'll go so deep into hell that you'll wave at Satan on your way down! So here's some help in getting you there!"

And with that, she threw a right forearm so vicious and martial that it would have cracked Warrick's jaw. Before her punch could crease his head, though, Tori Vaughan and Missy Crabolli both tackled her to the soft earth. Kicking her legs and screaming curses in Warrick's direction, Jill's voice died away in a bevy of tears.

Stu Krieger and a uniformed officer that had to be his pilot walked up behind them. Both female detectives lifted Jill slowly until she reached her feet. With slow, deliberate steps, they brought her to her brother's side. Ballack touched his sister's hand. The pilot, with a tag that read FELTON, crept up to Warrick's pathetic form. Krieger surveyed the scene.

"Geez, what happened to him?" the commander asked. "How'd he get laid out?"

Ballack shook his head at Hull, Crabolli, and Tori in turn. Tori winked. Ballack looked back at Krieger.

"Not a clue, sir," he sighed. "Not a single clue."

As he spoke the words, Jill dropped to her knees and buried her face in his forearm.

EPILOGUE

... and a Time to Build Up.

(April 13)

The sun had retreated behind the clouds in the distance, sending a blazing ribbon across the horizon. The potato skins and steak knives littered the glass table on the deck overlooking a freshly mowed backyard. Ballack took a long swig of his Beck's Light and peered at the western crepuscular glow. His mother had stepped back into the house to get dessert while he waited with Jill and their father outside. The early celebration was winding down none too soon, as they could see dark clouds racing in to overwhelm the orange-streaked gloaming with sheets of silvery rain.

"You're sipping from the opposition," Ballack remarked to his father, taking another draught from his own bottle and snagging a potato chip from a bag in the center of the table.

"Hardly the enemy. It's Denmark, son. Not Italy, England, or France," said Martin Ballack, tilting his head and opening his mouth to receive a few more ounces from his bottle of Carlsberg. "I have no reason to hate the Danes. Remember which tradition gave us one of the greatest literary treasures of all time in *Beowulf*."

"My father the cultural snob," sniffed Ballack.

"Your father the well-rounded beer connoisseur," Martin replied. His fingers gently danced on the neck of the green bottle as he looked at Jill across the table, giving her a tender wink. "The big surprise is that Thrasher there has already taken a couple of these down and she drinks only once every election cycle."

"I have reason, Daddy," she playfully slurred.

"That you do, Jilly," Martin smiled, though it was evident there was a twinge of agony in his voice. The press had descended on

Bellerive the night before like coyotes on a ravaged Colorado deer, and Martin and Marie nearly hit the ceiling when they watched the Fox 2 top story and heard their children's names in the crossfire of a shootout at the cemetery. Ballack apologized to his stricken parents when Martin called him and chewed his son out in blistering fashion. Thankfully, Barnes-Jewish West County Hospital was situated less than a mile up the road from the cemetery, an easy choice to transport Jill when she became crippled by shock. Despite Ballack's insistence things would be fine, his parents rocketed in from Saint Charles nonetheless and had been at the emergency room until half past two in the morning, when it was certain the medication had calmed her down. Tonight, in lieu of Valium, she was keeping pace with Martin on the Carlsbergs.

"The point is we made it, Daddy," replied Jill, who never tired of her childlike address for her father. "We're on this deck watching the stormheads roll in getting buzzed while Cam finishes the last bite of his filet mignon and I can put the turbulence of this past year behind me while perfecting my other talents. Like this." She set her bottle on the table and let out a repulsive belch.

"That'll wake the rabbits up from their nap. Great steaks, Dad, by the way," said Ballack, waving his final sliver of meat on his fork.

"Can't go wrong with Mannino's," Martin responded, collecting the used silverware and placing it on a tray in the middle of the table. "As soon as Jilly wanted to stay in tonight rather than go out, I zipped over to Cottleville to grab these on sale before anyone else scarfed them."

The sliding glass door opened, and Marie Ballack appeared with a massive homemade cheesecake christened with a caramel sauce and salted peanuts. The ripple effects of Jill's fear, the meteorological notations, and the commentary on Martin's meat-scoring run to Mannino's—all the banal common currency used to keep sadness from this natal sacrament—all died away as Marie cut the dessert into generous portions.

"If you want to catch a break from ravenous murderers, son," said Martin as he held the cake plate for Marie's meticulous knifing, "why don't you come with us to Florida in a couple months? Your old friends Rafael Billadero and Melissa Percy are getting married, and they asked me to do the wedding in Wellington."

"Back to the blanket-like heat, huh? Well, maybe Tori can use the break from me," Ballack replied.

"If she's confident enough in Paula's progress," chimed in Marie, "why doesn't Tori come with us? What could be the harm in that?"

"Not a fan of sixteen inches of cake icing, sister dear," said Ballack to Jill as he worked on his first bite, "so thank you for going esoteric on us with this."

"Frankly, I prefer eating outdoors at home to going out," Marie remarked as Martin got up to light the tiki torches on the two western corners of the deck. She looked lovingly at her daughter. "Happy twenty-sixth, Jilly. We're just relieved you made it, both of you."

"Trust me, I prefer the safety of my family to the psychosis of a certain counselor," said Jill quietly.

"Soon to be ex-counselor," admitted Ballack. "He won't be able to get a job emptying the mail bins at Centerpoint Hospital, if he ever sees freedom again."

"Dayspring won't recover from this," Jill uttered. "Several of my friends say they're packing up and can't bring themselves to attend church there anymore. Of course, that crowd includes me. They might lose half their membership."

"Not to mention what the aftershock will be for the counseling clinic," sighed Martin. "The loss of clients will be staggering."

"When can we expect his sorry self to go to trial?" asked Marie.

"Not for a while," said Ballack. "And I swear he'd better at least suffer in prison for the rest of his worthless existence, even if he doesn't get the death penalty."

"Suffering is too good for a savage who tried to kill our children," Martin said through his grinding teeth. "And who murdered two colleagues."

"I thought a man of the cloth such as yourself would hope for his spiritual redemption," half-joked Ballack, "rather than say you want him to burn in hell for the rest of eternity."

"I do think he's capable of redemption, Cameron, but my little demon inside wants him to burn in hell for eternity."

"I've never heard you wish that on anyone, darling," Marie said, squeezing her husband's arm.

"Just Hitler, Stalin, Idi Amin, and the New England Patriots at playoff time," said Martin, swirling the caramel sauce with a mass of cheesecake already on his fork.

"Sometimes I think the whole Christian landscape is headed there," blurted Ballack.

"I can't go there with you, brother, even now," said Jill, "but I can now see how someone would believe that."

"Seriously, everyone," Ballack continued, letting his fork drop with a clatter on his plate. "Come on, Dad. Think about all the crap you've experienced. And now I've viewed some unspeakable, unnatural, and practically unforgiveable things happen across the Christian spectrum. Adultery, neglect and murder at St. Basil's. Orthodox, obviously. Then you have the Catholic tradition soiled even more than usual with what we dealt with at the Cathedral Basilica last fall. Payoffs, murder, porn, and heaven knows what else we *didn't* stumble upon. And now, it seems our Protestant brothers and sisters can't keep their own hands clean."

"So what's the solution, son?" Martin's dark brown eyes looked up from his calorie-laden delectable. "Are we to overturn billions of years of human brokenness and misfiring efforts by giving up on people?"

"How do you endure it? *Why* do you endure it?"

"I can't answer how, because I don't even know the equation for that," said Martin, looking off in the distance as a stiff breeze whipped over the lawn. "All I know is that if I'm taking God seriously and what I read at face value, the Church at large is often spoken of in terms of marriage."

"Ephesians chapter five and the noble ideal," said Jill. "How often I've heard that."

"Because it *is* the noble ideal," frowned Martin, "and I'll be the first to tell you this: The Christian community can whore around and chase everything other than true honesty, integrity, and humility. I've screamed at God repeatedly about how the Church can act like a wayward slut that cheats on him left and right, to paraphrase Dorothy Day."

"I thought that was Augustine," replied Jill.

"No evidence he said that," Martin countered. "That quote actually originated with Ms. Day."

"And yet you remain in that community, to get back to the point," said Ballack.

"Yes, I do. Because just once in a while," his father said, his eyes misting over, "you get to be part of healing someone's soul, of being part of the solution rather than despairing over the problem. If God exists, then he loves people, no matter how faithless they are. There's a part of me that believes I should display at least a modicum of like patience."

"You sure it's not megalomania in disguise?" grinned Ballack.

"If so," breathed Marie, "then it's a noble version of it and I'll take it."

"I'll take you, babe," Martin replied, rubbing noses with his doe-eyed beloved.

"Good heavens," Jill wrinkled her face in disgust, "Why don't the two of you get a room while Cam and I walk off this feast for a few minutes?"

"No problem," Marie said, rolling her eyes. "We love clearing your messes off the table, as always. From six years old to twenty-six, little has changed."

She had to duck to avoid the potato skin Jill sent flying through the air with a raucous laugh.

Ballack rolled down the ramp in the open garage and motored into the driveway, waiting for Jill to get a jacket as the temperature had dipped into the low fifties. The slate wisps had fused together into a charcoal warhead of rain and fury, and he heard the rumblings of thunder in the distance, not as gentle as his own father's rumblings of worry as Ballack put a jacket on for the constitutional.

"You'll be okay?" Martin had asked.

"It's a quick out and back before the heavens open, Dad," he had answered.

"I mean everything else." The fatherly concern pulsated from his eyes.

Ballack shrugged. "I come upon a dead body in a harbor of emotional and spiritual calm, follow the clues through one shipwreck after another, then put on my back my team members who experience various clusters of severity, as well as my partner who finds out she'll be a grandmother before she's forty, followed by my own love life getting choke-slammed into the dust, getting shot at, and nearly emptying my bowels before seeing my sister is, in fact, safe." He popped out a singular chuckle and shook his head with a smile. "On the positive side, it's topped off by a delicious birthday dinner. All in a day's work. How would you feel?"

Martin squeezed his son's shoulder. "Stay dry."

Impatiently circling in the driveway as Jill took her time, Ballack felt the outline of a letter in his jacket, written on ivory-colored stationery in Dana's crisp yet elegant script. It had arrived that afternoon, and from the moment Ballack opened the envelope he could sense the discordant twins of love and fear rise from the paper itself. He leaned back in his chair as a bolt of fire streaked across the western sky as the memory of her words took hold.

Dearest Cameron,

I had promised myself that having been through the anguish of assault and betrayal, of apparent love and realistic coldness, I would never open myself up to the chance of loving someone and being loved ever again. Even when I first met you, when you scoured the frigid grounds at St. Basil's in search of the terror that stalked us all, I held back even as I knew instinctively you were different than all others, in every way. Never had I shared my nightmares with anyone. Never had I divulged my inmost sadness to another. You were the first to know my story, to see me—in slowly increasing measures—as I was and not as I presented myself to be.

And much to my happiness as well as my fright, you didn't run away. My heart has seen the backs of so many souls over the years, people who know about me but who sense something amiss, something deeper that they don't want to touch, and thus walked silently away. All that changed when you sat at the well of my heart and lingered with no pretension whatsoever. For the first time in my life, I felt completely and cleanly loved.

I know that you say you haven't changed, and though I can't bring myself to trust that, oddly enough I do believe that you are right. Despite the pain and crap of my life over the past several years, there is no doubt that you are the one who loves me truly and desires to love me deeper still. It is a failure on my part to be so unwilling to step out in faith and take hold of that love. I say that not to reject you, but to say that I am trapped in something beyond my comprehension. And as strange as it may be to hear this, my unwillingness to continue on does not mean I have stopped loving you. In fact, I know I can't stop doing so.

I feel shame for walling up my heart and letting you go. Even if I tell myself it is for my protection, I know that I can't continue with the storms in my soul. I have prayed so much to God to forgive me for hurting you, and I pray that at the end of this, that I will call for you and run to you one day, and you will be there to meet and love me regardless of my absence. I know I can't bet on that, nor can you guarantee you will remain and not move on. Nor should you have to promise that. But in this present darkness, it is the one pinpoint of light

I can keep in front of me, and I don't want this to be a "good bye", but a "one day yet."

Cameron, in a small way, you leveraged me out of a fiery chasm. And even if the long dark night of the soul is here, you have made me more hopeful that one day the morning will come. I can only hope against reason that you will be there when my sun rises.

I love you,

Dana

"Ready?" Jill's voice snapped him from his pensive trance.

Ballack smiled. "All set, Thrasher." They moved out of the driveway into the street and took a turn to the west down the sloping hill. For several minutes, neither spoke.

Steeling herself against the increasing breeze, Jill broke the silence. "Thanks for covering for me, by the way."

"You mean when you clocked him afterward?" Ballack chortled. "Why would I turn you in for that? After those haymakers, you deserve the Congressional Medal of Honor. Or a Purple Heart."

"Technically, it was assault."

"Krieger's pilot was still finding a place to set down by the time you were done with Ethan, and they never saw a thing. And you have your brother and three other detectives of unimpeachable character who will swear in a court of law that they saw no assault of any kind go on."

"And what would you tell the jury, dear brother?"

"That you and I were playing catch with a rock and I had an errant throw. As far as Ethan goes—wrong place, wrong time."

They walked in silence for several moments. Ballack heard an approaching salvo of thunder and felt a sprinkle or two on his hand as he steered his Quickie alongside Jill.

"And what indeed has the last two years with Ethan gotten me?" griped Jill as they turned right into a skinny cul-de-sac. "It seems like a colossal amount of wasted time."

"Because it ended in disaster?" Ballack replied. "Come on, Jill. Heartbreaks aren't throwaway moments. If that's all you get from them, you're not living through them."

"This isn't going to be a lecture, is it, Cam?"

"Not even an Anglican homily. Just think of this as an educational moment. You've discovered the type of guy you truly don't want. That's not a waste of your time, but a foundation for later."

"You've got a lot of confidence I'll grow from this."

"I've watched you make many mistakes, Jill. But to your credit, I've never seen you make the same major lapse in judgment twice. You at least consistently fail in a forward direction."

"Sounds like a lesson you've learned well yourself, brother."

Ballack felt the rustle of Dana's letter against his chest through his jacket lining.

"Still learning, Jilly. Still learning," he replied. They made the turn back toward home as the first drops of cool rain spattered comfortingly against them and the darkening sky lit up with jagged fingers of white flame.

LUKE HERRON DAVIS is the author of the Cameron Ballack Mystery series, of which *A Shattered Peace* is the third volume. He is a Kansas native now in his nineteenth year of teaching. Luke has taught in the ethics and religion departments in private schools in Louisiana, Virginia, Florida, and Missouri. Presently, he teaches Ethics and Church History while serving as the Bible department chairman at Westminster Christian Academy in St. Louis. Luke lives in nearby Saint Charles, Missouri, with his wife Christy, son Joshua, daughter Lindsay, and their retriever Gretel.

Other books by Luke H. Davis

Cameron Ballack Mystery Series
Litany of Secrets
The Broken Cross

The Merivalkan Chronicles
Joël

www.ingramcontent.com/pod-product-compliance
Lightning Source LLC
Chambersburg PA
CBHW050316030726
47505CB00003B/725